To

Judge David S. Bauscher

My "Big Brother"

and great friend to

his lovely wife Gloria

Bud

Ronald Bauscher II

DEADLY
CROSSING

ROYAL BOUSCHOR

authorHOUSE®

AuthorHouse™
1663 Liberty Drive
Bloomington, IN 47403
www.authorhouse.com
Phone: 1-800-839-8640

Published by AuthorHouse 04/14/2014

ISBN: 978-1-4969-0163-7 (sc)
ISBN: 978-1-4969-0162-0 (hc)
ISBN: 978-1-4969-0161-3 (e)

Library of Congress Control Number: 2014906036

For Royalynn and Tiffany

PROLOGUE

he long circuitous route finally ended at a highly secured parking lot of an old cement block warehouse. Mickey O'Leary looked out the heavily tinted glass of the van and wondered, *What the hell is this place? The director said his security clearance was going to up today, but where am I?*

The building looked to be several decades old with little chance of improvement based on the remote neighborhood and the slow economy. The building was about forty feet high and one hundred feet wide. The only identification was the well-worn and faded sign itself that said, *Sylvester's Warehouse and Storage.*

He eased his lanky six-foot frame out of the van and into an overcast chilly fall Virginia midmorning and straightened his black suit jacket that his kids called his CIA uniform. His quick green eyes rapidly scanned his surroundings. Something wasn't right here.

The old warehouse was brimming with multiple hi-tech in Motion cameras and "fish eyes" that continuously scanned the well-worn tarmac parking lot cluttered with old machinery and dated trucks. The yard was enclosed by a razor wire topped eight-foot cyclone fencing, much like the other buildings in the area, but the high-tech gadgetry appeared to be an overkill, watching a lot that was filled with old machinery and trucks with a variety of lot numbers on each unit.

His keen observation was broken when his driver led him through a gray steel door marked *Employees Only* and down a short hallway that was completely void of adornment and sound. He couldn't even hear his own footsteps as he entered into what appeared to be the business office.

Two well-dressed middle-aged women were fixated on an array of computer screens and comparing it to Mickey as he walked in. It was then that he realized he had just passed through a body scanner in the hallway to the office. His driver quietly disappeared.

One of the ladies scanned his CIA credentials as the other one picked up the telephone and made a quick, quiet call. He caught a computerized image of himself on one of the monitors just as a man quietly entered the room through an unmarked door. *Security* was inscribed on the dark blue baseball cap that sat on the bald head of an unsmiling stocky six-footer with deep piercing black eyes. The man's dark blue uniform was stretched across a powerful body.

"You're clear to go, Agent O'Leary. Officer Watson here will take you inside," said one of the ladies.

Mickey followed Watson into the cavernous warehouse and stopped dead in his tracks.

There were five dark blue heavily tinted twelve-passenger vans neatly parked along the right-hand wall. What caught his eye was the cement block building that was constructed within the warehouse; it was covered with satellite dishes on its roof, aimed through strange-looking skylights in the roof of the warehouse. There was another body scanner immediately in front of the inner building.

His guide, seeing O'Leary's concern, smiled and said, "Welcome to no-man's-land, Agent O'Leary.

"What in hell is this place, Watson?"

"It's a place that doesn't exist, sir. You're not even here. Just follow me," he said as he turned, smiling, and walked to the door of the inner building.

Watson punched a code into a handheld device and pushed open the handleless steel door of the strange inner sanctum. It led into a hallway that was as bland and unadorned as the gray cement box of the warehouse except for the brown camera bubbles that protruded from the ceiling.

Watson turned to Mickey and said, "Remember, Agent O'Leary, you're under surveillance at all times. Security is taken very seriously here. Keep that in mind."

Mickey was confused and just nodded. *Just what is this place, and what am I doing here?* His heartbeat jumped a couple of beats as he quickly thought of all the files he was working on to see if there was a connection. Everything had been pretty straightforward until now.

His guide stopped in front of an unnumbered door, glanced at Mickey, and said, "You're expected, Agent O'Leary." He tapped three times, waited for an electronic click, and pushed the door open.

"Thank you, sir," Mickey said as he walked into an expansive executive office suite. His attention was immediately drawn to the imposing smiling man walking toward him with a beefy outstretched hand. Today was nothing but surprises.

The big man walking to greet him was none other than Wade Walker, former CIA assistant director, head of Foreign Services.

His hair was different now, not the black military short cut that he had worn while in the agency. It was white and bushy now. He wore a well-seasoned dark brown leather sport coat with a tan shirt opened at the collar. His piercing gray eyes were in great contrast to his well-tanned face. He was still a trim six-foot Texas cattleman right down to his jeans and boots. There was no doubt that he was still a man of action, even in his seventies.

"Come in, come in, Agent O'Leary," he said with a big smile, shoving his beefy hand out to grasp the still dumbstruck Mickey's hand. "Have a seat. We met several years ago when I was with the agency and you were still running around the world, trying to get us into trouble."

"Yes, sir, Mr. Walker. I remember very well, sir. It's just that ... Well, sir, I thought you were retired," he stammered,

His smile and chuckle was genuine, as this obviously wasn't the first time Walker had heard this remark.

"Please have a seat. We have a vital situation we need to discuss," he said as he moved behind the big mahogany desk, which was covered with piles of various colored files, and eased into an oversized leather executive chair.

Shaking his head, Mickey settled into the soft leather wingback chair facing the big desk and gawked around the room like a tourist in a museum.

It was a twenty-foot square room covered in beautiful dark mahogany, with a ten-foot beamed ceiling. A heavy dark brown leather couch was pushed against one wall and surrounded by mahogany bookcases. A large coffee table sat in front of the couch, and a small conference table stood in the corner; they were all made from the same heavy wood. The dramatic contrast to the neat executive office was the organized clutter covering the walls—Walker's game trophies, antique weapons of many descriptions, and numerous photos of the man with various presidents and heads of states from all over the world. The room looked more like a man's den or "man cave" than an office. Not even the top brass had anything like this.

"How do you like my office, Agent O'Leary? By the way, can I call you Mickey?" he said with a smile. "I understand most people do, and you can call me just plain old Walker, if you would."

"What the hell is this place, sir? I mean, I've never even heard of it before, and I thought I was in the know. Sylvester Warehouse? My boss didn't fill me in; he said someone would do that when I got wherever I was going. This place is a hidey-hole. This is the greatest office I've ever been in."

The chuckle was genuine. "Hell yes, I know, Mickey. It's an inside joke. We call it the *Cat House*. Let me get right down to business, Mickey. I know you're a busy man, and so am I," he said. Then his smile disappeared, and his voice got serious.

"We have a situation that's come up, and you're just the man to get involved. I'm sure you've been apprised of your new security clearance. It's absolutely vital that you don't disclose anything relative to the Cat House. This place doesn't exist, and everyone who works here has a very different security clearance and pay grade than you ever thought existed. You wouldn't be here now or even know about this place if you weren't carefully checked out and didn't have a unique connection to this adventure. Need I say more?" he said, looking Mickey in the eyes.

"No, sir. I'm clear on that."

"We have a situation in Mexico. We need a man on the ground, and we need him now. Time is of the essence, and we don't have time to get anyone else involved, as we don't know where our leaks may be. We know we have some, and that's the problem," he said as he shook his head.

"Homeland Security can't do it, and if they could, by the time they got through all their bureaucratic bull crap, it would be too late. We can't get Mexico involved for the same reason: they have leaks just like us, and they're pissed about the wall the HLS was putting up that never got done. They have the same leaks on their border that we do, only more, and they wouldn't be of any use in this matter. They're busy fighting a drug war, and most of them don't even know whose side they're on. We can't use any of our agents already in Mexico for the same reason. We need a good man literally on the ground now, and we need him fast. I need a closed circuit here, Mickey, and you're that circuit.

"The damn border is a sieve. We all know that, and no one does anything of real value to seal it off. Hell, they come across in droves, and we only have a handful of men covering a couple thousand miles of border. We get all the garbage and the drugs. Only this time we have a rather interesting situation. They—who ever in hell *they* are— are smuggling a very dangerous Russian across the border."

"A Russian? Why in the world are they doing that? Russians come into the United States legally every day. That doesn't make a lot of sense."

"That, Mickey, is the sixty-four-thousand-dollar question. Who and why are they smuggling a Russian into the United States is what we want to find out. They smuggle people from every country that's an enemy of ours on a regular basis, including all the Arab nations. When we catch 'em, we just bus 'em back to Mexico for another try. It's ridiculous, but it happens daily. Sooner or later, more than 90 percent of them get back in. But for some reason, the word is getting around that this one is special. That's why we need to find out who the Russian is and what he's up to. Intelligence tells us that when he gets into the United States, the country will change forever. We need to know what in hell that's all about."

"How do I fit into this?"

"You have an old partner by the name of Sinclair who has a place and lives part-time down in Sonora. I know all about him, Mickey. He speaks the language, he's a hunter, he knows his way around the Sonoran outback, and he's a damn clever man. Hell, he was one of our best. He was one of the few who could think outside the box. He's a survivor."

"Sinclair's supposed to be retired, sir. Like me, he's fifty-two years old."

"Hell, Mickey, I know that," he said with a quick grin. "But I also know he's got a clause in his retirement package that says we can call him in for a national emergency, and this is exactly what we have. We don't have time to hunt up someone else for the job, and presumably it's taking place in his backyard."

Walker leaned back in his chair, staring at Mickey, and then said in a conspiratorial voice, "Look, Mickey, I know all about the business where he got sold out to the enemy in Southeast Asia when he was doing recon. I know the senator who was involved got himself shot and died. I know Sinclair wasn't directly involved; he had a good alibi. Hell, if it was me, I'd of shot the bastard myself. That's behind us. We need a good man on the job down there, and Sinclair's it. Let's face it; he was a legend around the agency. I know that after his wife got shot, he became a loner and transferred back into special ops and took all the most dangerous assignments. Hell, Mickey, many were suicide missions—and he survived.

"They sent him everywhere—Southeast Asia, Central and South America, Africa, you name it," he said, waving his hand. He did everything, and he came back. That's the kind of a guy I want now, and you're the guy who's going to put it together. You're going to run him just like you've run moles in the past. You're going to be his handler. You're the only guy who can do it, and you and I know it. You two go way back, I know. You were partners in Russia and France when you were undercover; you two are practically family. I've checked him out. From what I know, he's in good shape, still damn sharp and clean. He's not a leaker. This doesn't require him to use his old skills. This is just an observation job. Hopefully," he said as he glanced up at the ceiling.

With that, he leaned back in his big brown leather Texas-style chair and analyzed Mickey's reactions with his cool gray eyes as he let it all sink in. There wasn't an option here, and Mickey realized this immediately. What was going on, he had no idea, but he and Zack Sinclair were going to be involved. They hadn't sent him here for a rejection. He and Zack were in.

Yes, they really were like family—only closer. They had trusted each other with their lives on many occasions. At Langly they were known as Mick and Mack, derived from Mickey's Irish and Zack's Scottish heritages. When Zack told the office staff that his Sinclair ancestors had settled with the Mic-Mac Indians on the northern East Coast of America a hundred years before Columbus even got to America, they had been promptly just referred to as "the Indians."

"Holy balls of fire" was all Mickey could mumble. "How do you fit into this, sir?"

"I'm off the radar here, Mickey," he said as he leaned forward, put his elbows on his desk, and looked around the room. "You've never been here. This place doesn't exist. When the shit hits the fan in numerous agencies, they call us to clean up the mess. We're known as the bottom line. When bureaucracy gets in the way or when time is of the essence—like now—they call on us. We're an indispensable agency that solves difficult problems the government doesn't want to know about or be involved in. It's as simple as that.

"It's just a refinement of several agencies putting this team together and eliminating undesirable parts of their organizations. If there were more time, I'm sure the CIA, Homeland, or whoever would, and could, put something together. But because it's Mexico and because we have a liberal government that can't make sense of anything and is not too interested in solving the border problem, we are the problem solvers. Washington may never learn about this project, and if they do, it will be when and what the agency wants them to know."

Shaking his head, Mickey had trouble digesting everything he'd just heard. A clandestine agency within multiple agencies? A special operation agency? A black operation agency? *What the hell am I getting into?*

"Look, Mickey, I know this is hard to get your head around right now, but you've been with the agency long enough to know that there must be organizations like the Cat House that handle things off the radar. We're legit, and your ass is covered. Your boss wouldn't have sent you over here if he didn't know it wasn't damn serious. Now let's get down to business," Walker said in a serious tone and then opened a file on his desk.

They knew the location in Sonora where a large drug deal was going to happen in the desert, and this drug deal was the payoff to get the Russian into the United States. He might be on sight and involved, and yes, it was in an area where Zack hunted and knew well. They had chosen the right man for the job.

The whole scenario had started innocently enough when two radio interceptor-translators had picked up a signal.

They had gone to their NSA boss, who blew them off until Monday because she was leaving for the weekend and all the brass had already left or were preoccupied.

They had thought their discovery was important enough that they talked one of their pals who worked for the CIA to introduce them to one of the CIA assistant directors.

The message had originated in Afghanistan and was answered on a cell phone in Guadalajara, Mexico, that they knew belonged to a Mexican mafia family. It discussed in vague terms that the translators had long ago learned to translate: a large drug sale was going to happen very soon in a particular place in Sonoran Desert the operators thought they had identified. It had something to do with smuggling a Russian into the United States. The frightening thing of the message was that it said when the Russian arrived in the United States, things would never be the same again. It was happening now, and time was of the essence.

"He doesn't have to get involved in any way, Mickey. We just want him in close enough to observe and tell us what's going on and when and where they plan on smuggling this Russian into the States, if possible.

"I know his reputation, and he's damn capable, but we don't want him to shut down the operation. We just want him to tell us what in hell is going on down there if he can and when and where this guy thinks he's going to get into the United States. Get us some ID or photos if possible. If he can't get too close, then we'd like his best estimate of what we are dealing with. He can track 'em and call you as they go.

"Don't worry about packing a bag, Mickey. The plane is loaded with everything you and Sinclair will need. You can buy what clothes you need when you get there or bum some stuff off your pal. The plane is waiting, and you're gone."

He pushed a 4G Apple iPhone across the desk and said, "I'm the only one you report to now, Mickey. Here's a special encrypted satellite cell phone that you can call me on 24-7. The number is in the memory. Here's another one for Sinclair. Your cell phone number is in memory as well. You can add any numbers you feel necessary, and here's a camera that is already logged into Sinclair's phone for transmitting photos.

"You're on our expense sheet now, Mickey. We don't quibble about necessary items you think you need," he said as he stood, walked around the desk, and grasped Mickey's hand.

"He's your man, Mickey. He's perfect. He's off the radar. He belongs to no one. We don't even know him. We need him, we want him, and we want him now!"

The last remark frightened Mickey as he walked out of the office. Was Zack just a pawn in this operation? *He belongs to no one? Is he expendable? Am I?*

CHAPTER 1

Just as Zack Sinclair reached a small ridge, a soft breeze carried an urgent sound on its breath, a sound that didn't belong in the desert.

It was his third day in the hot Sonoran Desert after Mickey had sent him on this damned wild goose chase. He'd wandered all over hell on the hard sun baked ground, which offered little shade, and gone shooting a few doves just to make it look good, but all the time he was looking for something that wasn't there. *Now at last, where are you?*

He wore the well-worn camouflage clothes of a hunter. They almost matched his rugged tanned features. He appeared every bit the recreational bird hunter.

Well-ingrained life-saving instincts jumped into play. He quickly moved into the heavy shadow of a mesquite tree and then rapidly scanned the immediate vicinity. The sounds he had heard were angry voices that didn't fit into this isolated area.

He opened the breach of the superposed twelve-gauge Browning shotgun, pulled out the two 7½ shot birdshot shells, and replaced them with the heavy double ought buckshot rounds that could knock down almost anything. He was all business now as he cocked his ear to pick up any sounds that might indicate the direction and distance of the sound.

Ah, there it is again, he thought as he directed his vision in the direction of the sound's source.

He was in his element now. He smiled to himself as his ice blue gaze raked across the desert to determine his next move. It was time for the stalk. God, how he loved the stalk.

He knew the stalk well; he'd been doing it as long as he could remember. His first instructor had been a grizzled old poacher Zack followed into the Minnesota woods early one day when he was ten years old. He had wanted to see where the old man went in his homemade camouflage hunting clothes that were a work of art of burlap tatters and fabric fragments sewed into a shaggy ensemble. The neighbors called it his Raggedy Ann outfit.

Trying not to be seen, Zack had followed the old man through brush and forest, sometimes so thick the sunlight never touched the ground. The old man had eased around a bush and disappeared right before his eyes, and as Zack had hurried ahead to search for him, he had heard the old man say, "Whatcha lookin' fer, Zack?"

Zack had whirled around to find a smiling weatherworn grizzled old face that was cracked like a county road map. Around his eyes, the deep squint lines contained the dust of decades, and a perpetual tobacco stain hung from the left side of his mouth like a brown Cheetah teardrop. The old geezer's pencil-thin frame was standing ten feet behind him.

"Gee whiz, Mike. How'd you do that?"

"Do what?"

"Disappear like that."

"Din't disppear, Zack. Just blended in," he had said in his slow woodsy drawl as his crinkly eyes squinted at Zack from his well-worn face.

"Boy! Show me how to do that, will ya, huh?" Zack had pleaded.

The ultimate stalk in the North Woods was to sneak up and touch a deer. It had taken Zack two years to do it and that was only after he had learned the most valuable lesson of his life: the stalk.

"Ya gotta learn the animal your huntin' first," the old man had lectured. "Ya gotta learn his habits, how he moves and thinks. Ya gotta unerstan his capabilities, ya know, his strengths and weakness.

His little nuances, I think ya call it. When ya do that, well hell, you can stalk anything, man or beast."

The old man had died three years later but not without teaching Zack everything he could about the woods, the animals, and the stalk.

After graduating from the University of Minnesota with a degree in economics, Zack had known what he wanted to do. He wanted to hunt—hunt anything—so he had signed up in the army as a recon candidate. His marksmanship and skill in the field hadn't gone unnoticed by the sergeant, who had called him over after completing his basic and said, "Young man, I think you should go to graduate school."

His inherent stalking ability virtually made him invisible in the sniper ghillie suit, which was a dramatic improvement over the Raggedy Ann outfit he had used in Minnesota. He had enjoyed disappearing around the new lieutenant when they were on exercises and had driven him nuts until he was reported for insubordination. The day before he was to see the captain, two men in civilian clothes had shown up to talk to him about his shooting skills and disappearing antics.

They had talked to the commanding officer, and instead of a reprimand, he suddenly had a new boss: the Central Intelligence Agency. They had sent him to a base in Texas for training with the special forces. There he had trained in hand-to-hand combat and sniper school. They had left nothing out. Just when he had thought he was really getting good at something, they had moved him to another type of training.

When the pros were done with him, he was a chameleon—a deadly chameleon.

Zack knew he was right above the ongoing argument now. The slope to the ravine below him rolled in such a way that he couldn't see the bottom or the men in the heated discussion.

His sixth sense told him there were more than just the two antagonists; he just couldn't see them.

He worked his way slowly down the slope from one bush to another before moving under a mesquite tree and slowly standing up among the branches. He could see the top of an automobile. *This is a long way from the roadway,* he thought. *This could be what I'm looking for.*

A young Hispanic male wearing black slacks and red golf shirt stood in front of the car Zack had seen from farther up the slope. The Ram Charger was covered in red desert dust. The young man was lean and probably in his thirties. He was yelling at an older Hispanic gentleman who appeared to be in his sixties. The older man was dressed in dark blue slacks and a long-sleeved white shirt. Neither of them belonged in the desert. They were city boys.

The subject of the discussion was an aluminum valise on the hood of the Ram Charger. It was open and full of white plastic packets. The argument was about the payment for the valise.

Between the two men was an open duffel bag that had bundles of dollars and peso notes falling out of it and onto the ground. This was apparently the source of the argument.

From what Zack could understand, the payment was in dollars and pesos. This was the result of the banks of Mexico restricting the acceptance of US dollars for deposit or exchange in an effort to control drug trafficking.

Dollars were hard to come by, and part of the payment was in pesos. Whatever the currency was to be used for, pesos apparently wouldn't satisfy the seller.

Behind the older man, a black Lincoln Town car was parked on the same desert trail. It was facing the Ram, so it had entered the desert from the opposite direction. Zack could see a man behind the wheel of the Lincoln, and his instincts told him there were others in the immediate vicinity; he just couldn't see them from this vantage point.

His instructions were clear: don't be discovered, get photos if possible, get information if possible, and for god's sake, don't create any problems. The big boss, whoever in hell he was, had made that clear. There was to be no international incident.

Just as Zack started to take photos of the area and the two men, the driver of the town car emerged. He was a swarthy, powerfully built, balding man in his midthirties. He wore a blue sport coat and white shirt that was opened deeply in the front, exposing a heavy chest. Dark sunglasses hung on his expressionless face. This was a man of action.

Without hesitation, the man reached into his sport coat and produced an automatic handgun. It was a no-nonsense gun, a large 1911 Colt .45 automatic. He held it with both hands, raised it straight in front of him, and lowered his head so that his gaze met the sighting plane along the top of the gun, all in one smooth conditioned movement. He held the gun between the door and the car itself and took careful aim at one of the antagonists. His deliberate motions gave the unmistakable impression that he was going to shoot some one, and right now.

Another man's head, covered in a baseball cap, appeared at Zack's lower right, facing the driver. The man was about fifty feet away, and he raised his hand and pointed it at the driver of the Lincoln. He was holding something that looked like a black crackerjack box with a small pipe sticking out of the end. Zack recognized it as one of the foreign-made machine pistols that had made their way to the West.

Everyone and everything was moving rapidly now as Zack clicked away, but the unexpected, unreal aspect of the event gave Zack the feeling he was watching a movie in slow motion. He stood transfixed and wouldn't have moved if he hadn't been jarred out of his intrigue as an observer by the rapid explosions that suddenly took place. It was like a crack of lightning followed by a turbulent desert monsoon.

The older man turned with a panicked look on his face, and with his thick legs churning, he ran for the Lincoln.

The younger Mexican jerked a gun out the waistband of the back of his trousers and fired point-blank into the back of the retreating runner. The impact propelled the man forward, and he dropped without moving. The driver of the Lincoln fired the big gun almost in the same instant as the man in the red shirt fired, but he was too late to save the runner. The .45 roared, and the big automatic jumped with each shot.

The first round slammed into the red-shirted Mexican, slamming him against the Ram Charger. The second explosion followed so closely that its impact almost lifted him onto the top of the hood, shattering and spraying the windshield crimson. He slid off the hood, leaving a red smear after him, and crumpled to the ground.

While Zack was watching the driver in fascination, clicking away, the windshield of the Lincoln exploded, a headlight popped, and pieces of paint and debris jumped off the hood of the big car. The driver's shirt erupted with several red spots, which didn't appear to affect him in the slightest as he continued to hammer away with the big gun. He had changed targets after dropping the man in the red shirt; he had moved to the man with the crackerjack box gun, whose amateur shooting continued hammering and spraying the area in a rapid staccato, trying to tear the Lincoln and the driver to pieces.

The crackerjack shooter was slammed backward by shots from the driver's heavy gun and disappeared from view. All hell had broken loose that quiet afternoon. The Ram's windows exploded in a hail of bullets that came from out of sight to Zack's left, somewhere in front of crackerjack. Close to this gun were two other different sounds of muzzle blasts.

There was a lot of lead in the air at one time, all generated in the space of a few seconds, and Zack had the feeling that bullets were flying everywhere without apparent control or design. The trees around the area were dropping small branches and twigs as the bullets crashed and whined through the air. It all started so fast, and he was so mesmerized as an onlooker that it took a few seconds for his instincts to kick in. Finally, he dropped to the ground, hoping a stray bullet wouldn't hit him.

The shooting was easing. Men were yelling and swearing in English, Spanish, and another language Zack didn't understand as they screamed or grunted in pain. In any language, Zack knew what that was about. He had heard those same cries many times in a jungle near a stinking, rat-infested and sluggish river many years ago. Zack hugged the hard desert surface while the shooting and shouting eased. It seemed to go on forever, but it actually only lasted fifteen to twenty seconds, enough time for several hundred rounds to be fired.

Then it stopped as suddenly as it started. The silence was deafening. It was as if everyone and everything was in awe at the noise and destruction that had exploded in this quiet ravine. The only sound was that of the unrelenting soft sigh of the afternoon breeze as it slipped through the trees.

Zack waited and counted the minutes. Damn, he was back in the game. The duffel was still there with the money, and the bodies were still in place. It was quiet—deathly quiet.

His mind was made up. He quietly eased down the slope and covered the ground between his cover and the carnage.

He stopped two feet short of the dry river bed, or arroyo. To his right was crackerjack and a companion, crumpled on the ground, covered in blood, and two more to his left, all unmoving and silent.

Just as Zack was about to step into the sandy wash, his heart jumped in his chest as he heard a wheezy cough to his left. He froze, looking for the source, afraid to move a muscle. His body broke into a cold sweat, and he could feel the little rivulets of sweat start running down his neck and back.

An immense black man started to move in the wash to Zack's left. He was gagging and spitting as he struggled to his knees, searching for a gun. He picked up a large-caliber revolver, which looked puny in his huge hand, and slowly staggered to his feet. His small waist accentuated the tremendous width of his shoulders and the girth of his chest. His huge frame was topped off by a head that was bald and shiny and so small compared to his bearlike body that it appeared like it belonged to a small boy. The man was facing the other way after retrieving the gun and reloading. Zack took advantage of the short time to duck back and hide as best he could by squatting behind a small bush. The cover was terrible, and he was sure he would be seen. If he was seen, he would probably have to shoot the big man.

The giant's yellow golf shirt was so bloody that it seemed impossible he could be alive. When he coughed, bubbles foamed out of the back of his shirt with an ugly hissing noise. He turned slowly and looked around the entire area. He seemed to see the others on the ground, and his gaze actually passed over Zack. For an instant, it seemed they had actually made eye contact.

Zack tracked the man carefully with the barrels of his shotgun, keeping the safety off, thinking that perhaps the man had actually seen him and was just waiting to get into a better shooting position. The giant laboriously made his way out of the wash toward the cars, which were about fifteen feet away from him, parked slightly higher than the arroyo bed.

Wheezing loudly, the large man made his way to the two men lying between the cars. With a grunt, he kicked each of them not too gently in the head to see if he would get a reaction. Staggering with difficulty to the Lincoln, he looked inside, and with a voice that matched the size of his big body, he said with a growl, "Get out, bitch."

Zack was shocked to hear the man talking to someone apparently still alive after the carnage. How could anyone have remained so quiet all this time or even survived this bloodbath?

A whimper came from of the backseat of the Lincoln. A small female voice said in English, "Please, Mongol, don't hurt me." Mongol put the hand with which he was holding the gun on top of the Lincoln and with his other hand reached inside to haul a woman out of the backseat like a rag doll. It was impossible to see her face, as it was shielded by reddish-blond hair that covered her head and shoulders. She was young, slim, and wearing a light blue spandex type mini dress and high heels. He dragged her out of the car and pushed her, stumbling, onto the hood of the car, where he roughly slammed her facedown. She was crying the whole time and begging for Mongol not to hurt her as he was calling her a bitch.

Zack was amazed at the strength the seriously wounded man demonstrated. He pushed the woman around as if she put up no resistance at all. "You fancy bitch, you make one move and I'll kill you on the spot," he said as he staggered over to the Ram Charger. He looked inside and then walked over to the crackerjack box man and his companion.

There was nothing between Mongol and Zack at this point. They were in clear view of one another, and less than twenty feet separated them. If he glanced in Zack's direction, he would easily see Zack and would sure as hell shoot.

Zack covered Mongol's slow progress with the superposed barrels of his shotgun. He was wet with perspiration, and his heart hammered away in his chest. *I've been out of this too long*, he thought as the short walk seemed to take Mongol forever.

He finally reached the two men and kicked each one in the head. With a grunt he turned and started back toward the Lincoln.

Zack froze as Mongol turned his head slowly to face him. They were looking at each other, now less than twenty feet apart. Mongol had the meanest sneer Zack had ever seen, and it turned into a mean, angry snarl.

"Howdy, Mongol."

The girl was stone quiet.

Mongol snapped his head the rest of the way and stared at the muzzle of the shotgun. Then he slowly and deliberately raised his coal-black eyes and looked directly into Zack's eyes. This was a bad man.

The big man said, "Well, well, what have we here? A sightseer?"

"Drop the gun, Mongol, and turn around real slow or I'll kill you where you stand."

The big man laughed, making his shirt bubble, and said, "You're going to kill me? Hell, I'm already dead, man. I just ain't fallen over yet."

With that, the big man moved faster than Zack thought possible; he turned, lunging backward, trying to get out of the line of sight of the shotgun while attempting to swing the big revolver into play.

The shotgun aim traveled smoothly with the man, and the blast at close range caught the giant full in the chest, shoving him backward. The second round hit Mongol in the neck and flipped him over on the ground.

The woman was screaming and convulsing in terror. Then she shuddered and lay limply on the hood, making a soft mewing sound.

Zack quickly snapped open the breach of his gun, which propelled the two ejected cases over his right shoulder, and slapped in two shells he had between the fingers of his left hand before slamming it closed again. He kept the gun pointed at the back of Mongol's head as he walked up to him. When Mongol didn't move immediately, Zack kicked the revolver away.

With Mongol dead, Zack walked over to the Lincoln and took a good look at the woman for the first time. She was still lying on the hood of the car, continuing to sob. Then she attempted to get up and turn around.

Zack put the barrel of the shotgun on her back and gently pushed her back down on the hood of the car. Hoping to keep her quiet, he said, "Look, lady, I just saved your life. Stay where you are and don't look around, and you'll be all right. Do you understand?"

"Oh god, please don't hurt me. Who are you?"

"Be quiet and stay where you are."

"Oh please, oh please—"

"Just stay where you are and don't turn around. Do you understand?"

"Yes, I understand."

"Good," Zack assured her. "Just follow directions and you'll be fine. Don't look at me."

Zack looked around and counted seven people lying on the ground, and he knew he had to check to see if any of them were alive and still a threat. He needed photos of everybody and as much ID he could get. He thought about the girl and thought he'd pass on her. She certainly wasn't a player in this mess.

Starting with the Lincoln, he put two more shotgun shells in his left hand and peered into the front of the car, looking down the twin barrels. The big car was empty, and the driver was lying on his back, legs askew and arms stretched in the shape of a crucifix alongside the open driver's door.

Zack approached the man carefully and touched the muzzle of the shotgun to the man's open eye. No movement.

Next he went around the front of the car and walked over to the men he had thought were the buyer and the seller; he followed the same process. The two men lying between the two cars, obviously the lead players in this game, were both dead.

Zack poked the barrel of the shotgun into the Ram. It was empty.

The crackerjack operator and his partner were both dead. They lay in the hot sand amid spent shell casings and magazines. Zack picked up the crackerjack box gun, ejected the magazine, and upon finding it half full, jammed it back in. He put the safety of shotgun on and let the gun hang in its sling. The small automatic would be a lot easier to carry and give Zack a lot more firepower if he needed it. Both of these men looked Arabic, not Hispanic.

There were a lot of people dead—all killed in a hail of bullets in a matter of seconds.

The man crumpled on the ground where Mongol had risen was an American, a gringo for sure.

He walked back to the Ram, keeping a close eye out for any movement. On the hood of the Ram was a large hard-sided black Samsonite briefcase, and next to it lay the aluminum case with the white packages. He opened the briefcase. It was crammed with bundles of hundred dollar bills in bundles of one hundred.

The aluminum case was an expensive watertight grip that held several dozen tightly wrapped plastic bags filled with a powder; it had the consistency of white talcum powder. Zack hefted one and guessed it weighed a couple of pounds, probably a kilo.

Zack knelt down beside the duffel holding the pesos. The peso bundles were made up of one hundreds, two hundreds, and five hundreds from what he could see. The US dollars were all in one hundreds. How much the duffel bag contained he couldn't even guess. He just knew he wasn't going to leave any of this behind.

Zack walked around the Ram again, looked in the back baggage area, and saw another small black leather valise lying on the floor. The tailgate window was open, so Zack reached in and took it out. He popped both snaps and opened the case. It contained more plastic bags of the white powder. He had never seen street drugs before, but these were not going to make the street if he could help it.

All the Hispanics were heavily jeweled. The gold chains around their necks were laden with crucifixes and other religious symbols. They also wore Rolex watches and diamond rings. Zack walked around and examined the other men on the ground and found they had no jewelry or identification.

He carefully photographed each of them. He got a full-body shot and a close-up facial shot of each of the seven men. The only identification was on the two principals; he photographed them as well.

He wasn't sure how he was going to explain this to Mickey and the company, but he would try.

Zack dumped the contents of the valise filled with dollars into the duffel with the pesos. Then he scooped up the bundles of pesos lying on the ground and threw them in also.

Throwing the now empty briefcase aside, he zipped up the bag and set it aside.

The several bags of white powder that were in the Ram, Zack dumped into the large suitcase with the other bags and forced the lid closed. He snapped it shut and hefted the case.

A plan was forming in Zack's mind. Sonora's hills and mountains were littered with caves of all kinds, worn by the receding sea millions of years ago and the winds of time. The aggregate type rock was easily turned into caves and spectacular pinnacles by nature and time. He would stash the case of drugs in one for now. He wouldn't leave it for another to find and put on the street.

Zack slung the duffel bag shoulder strap over his shoulder, grabbed the suitcase in his right hand, and walked back to the Lincoln and the girl.

"I'm going to leave now. You don't know me, and I don't know you. Let's leave it at that. Count to five hundred. Then get in the Lincoln and drive off. Don't look at me or attempt to follow me. I saved your life once today, but don't press your luck. The keys for the car are still in the ignition. Do you understand?"

After some hesitation, the girl said, "Yes, I understand. Thank you, thank you."

Heaving a sigh of relief after a long walk, Zack dropped the heavy duffel in the wash near a deep dark cave. Then, after crawling in on his hands and knees, he dragged the aluminum case inside. The cave held no signs of being used by any desert dwellers except an occasional passing squirrel or pack rat. There was a cleft in the floor of the cave toward the back. Zack dropped the bag into the crevice in the rocks. He carried in broken limbs and rocks and covered it so no casual observer would see it. He then set a visual trap outside the cave so only he would know if anyone had breached it. Then he headed for the truck.

CHAPTER 2

H e unlocked the camper shell on the bed of the half-ton Ram Charger pickup he'd driven into the desert in the early morning and opened it. He laid the shotgun on the tailgate, stuffed the machine pistol in the duffel bag, and threw it in the back of the truck as far to the front as possible.

Just as Zack picked up the shotgun and started to walk around the truck to get in the cab, he heard the sound of an approaching vehicle coming on hard. He could hear the stones and dirt bouncing off the underside, announcing the vehicle's approach long before he could see it. It was coming from the direction of the Lincoln and the Ram Charger.

Looking frantically to see if he could hide and not be seen by the approaching car, he realized the cab and back of the truck were open and anyone would know that someone was there.

Trying to be casual, Zack walked back to the rear of the pickup and put the shotgun sling over his shoulder again with the breach open. He dropped in two more heavy buckshot rounds and acted like he had just arrived at the pickup.

A black four-door car approached, trailing a plume of brown dust and snapping gravel off the dirt road as it came into view and began to slow down. It was going to stop in the road parallel to Zack's pickup, which was parked off the road by a big earthen water tank.

The dust settled slowly as the car finally rolled to a stop. Zack watched, feeling the sweat run down his back in small rivulets. He had been watching the car all the time through the side of his dark sunglasses. He was trying to act as casual as possible. This was not a police car.

It was a dusty black Buick with heavily tinted windows. The driver lowered his window and looked over at Zack. Zack could see two men in the front seat and two or three more in back. These men were not farmers or ranchers. They wore city clothes and sunglasses, even in the fading light. The driver had an expression like a tombstone.

"*Buenos tardes, senor. Como esta usted?*" (Good afternoon, mister. How are you?) the driver said. Tombstone was a Mexican of medium build, about thirty years old, with a full head of black hair and a mustache. He snarled when he talked; this was a mean man. The man alongside of him was an American with light brown or blond hair; he was of medium build and was smiling from ear to ear. Zack's heart accelerated as he noticed the heavy gold chain hanging on the driver's chest, under his open shirt.

From the backseat of the car, Zack could hear a muffled woman's voice. It sounded like the woman at the shooting. She was speaking in Spanish to one person and then English to another. She was talking to a man in Spanish who was asking her if this was the man. She was saying she didn't know. It sounded like she was near tears and was being pressed for an answer. She continued to say, "No se. No se" (I don't know. I don't know).

Zack played the role of the dumb gringo who couldn't speak Spanish and said, "Howdy, amigo. Sure is a nice day, huh?" If he spoke Spanish, he knew the driver would know he could understand what was going on in the backseat of the car.

Everyone in the backseat was talking in hushed voices now, and he knew he was in trouble. If these men were to start something or get out of the car, he would be one against four or five. If they were like their friends, they would have a lot more firepower than he did, and it would probably be a lot more deadly. He did have the two double ought rounds still in the barrels. As casually as he could, he got the last two double ought rounds out of his vest and palmed them both in his left hand while he was making small talk in English to the driver and casually moving toward the car, acting as if the driver could understand everything he was saying, which he probably could. He had to get out of here without raising their suspicions.

Things had changed in the backseat. The woman now answered, "Si. Possible," meaning yes it's possible it's the man.

Zack casually glanced at the driver, and saw the expression on his face change from not too friendly to damn unfriendly.

Zack thought, *Oh shit. Here it comes.*

Pretending to look away from the car and down the road in the direction from which the big car had just come, Zack carefully watched the driver out of the side of his sunglasses. He knew the driver couldn't tell if he was being observed or not. As Zack pretended to look down the road, he turned his body ever so slightly so that the shotgun, with its breach open in an unthreatening manner, was lined up directly with the driver side window.

The girl was now openly crying in the backseat, and the men were trying to muffle her.

Zack nodded down the road in the direction in which he appeared to be looking and said, "Where does this road lead to?" As he was talking, the driver very slowly and very deliberately raised an automatic handgun up and over the windowsill of the car.

Zack had no doubts that he was going to be shot, and while the driver was being slow so as not to attract attention, Zack did just the opposite. He snapped the breach closed, which brought the barrel directly in line with and inches away from the driver's face, and pulled the trigger.

The shock on the driver's face as he looked down the twin barrels and knew he was about to die was the only indication that anyone in the car knew what was happening. They were complacent in the fact that they knew the driver was about to shoot Zack, and the sudden change in events caught them all off guard.

At point-blank range, the double ought caught the driver full in the face, driving him across the front seat and turning his facial features into a crimson mess. Zack adjusted his aim a couple of inches and squeezed the trigger again, firing directly into the blond head of the smiling American.

The car exploded with activity. Both back doors burst open simultaneously, and the occupants were scrambling to get out.

Zack snapped open the breach, ejecting the shells over his shoulder, and in a practiced motion brought up his left hand with the two spares. In his eagerness, he banged his hand on the barrel, jarring the two shells and almost losing them both. He knew he had to stay in control and couldn't slow down. He couldn't possibly run or duck without being cut down in the middle of the dirt road by the others.

There were two men piling out of the back of the car, and he was still trying to get the shells into the shotgun. It was like a bad dream in which he was running in deep mud, trying to escape something bad, but he just couldn't move fast enough. A gun was starting to line up on Zack from the rear of the car. It was an assault rifle and too big to maneuver in the backseat, and the man was trying to get out with it. Zack could see a head of black hair above a pair of sunglasses behind the gun, and the man's head was starting to appear over the door.

Zack finally got the cartridges lined up, jammed them into the breach, snapped the shotgun closed, and with the barrel pointing at the window of the door, pulled the trigger. The impact tore a golf-ball-sized hole in the rear door window, and the gun fell out of the man's hand as he bounced off the doorjamb.

Zack quickly moved to his left. While aiming through the driver's window, he saw the other man just exiting the car. He pulled the trigger.

Zack knew the two in the front seat had to be dead, but the others, he didn't know, and he couldn't stand around to find out, so he turned and ran. He sprinted around the far side of the pickup, reloading the shotgun with light birdshot as he went. He put two more in his hand and came around behind the rear of the pickup at full tilt, making himself as difficult a target as possible.

The man he shot through the window was on the ground. He wasn't dead but was gaining on it. He was reaching for the AK-47 assault rifle he dropped when Zack had shot him through the window. He had one hand on his huge bubbling wound and was groping with the other for the automatic. He was pawing it into his hand when Zack shot him twice.

After reloading, Zack slowly peeked around the rear of the car and found the other passenger dead on the ground with a 9 mm Glock automatic in his hand.

Zack went back to the door where he had just shot the man with the assault rifle and pushed the tip of the barrel of his gun into the rear compartment. He could see the girl lying in the backseat but couldn't tell if she was dead or alive.

He stepped back from the door and said, "Come out with your hands on your head." He had to repeat it twice, but he finally got a response.

"Okay, don't shoot. I'm coming out."

Zack backed away from the car and stood toward the rear so that he was protected as much as possible. Then he said, "Put your hands on your head and come out on the left side, and come out real slow."

She had to reach out and grip the top of the door to steady herself as she stepped over the man on the ground. She stood facing Zack with her knees locked together and her hands on her head.

She was a mess; her face, contorted in horror, was swollen and puffy from crying and being knocked around. This was the same girl he had seen earlier all right; she had on the same blue dress, but her long blond hair was disheveled and matted, and the dress splattered with dark red blotches. She was shaking and sobbing uncontrollably, but it was her.

This was the first time he had really looked at the woman. She could really be a looker under different circumstances. Her trim, voluptuous body was obviously well cared for. Her hands were narrow and delicate, ending in long scarlet well-kept fingernails.

There was also something in her that shined through, something that showed she'd had a hard life.

"Walk over to the pickup and put your hands on the hood," he said. "Don't even think of putting your hands anywhere else."

She stood in shock as Zack repeated the demand and motioned with the shotgun for her to move.

She blinked a couple of times as his demand slowly registered. With her knees still pressed together to keep her from falling, she whimpered and staggered over to the pickup. With utter exhaustion she put her hands on the hood and leaned on the truck.

He put his boot between her ankles and nudged her. "Stand with your feet apart."

Keeping a close eye on her, Zack went back to the Buick and picked up two Glocks. It seemed all the men had one. He put the safety on one and pushed it into his game pouch in the back of his shooting vest. He checked the magazine of the other and kept it in his hand. Then he put the shotgun on safety and let it hang in its sling before he approached the girl again.

He put the hand holding the Glock on her back as he reached around her with his other hand to pat her down.

The tight Lycra dress she was wearing didn't leave much to the imagination, but he wasn't taking any chances. He ran his hands completely over her body, including her full head of hair, while she sobbed and shivered.

Convinced she was unarmed, he looked at the shot-up Buick automobile. Its engine was still running where it sat in the middle of the dirt road. Someone could come along at any time, and he had to do something and do it fast.

Zack told the girl to get in the backseat of the pickup and that he was going to reset the alarm. "If you try to open a door, the alarm will go off, and you don't want to do that," he growled.

Zack had parked his pickup in the early morning under a mesquite tree near a big stock tank, a man-made watering hole for cattle. He ran to the top of the large earthen works that had been bulldozed to catch runoff when it rained, and he saw it was about two-thirds full of slimy murky green-black water. The tank was about seventy-five to one hundred feet across, and he guessed about fifteen feet deep.

A plan was beginning to take shape in Zack's mind as he hurried back to the pickup and turned off the alarm. He unloaded the shotgun and put it in its case. Then he took off his vest and put it in the back of the pickup. After that, he closed the tailgate and reset the alarm. He kept one of the 9 mm Glocks.

With his little digital camera, he took pictures of the scene and the four men who were the occupants of the car. He was mumbling to himself as he worked. "How in the hell am I going to explain this one to Mickey?"

When he had several pictures captured, he started to lift the bald man, who appeared to be Mexican American, into the backseat of the Buick. When he was pushing the man into the car, he spotted a plastic grocery bag on the floor by the backseat. He reached in, hauled it out, and looked inside. They had collected all the watches, jewelry, and wallets from the shooting scene. They had ransacked the bodies for anything of value or identification. He rapidly took several photos of the bag's contents and the identifications.

As Zack was lifting the big man, he felt an all too familiar shape in the man's back pocket. He boosted the man into the seat, rolled him over, and emptied the pocket. Handcuffs. Zack didn't have to look far for identification. A United States Border Patrol badge was in his side pocket. The man who had tried to kill him was a Border Patrol agent. Officer Rodriquez was in the drug business. That probably explained the blond man in the front seat as well, he thought. He slammed the door closed, turned to the pickup, and saw the girl watching him.

The other rear seat passenger was thin and dark skinned but too angular and heavily featured for a Mexican. He carried no identification but had a Middle-Eastern look about him that Zack noticed as he jammed him into the backseat. Then he hauled out the woman's big purse from the floor and threw it over by the pickup.

He pushed the driver aside, over on top of the other man in the front seat. There was too much gore for him to want do any body searches. "Hell, I didn't sign on for this," he muttered as he put on shooting gloves and began digging in the men's pockets. Officer Wilson was also in the drug business.

He turned the pickup's alarm off, got an old rug out of the truck bed, and threw it on the driver's seat of the car to cover the glass and blood. He got in and drove the car off the dirt road and onto the sidetrack that ran up the side of the big water tank, the one the bulldozers had used to build the tank. He turned the car so it faced into the tank, backed up about thirty feet, and put the car in park. Both the right front and left rear windows were shot out, so it would sink fast. He jammed the driver's foot down on the accelerator, got out of the car, and held the door open as he pushed down on the brake pedal to release the gear. He reached in, pushed the gearshift from *park* to *drive*, and jumped back as he slammed the door.

The power of the big car spun the tires on the desert surface before digging in and hurtling the car down the slope and into water. The car hit the water with a tremendous splash. The momentum carried it about thirty feet into the tank before the engine died and the vehicle slowly drifted and began to sink. Within seconds the slime-covered car sank, leaving nothing but green belching bubbles on the water's previously smooth surface.

Zack hurried back to the truck and turned off the alarm. After reaching under the front seat, he slid out a machete he used for camping.

The girl began to whimper when she saw it. Zack said, "Get out of the truck. I have a job for you. Just don't try anything foolish, and move it fast."

The girl started to become hysterical and spoke to him for the first time, begging Zack not to kill her. "Are you mafia or police?" she asked. "You must be American mafia because you aren't a Mexican for sure, and you don't act like the police. Please don't kill me. I'm only the girlfriend of Nicholas," she rambled, staring at the machete.

"I'm not any of those. I'm just a guy out bird hunting who was in the wrong place at the wrong time. But remember, as far as you're concerned, I was in the right place at the right time, and don't forget it. I'm not going to kill you. I just need your help because it'll be dark soon, and we have some work to do before then. If I was going to kill you, I would have done it when you were on the Lincoln. Now get out of there," he said impatiently.

"I'm sorry. I appreciate what you did for me. I won't forget it. But please don't hurt me."

Zack cut two large branches from a bushy creosote bush near the tank and gave her one. "Use it like a broom and brush out all the tire marks and footprints of everyone, including yours. Start in the road and work your way toward the tank."

She hobbled off to where Zack indicated. Once she got started, Zack got into the pickup, started the engine, and moved onto the roadway. He caught sight of the woman out of the corner of his eye, standing and staring at him with a fearful look on her face.

"What the hell's the matter now?" he growled.

"You're going to leave me out here in the desert with all these dead men. I don't even know where I am. I'll die out here." The panic in her voice was obvious.

"Damn it, woman, I'm not leaving you here, but if you don't get busy, I may. I'm moving the truck so we can wipe out the tire marks from where it was parked."

She looked relieved and frantically began sweeping the desert floor.

With the two of them working, it only took a few minutes to finish. Zack walked over everything. He checked where the pickup was parked and where he had moved it, the tank sides, the approach, and everything in the area of the shooting. He brushed dirt over the bloodstains on the road, picked up and counted the shotgun shells, and examined the whole area closely.

The girl had calmed down now. The exercise had worked wonders; she was no longer shaking, but her tear-streaked face looked tired and strung out. He poured a cup of ice water from the big jug in the pickup and offered it to her, but she was hesitant to accept it. Zack took a swallow and then handed the cup to her.

"Don't worry. It's all right. Why did you ask if I am police or mafia? Who are you people, and where do you all come from? Earlier today I was just a guy hunting. Then I ran into you crazy people. I thought at first that maybe someone needed help. I made the mistake of going to find out. Why do you ask if I am mafia?"

She hesitated, looked around as if expecting to see someone, and then looked Zack directly in the eye as she said, "Because you kill like a professional. You've done this before. I've been with Nicholas for a long time, and I've seen your kind before."

Zack's gut reaction was surprise before he conceded that what she said was true. She was traveling with dangerous people and had probably seen a lot, but she didn't appear to be the type who could lie very well.

Avoiding a response, he said, "Okay, get in the truck, on the backseat, and lay down out of sight. I don't want to see your head above the seat until I say so. You speak very good English. I want you to talk to me in English all the time."

While she crawled reluctantly into the backseat, Zack took a clean towel and wrapped some ice from the cooler in it for an ice pack. Then he handed it to her and told her to use it on her face.

Her surprise showed on her face, and Zack said, "I want you down all the time, and don't get up unless I tell you to. You be fair with me, and I'll be fair with you. Do you understand?"

"Yes," she said as she curled up on the backseat, held the cold pack to her eyes, and let out a moan.

Zack dug in the cooler for a Tecate beer, snapped the tab, and drove off into the rapidly dying desert light, grumbling. He had to get out of here, and now.

CHAPTER 3

Driving through the night was like driving through ink. It took almost an hour to find the main road in the tangle of little trails that finally brought him out. The girl began to talk in a release of nervous energy, and he just let her ramble on. He wasn't really listening or interested in a lot of what she had to say; he was intent on driving and trying to figure out what to do with her. The guns and jewelry, he had sent down with the Buick except for the two Glocks and all the clips he could find, but the money he had in the back of the pickup.

The woman was a burden. Without her he could go on his way, but he couldn't just drop her off anywhere. She knew what he looked like and could and probably would tell someone. Then he would be the hunted.

Her name was Veronica, and the people in the desert, she referred to as the Nicholas family. The built-up nervous energy bubbled out of her like a fountain, and she liked to talk about herself. Zack was going to hear her whole life story if he liked it or not, so he just let her ramble. Maybe he would learn something.

Nicholas, her lover and protector, called her Veronica during tender moments, but she normally went by the name Goldie. The woman she called Rosa had given her the name Goldie when she "bought her contract" from Veronica's father. Rosa called Veronica "mi puta de oro" (my golden whore). Rosa would be in charge now with Nicholas gone and so many of the family unaccounted for. The family was made up of only fifteen or so regular members, and the rest where hired on for specific jobs. Nicholas, the headman whose blood was soaking into the desert sand, was the heart now cut out of the family, and Rosa would fill the void.

Zack asked, "What do you mean when you say she bought your contract from your father?"

It sounded like her life had started out innocently enough, but after being raped by an uncle and then dealing with a pregnancy, a botched abortion, a hospital stay, and bills, her life had rapidly gone downhill. This Rosa character had simply purchased her from the family. No magic, no problem.

She told her tale without emotion, as though it happened every day.

"She paid the hospital, the doctor, and my mother a lot of money. She bought me. I was to be a household maid. I was weak and tired, but Rosa seemed to be a nice lady and promised to look after me. I thought she must be very rich, and she made all the arrangements to move me by car to her home in Guadalajara. The doctor agreed, my mom agreed, everyone was paid, and I was set up for a different life."

"Wait a minute," he interrupted her. "What was that white powder in the suitcase?"

Without hesitation, she admitted, "It's heroin. Or you Americans call it horse."

"You were in the heroin business?"

"No, not really," she stammered. "I mean, Nicholas was only a banker. He was the middleman. He financed the people who brought the drugs into the country and made arrangements to find a buyer. He handled all the money. The people who brought the drugs into Mexico had some big project they were financing, and Nicholas helped them to get into the United States."

"Where did the heroin come from?"

"From Afghanistan. They're the largest producers and suppliers in the world, I think," she said in a singsong voice. "They bring it into Mexico easily, and then that's where Nicholas comes in. He finds a buyer and gets them into the United States if they want to go."

Incredulously he asked, "You mean he gets people from Afghanistan into the United States?"

"Oh sure. Lots of people go into the United States."

"Did this Nicholas ever deal with the Columbians or get drugs from South America?"

"No, he said they were too violent and couldn't agree on any procedure. Every day was different."

"Did you know the guys in the Buick?"

"Sure. The two border guys have worked with Nicholas a long time, and the other guy in the backseat was Omar something or other. He was one of the guys who brought the drugs in. He was going to the United States, and the driver was one of the Tijuana group that was buying the heroin. They were waiting for us to drive out, and when we didn't show up, they came looking for us."

"Why did Omar want to go to the United States?"

"I don't know. He was just one of the men who brought the heroin in. Nicholas has moved a lot of those guys into the United States. They pay very well to be transported without a passport."

"Isn't it hard to get them across the border?" he asked.

"Heavens no. The border is just a rat hole. Did you know they even have tunnels across the border in the cities? As long as you have the right connection, it's a cakewalk. He never got involved in actually moving the drugs or people across the border. He just set them up with the people who could do it. They crossed with the Mexicans that the coyotes were moving."

"Was Omar from Afghanistan?"

"I don't know, mister. Those Arab types came from all over the Middle East. I don't know where he came from."

"Did a lot of these Arab type people cross into the United States?" He continued to press.

"Oh sure. They've been crossing for at least four or five years that I know of."

"You don't think that maybe they might be terrorists or something?"

"Heavens no. They're in the drug business," she muttered under her breath.

Zack could tell he'd hit a sore spot. She was getting hesitant in talking about it now. In an attempt to keep her talking, he rapidly changed the subject back to her. She liked talking about herself.

He asked, "Where did you work in Guadalajara?"

"I told you. I lived with Rosa in her house. The first year or so I was working as a maid. She taught me how to clean rooms and care for her. She was very good to me for those first couple of years."

"What was Rosa's business? Why did she want you there?"

"Well, she changed my whole life. She taught me how to act like a lady. I thought all this time that she was doing this because she was genuinely fond of me, as she started taking me places with her. She was in the agency or escort business for escorts and high-class girls for businessmen. It fit in well with what Nicholas was doing. I have to rest awhile," she said as she yawned.

In Mexico, he knew, police would stop everyone when they were watching a region. He had to get himself and the girl away from this area as far and as fast as possible and undercover before daylight. The territory where the shooting had taken place had all the earmarks of a drug deal gone bad, and they would be looking at everyone, searching every vehicle for people, drugs, guns, and money.

When Zack heard Veronica stirring, he said, "There isn't much traffic here, so you can sit up for a while." In an attempt to keep her talking, he said, "Who is this Nicholas person you talk about? Tell me about yourself and the family."

She yawned and said, "Nicholas was the don, the big boss, the bank, and he made all the decisions. Rosa was his right hand back then, but Nicholas was the person who made it all happen. Nicholas would let Rosa romance the men who came to town as investors in different business deals they made. She was good at it and very beautiful." She hesitated and said, "When I talk about it now, it's kind of embarrassing."

"No, no, go ahead. I'm not embarrassed, and you're a professional, so tell me about yourself. I think your story is fascinating."

"I did everything. Rosa even had me on at the club, or her disco, for a month. That was a tough time, I can tell you, but it got a lot easier as time went on. The hours were long and late, the smoke was terrible, and I had drunk men pawing all over me while I tried to work them for drinks. Those girls who work there have a hard life. They earn their money. I kept away from the Arabs who bring in the drugs. They hang out there all the time. They had tons of money, but they treated the girls like their goats. Christ, they were terrible."

"The Arabs went to the disco? I didn't think they could do such a thing," he said.

"When they were in town, they were at the disco a lot. Rosa brought them in, and they liked what they saw. They liked what was available. She knew how they were, and they threw their drug money around like it was just paper. Rosa made a fortune off those guys."

"If they were throwing money around, why didn't you stay in the disco?"

"No way! They treated the girls like there was no tomorrow."

"What happened?"

The stories she told were descriptive and described the dramatic life of a high-end call girl. She was very physical and proud of her work and her connections. She talked of drugs and smuggling with the ease of someone explaining his or her job at the Dairy Queen. This woman knew a lot about what was going on in the smuggling and drug business. She was completely unemotional about it. Maybe that was why she showed so little emotion about loosing Nicholas, he thought. In an attempt to get her back on the subject of the Arabs, as she called them, he asked, "How often do these Arabs bring in heroin?"

"Oh, four or five times a year they come to Guadalajara, and that's when Nicholas gets involved. I don't know who else they deliver to."

"Guadalajara? That's a long way from the border. Why Guadalajara?"

"Drugs come into Mexico, into the big cities through ports on both coasts. The big cities are where the business is done. The border states only facilitate the movement to the States. All the arrangements are made in Guadalajara, and the movement starts from there."

"Do the Arabs always cross over with the heroin?"

"Oh no. It goes by itself mostly, but the Arabs come in and cross at different times. They come into Guadalajara, and Nicholas sends them to a tutoring school that teaches them enough Spanish and English to get along. That way they can blend in with the Mexicans going north. It's standard procedure. Guadalajara is a big city. You can get anything done there."

"Why do they want to go to the United States?"

"How would I know, mister? I don't get involved. I just see it all happen."

"Did this Nicholas facilitate the movement of anyone else other than the Arabs you talk about?" he asked in hope of broadening the discussion and digging a little deeper.

"I don't really know. I just know about the ones Rosa got involved with. Generally these people throw their money around, and that's where I came in," she said with a chuckle.

"How about Europeans or Russians?"

"Oh, I'm sure that sometimes the people he handles come from Europe. I usually don't ask too many questions, you know."

"Gosh, you really lead an exciting life, Veronica. Have any Russians come in lately?"

"I don't think so, but there is one in Guadalajara right now, I think. I heard some of those people talking about him. I haven't seen him, only heard his name mentioned."

"Oh, what's his name?" he said as his interest perked up.

"They just call him Little Ivan. He's going up for the holidays. That's all I know," she said with the ease of someone talking to a close friend.

Zack realized he'd struck gold with this woman. He couldn't have asked for more. The problem was that the action was in Guadalajara and not in Sonora at all.

"This Ivan guy, is he hanging out at the disco like the rest of them?"

"I don't know, mister. I told you, I don't get to the disco that much now that Nicholas has taken me in," she said with some hostility. "Why the hell you asking me all these questions anyway?" she said.

"Hey, Veronica, I'm really excited about your lifestyle, that's all. I think you live a really exciting life. My life is boring as hell alongside yours. I'm just interested. It's not every day I get to save the life of a beautiful woman who leads such an exciting life. I think it's great," he said with as much enthusiasm as he could muster.

"Well, I guess it is at that. I've had a great time, but Rosa and I are kind of on the outs, and she's really pissed that I moved in with Nicholas and left her." She sighed. "She had a good thing going with me. I made her a hell of a lot of money. I'm not complaining, you understand. I made a lot of money with her too and got expensive gifts and big tips. Hell, I did real well. I could make as much in a week with her as I could with a really good job in Mexico City in a year," she said with a proud attitude.

"Are you going to go back to Guadalajara now? It looks to me like you may be in some danger after what happened out there in the desert."

"I'm through in Guadalajara. I can't go back there to live. If I went back to Rosa, I'm afraid she'd hook me up on drugs and dump me in a disco. I'd die there. No, I'll move on. I think I'll go to Spain."

"How do you plan to get there? Do you have a passport?"

With a chuckle she said, "Mister, I've got three passports. I've squirreled enough money away to take me just about anywhere. I'm okay. You want to go?"

"Gosh, that sounds like a lot of fun, but I'll pass. I've got a little business to take care of, and that's how I eat, you know. Some of us are working stiffs. I'd love to live your exciting life, but sorry, can't make it."

"Oh well." She yawned. "Look, I'm really worn-out after all that mess today. That's as close as I've ever been, and I don't like it. That's it for me," she said as she squirmed down in the seat.

CHAPTER 4

Zack drove slowly down the cobblestone street and then pulled into the stylishly covered six car parking area, which served as the roof for his little casa that overlooked San Carlos Bay. He killed the engine and sat in the truck for a long moment, waiting and listening. The heady scent of magnolia trees lingered in the late evening, and the gentle breeze swished the leaves of the oleanders, casting long flittering shadowy shapes into the deserted street. There was no one about, and the bay was calm and smooth as glass. The lights from the homes on the far side of the bay reflected across the water in long yellow and white streaks. Some twinkled like diamonds, all a mirror of the landscape, climbing out of the water in the big sailboat bay, completing the double image.

Zack got out of the truck and rolled the seat forward to check on the sleeping girl. She was curled up on the backseat, still sound asleep. He looked up and down the dark cobblestone street to confirm it was deserted before he woke her. Startled from her sleep, Veronica looked around wildly with a panicked expression on her face. She swung her arms wildly before her eyes settled on Zack's now familiar features. Reluctantly, she nodded to confirm his hand movements urging her to stay quiet as he literally hustled her out of the truck, down the stairs, and through a sliding glass door. Once she realized she was being offered a sanctuary, she moved and responded without hesitation, displaying a trust that surprised Zack, as if she always did exactly what she was told.

After showing her the layout of his little house, Zack took her through to the bathroom and the only bedroom, tossing towels and a bathrobe on the bed as he went.

"Take a shower. You can use this robe. I'll fix you a drink if you'd like. Maybe it will help you relax. You're safe now. You'll be okay here."

"No thanks, I just need a shower."

Once she was in the shower, Zack went back out to the pickup and unloaded all his gear. His shotgun, he left in the pickup, but the two Glocks and the magazines he took into the garage and stashed in an empty box. He jammed the duffel bag into a big Igloo cooler and wedged it into the corner of the storage area under a bunch of fishing gear.

Back inside, Zack fixed himself a Canadian Club and went outside to sit on the patio. He needed to collect his thoughts to determine just what he was going to tell Mickey when he called him.

If this girl was known to the police, or picked up by the police, then he had a real problem. The "family" posed a whole new enigma. The more he could find out about them, the safer he would be and the better he could plan. They were a ruthless bunch, dealing in just about anything that was illegal.

He walked back into the house and saw her sitting on the side of the bed, wrapped in the bathrobe, looking worn-out and puzzled.

"Okay, so you got me here in this little place. Just what is it, and what do you plan to do with me now?" she said with the first real concern he'd heard all evening from her.

"I don't know," he said. "Let's just take it one step at a time. Maybe tomorrow we can look at the whole picture a little clearer."

She nodded and said, "I don't even know your name or why you're helping me—"

"Look, we'll talk tomorrow. My name is Zack. That's all you need to know. Right now what we both need is rest. Go to bed. We'll talk in the morning."

She couldn't leave the apartment without going up the stairs and through the carport where the truck was, so this seemed like the best place to call Mickey, as she couldn't hear him talking.

He attached the camera to the satphone like he had been shown and dialed Mickey. It was after midnight on the East Coast, and it took three rings to get Mickey to pick up.

Without any salutation, Mickey said, "Where the hell have you been, Zack? You were supposed to call in hours ago. Hey, Zack. You okay?" he said with obvious concern.

"Hi, Mickey. I just got in from a delightful dove hunt. I'm sure glad you dragged me into this thing. It's a thrill a minute here. I have some interesting pics for you guys to review. You ready to receive?"

"All right, Zack. You're my man. Hold on while I get to my computer."

Zack could hear Mickey's wife asking what was going on and Mickey telling her that Zack couldn't tell time. She told him to say hi for her as he raced to his computer.

"Okay, Zack. I'm back. I'm plugged in, and old Bertha is warming up. What do you have?"

"Here they come, Mickey. I'll try to identify each one as they come with the information that I have."

Zack forwarded each picture he had taken in turn and told Mickey everything he knew about their identity that he had learned from Veronica or from the identification some had carried. When they had all gone through, he waited … and waited.

Mickey was silent.

"Hey, Mickey. You getting these?" he said, holding back a chuckle.

When Mickey finally found his voice, he stammered, "Christ, Zack, these guys are all dead. Some are shot completely to hell. Oh my god, what the fuck is going on down there?" he stammered.

"Hell, Mickey, they wouldn't hold still. That's the only way I could get photos for you guys. You were so intent on photos, I did the best I could," he said, doing his best to keep from laughing. It was no laughing matter, but he thought it was time to jerk his pal around a little.

"Jesus Christ, Zack. Have you lost it?" he yelled. "How in hell am I going to explain these? Jesus, Zack, tell me this isn't true."

"You're right, Mickey. It's not quite true."

Zack went on for a half hour, giving Mickey the details of the day and answering questions Mickey hammered at him. When Mickey was finished asking questions, Zack thought perhaps he'd lost contact as the phone went silent.

"You still there, Mickey?"

"Oh yeah." He sighed. "I'm still here. What the hell have we got ourselves into, Zack?"

"I really don't know, Mickey, but this woman is a fount of information, and if I can keep her talking, we can learn a lot. This thing is leading to Guadalajara, and we need a Guadalajara plan, and we need it now. You had a job down there once. As I recall, it was a few years back. Do you still have any connections?"

Mickey had developed a relationship with an assistant district attorney in Guadalajara four years ago when he was acting as an undercover DEA agent for the CIA. There had been some dramatic shootings in Guadalajara that the CIA was interested in, but they didn't want the CIA exposure, so Mickey posed as a DEA agent with full authority.

They worked out the semblance of a plan that would change as needed, but he would call his connection, who he felt was reliable, and introduce Zack as a DEA agent who happened to be in possession of a great deal of drugs and wanted to get them off the street. He felt he could rely on his contact to help Zack. They couldn't disclose their mission, but he felt the attorney general had enough clout to help him out.

"This is one hard woman, Mickey. The way things are going, I think I can get what we need. I think I'll offer her a 'go home free card' from the DEA and see if that works. Time is of the essence, and we can't spend time fooling around trying to get her to talk. By the time that works, if she ever would, it would be too late. There are too many people involved, and something tells me that this is big, Mickey."

"Damn. I hope you know what you're doing, Zack. This is a real mess. The 'go home free card' sounds good. I'll get you some authority on that. I'll talk to the man and tell him what's going on. I'll pass the Little Ivan thing along and see if he can help. You could be right. Keep me informed. Call on schedule, please. I worry about you. And Pat says hi."

"Give her my love, Mickey, and tell your boss that I'm moving on with this thing. We don't have time to fool around with protocol. Something just isn't right here."

CHAPTER 5

Mickey was so apprehensive about reporting to Walker that he was starting to break into a sweat.

The door finally opened, and he faced the man. *This is going to be damn difficult*, he thought as he glanced around the room to make sure they were alone as they sat down.

When he finally finished his report, the old man's bushy eyebrows got lower and lower until they almost covered his squinting eyes.

"You mean to tell me, Mickey, that there are a whole bunch of dead drug runners who killed each other except for the assist by your man Sinclair and that there is a car full of drug runners, illegal Arabs, and a couple of dirty US Border Patrol agents, all of whom planned on sneaking into the United States along with illegal drugs, and that some of them have just flat disappeared. Is that right?" he growled as he leaned forward on his desk.

"Yes sir," Mickey stammered, squirming in his seat.

"And yet, as a result of all this, we somehow avoided an international incident, no one knows we were there, we've identified a bunch of people, and we got the drugs and a whore to boot. Is that about the size of it?"

"Yes sir." He gulped.

Walker leaned back in his chair. A big smile crept across his face as he gazed up at the ceiling, shaking his head. "Damn, I love this guy, Mickey. You guys were right; he's a hell of an agent all right.

Let him follow up on his hunch about the woman and Guadalajara. I'll take care of the 'go home free card.' I think that's a great idea. He's been right so far. See what he can do down there. We've got zero hard info and zero time, but we've learned one hell of a lot so far. This Little Ivan guy thing doesn't give us much to work on, but I'll look into it. I'll get one of my researchers on it right away and see what he can come up with.

"Damn, I love that guy. I've got to meet him, Mickey," he said, shaking his head. "I wish we had a whole bunch like him. The old 'Independents' are gone forever, but boy how they could think, act, and put things together. Hell, Mickey, nowadays they have to have a congressional committee just to tell 'em when to pee," he grumbled. "We're bogged down with bureaucracy."

"Okay, follow up, Mickey. Move as fast as you can," he said, dismissing him as he leaned forward on his desk, shaking his head with a smile, and picked up a thick report. "Keep me posted," he mumbled without looking up.

Mickey made his way to the door without looking back or saying a word. He had to figure out what had just happened. Walker's voice stopped him as he opened the door.

"Hey, Mickey. Good job, man. Good job. I know you got that horse on a loose rein, but don't let it get too loose," the old man said with a smile on his face and a glint in his eye.

CHAPTER 6

Zack hustled through a hot shower, and after checking to make sure the woman was in bed, he lay down on the well-worn leather living room couch. He had placed an empty beer can on top of the doorknob of the bedroom. If she turned the knob, the can would hit the tile floor and wake him up, so he allowed himself to drift into oblivion as he watched the twinkling reflection of the lights in the bay beyond the open drapes.

At twilight he got up, removed the beer can, and started a pot of coffee. His mouth tasted like the bottom of a birdcage, and his eyes felt like they had broken glass in them as he staggered down the hall to the bathroom and pushed the door open. Veronica was standing in front of the vanity with her back to the door. She was combing her hair without the bathrobe on, displaying the golden curves of her voluptuous body.

He mumbled softly, closing the door as he exited and took in the heavily perfumed womanly scent she left behind. He thought about her lifestyle.

Veronica was in the white terry robe and lounging on the terrace overlooking the bay with a cup of strong Combate Mexican coffee when Zack got out of the shower. He sat opposite her and said, "Okay, let's talk. We have a problem, and I just may be able to help."

Veronica didn't respond for a long time. She nervously shuffled her feet back and forth and then said, "I think I told you too much last night as it is. I don't know what to say."

"If you expect me to help you, then you'd better come clean with me so I know exactly what's ahead for us and we can plan accordingly. You told me Rosa was probably running the affairs of the family. Why don't you just call her and tell her what's going on?"

"Okay, I'll be straight with you," she stammered. "I can't go back to Rosa, period. I've been living with Nicholas for the last few years. I just can't go back."

"So you don't want to go back and work for the family?"

"Oh no. Once you're in, it's pretty difficult to get out. I would like to do something else." She hesitated for a while and then said, "Maybe this is my chance." "When I first found out what was really happening, it was too late to make an easy exit, so the best I could do was to keep away from the really bad stuff, the dealings, and the other problems. It just hasn't turned out that way."

"Nicholas said drugs or booze, what's the difference. They were all controlled substances at some time. He just helped supply the demand. He has so many legitimate investments that he was looking to get out of the business. The only people he was working with now were those Arabs. He moved them in and out of the United States and financed their drug sales. When he was finished with them, he was getting out of the drug business. This was supposed to be his last deal. 'The Project,' whatever it was, was going to be the last of it. There was big money in it for him, so he was out," she said with a sad sigh.

"Isn't that always the way of it? I don't know what all it involved. It was complicated. He took me along; otherwise, I would not have been anywhere near there. He said this was it and we were going to go on a long vacation, just the two of us."

"What kind of a project was he working on?"

"I have no idea, and I didn't ask. I never got involved in Nicholas's business. I was just his woman, nothing more. All I know is that they were moving these Arab guys in and out of the United States just like everyone else Nicholas moved. They did haul stuff with them from time to time."

"What kind of stuff did they haul with them?"

"I really don't know. I know they had a big argument a couple of weeks ago over something they wanted to take to the United States. For some reason they couldn't agree on it."

"Look, Veronica. Maybe I can help you disappear. I used to work with the DEA in the States and have a lot of contacts there. If you help them, then I can help you. I can get you anywhere you want to go without anyone ever knowing about it."

The woman just stared at him with fear in her eyes that she could not hide.

"You are DEA for god's sake?"

"I used to be."

"Oh my god. Are you going to arrest me now or something?"

"No, nothing of the kind, Veronica; I'm on your side. I want to help you. Believe me. I want you to think about what I said. I can help you, but first I'll go into town and get you some clothes and shoes. Then I think we should head for the border. I don't want you seen in public if at all possible. I'd like you to talk to my friends in the United States about all this. They can help you a great deal."

Veronica nodded and said, "Zack, the first thing that I want to do is call my girlfriend Carmen and find out what's going on in Guadalajara. She knows pretty much what is happening because Rosa hangs out at the Crystal Disco a lot now. She knows I went with Nicholas to the desert, and I haven't called her. She needs to now what's happened so she can make her own plans."

"Then can we head to the border?"

"I've told you before, I'm not getting involved with any of this government shit. Nicholas was involved with government officials. Hell, all government officials are crooks. I don't want to have anything to do with them. If the government in Guadalajara hears about Nicholas and they hear I'm alive, my days are numbered. I'm out of here, Zack. I'm gone. You want to help me get out or not?"

"Look, Veronica. I stuck my neck out and saved your life. You owe me. There's no two ways about it. I need to know as much information as you can tell me, as now my life is on the line as well as yours. Remember me? I'm just a guy out bird hunting who was in the wrong place at the wrong time and risked his life to keep you alive. Now to keep me alive I need to know what is going on so I can dodge the bullet. Do you understand what I'm telling you?"

"Yes, I understand, but we're not going to the border. I'm not talking to any of your friends. If I'm in the States, these people can and will find me; then I'll be dead. Your government leaks like a sieve too, you know. I need to get to Mazatlan. I can handle it from there; you with me?"

"Yes, I'm with you, and I'll help you, but you must tell me everything you know about this last deal. It's damn important, Veronica. Your life and mine may damn well depend on it. I want to hear it, and I want to hear it now."

Veronica retold her story but added that there was something funny about this Russian they were bringing in. Apparently he was a small person, because they called him Little Ivan. It related back to the argument they were having about crossing the border. They talked about bringing Ivan into the United States in a box or suitcase. He wasn't walking. That didn't make a lot of sense to her, but it was a big deal.

"Hell, that guy can't be that small, can he? Another thing, those Arabs said they were all brothers. I know damn well they were not brothers; they didn't even look alike. I don't know why they would say that, but it was real important to them."

He stared out across the bay, watching the sport fishing boats move out for a day of fishing as he mulled over what she had said. Something wasn't right here for sure. The bit about Little Ivan's travel plans didn't make any sense at all.

"Okay. I'll take you to a long-distance telephone service in Guaymas after I get you some suitable clothes. It's only fifteen minutes from here, and it'll be a lot safer in case the call is traced. You stay here and don't go outside while I'm gone. Remember, your life depends on it. I'll go into town and get you some jeans and shirts to wear, maybe a wig or a baseball cap. When I come back, we can go to Guaymas, and you can call your girlfriend. We have to be damn careful that you aren't seen anywhere."

CHAPTER 7

Zack pulled into a Leys supermarket parking lot and told Veronica where the pay phones where. He could see them from the pickup. While she was on the phone, he called Mickey.

Zack had to let Mickey know that there was no chance of getting the girl to the United States or having him or any other government agent talk to her. She'd made her position very clear. He told him everything he knew so far and how they crossed the border.

"I know they've found dozens of those tunnels you talk about, Zack. How they dig them without being caught is beyond me."

"Get me set up with the DEA in Guadalajara, Mickey, ASAP. That's where I need to be. I'm going to take her to Mazatlan. She has connections there, and maybe they can help.

"She tells me the Russian called Little Ivan that she told me about isn't going to be walking across the border. There was some argument as to how he was going to cross, and they discussed putting him in a box or a suitcase. You know, Mickey, maybe Little Ivan isn't a person at all. Maybe it's an object of some kind, and it sounds like it's probably in Guadalajara. She also said that the Arabs all referred to each other as brothers, but they obviously were not related."

"Okay, pal, I'll pass that on. I hope you know what you're doing. I'll get the DEA set up for you in Guadalajara. You're going to have to move fast, as it sounds like you may have some people out there hunting for you now."

"I think you're right, Mickey. That's why we're on the move. Get me all the satellite info you can on that area. See what you have. Someone has to have been there by now. She's coming, Mickey. I'm shutting down."

"I'll do what I can."

CHAPTER 8

When Nicholas hadn't called Rosa by midnight, she knew something was very wrong and called one of the family's contract workers in Obregon Sonora, which was located about an hour from the meeting place where the trade was supposed to be made. Jesus knew where the exchange would take place, as Jesus had been there in the past with other family members and Rosa made it clear he was to leave immediately, find out what happened, and call her back, regardless of the time.

It was almost three o'clock in the morning when a nervous chain-smoking Rosa picked up the telephone on the first ring. She could hear the bad connection of a cellular phone that was out of range.

"Holy Mother, Rosa, they are all dead out here. There's nothing here but two cars and a lot of bodies. I don't even know most of them, but Nicholas is dead. Rosa, what the hell is going on?"

"I don't know, Jesus, but I'll sure as hell find out. Tell me who's there. Are you sure it's Nicholas?"

"Hell yes it's Nicholas. I know him. What's going to happen now, Rosa?"

"Don't worry about that right now, Jesus. Just tell me how many people are there and who they are if you can. If you don't know them, then describe them for me. Is the stuff there?"

"There's nothing here, Rosa. The bodies and the place have been picked clean. Everyone's been shot, and there's not a gun in sight. Your stuff isn't here either. All that's here are bodies."

He gave Rosa a body count, identified those he knew, and described the rest. When he had finished, he said, "Look, Rosa, I'm getting the hell out of here. I don't want to be seen anywhere near this place. The varmints are already here, and the police won't be far behind. You do what you want." With that, Rosa's phone went dead.

Rosa couldn't believe that their man Chuy could be involved in a rip-off; he wasn't even that smart. Steve, that other border guy, and that Arab—she could never remember his name—could do it. Those bastards very likely may have decided to go into business on their own, but the Arabs needed the money. That just didn't make sense.

She called the Crown Plaza Hotel for the four Arabs who were waiting, like herself, and called a meeting.

Rosa had finally calmed down enough to organize her thoughts by the time the four men made their way into the dimly lit disco. The early morning music was loud and pounding, and the smoke was stale and thick as they passed unnoticed by the gyrating naked girl on the dimly lit stage. Men of all ages and descriptions ogled the bored girl, who did her best to act like she was enjoying her work. The Arabs made their way up the narrow dimly lit wooden stairs to Rosa's office, which overlooked the smoky dance floor through a one-way glass window. They pushed the door open without knocking.

"Okay, Rosa, what's going on? Why'd you call us down here in the middle of the night? Something must be wrong. Nouri didn't call us tonight as planned," said the thin man who had declared himself the spokesman. He was shorter than Rosa's five foot six inches, poorly shaved, and dark skinned like the rest of the Arabs. They were all dressed in wrinkled slacks and a variety of golf shirts.

Rosa told them everything she knew and watched them closely to see if they knew more than they put on. She knew men and could read them like a book, even the Arabs.

A half hour later, when the heated discussion had died down, Rosa agreed to take them to Sonora and introduce them to people she assured them they could trust. They would check with their contacts to see if they tried to cross the border and would put out a watch for the backup car. It was probably a worthless effort, she knew, but it was worth a try.

"I can do more here in Guadalajara than I can in Sonora, so as soon as I get you set up, I'll come back and try to rally some people to help us out. You follow exactly what the men I introduce you to will tell you, and stay out of sight as much as possible. We can't get you across the border if you get picked up for something in Sonora, so be careful."

Habib, the skinny, shabbily dressed, self-appointed boss of the team, said, "Rosa, I don't like this. Where are the others who were with them? There is something going on here that we don't know about, and I don't like it at all. We should have heard from our people. They would have called no matter where they are. This is a bad omen. I feel it," he said as he bowed his head.

CHAPTER 9

armen told Veronica that Rosa was upset and charging around the disco like a wild person. There was nothing on the news—nothing. Veronica said Carmen was very disturbed to hear about the deaths and that she would keep her eyes and ears open and would report to her when Veronica called her. Carmen would stay in her room, as it was easier and safer to talk on her own cell phone. She told Veronica that Rosa was busy calling everyone and was being pressed by some of those Arabs that hung around the disco. They had chartered an airplane and were going to fly to Sonora.

Instinct told Zack to stay out of sight. If Carmen were right, Sonora would not be the place to be. Once they found the bodies, Sonora would be searched and the border closely watched.

"Veronica, tell me exactly what you said to Carmen," he demanded as he pulled the truck into traffic. "Repeat the whole conversation exactly, word for word, and leave nothing out."

When Veronica was through, he knew it just didn't sound right. He should have been in the telephone booth with her. He'd forgotten the cardinal rule: trust no one. He'd been out of the business too long.

"Where did you tell her you were?"

Veronica hesitated too long, and Zack knew he was in trouble. "Damn it, Veronica, where did you tell her you were?"

"Oh well." She sighed. "I told her I was with you, but I didn't tell her your name. Honest, I didn't."

"Where did you tell her you were?" he insisted.

Veronica knew she was in trouble now. She looked away from Zack and hung her head as she looked out the window. "I told her we were in Guaymas Sonora. Gee, I'm sorry. I didn't think. She's my friend, for god's sake. If I can't trust her, who can I trust?"

Zack just shook his head as he rubbed the back of his neck again. There was no need to explain. It would fall on deaf ears anyway. "What did you tell her about me?"

"Nothing. Well, I mean, I said you were a gringo and you came along and saved me from Mongol, and you had … Carmen hates Mongol. He hurt her once. She hates him."

"What did you tell her? Our lives depend on it, Veronica. Don't you understand that? What were you going to say when you said that I had … and then stopped? Let's hear it, Veronica, and now!"

"I told her you killed Mongol, that's all."

"How did you tell her we were traveling?"

"In a red truck."

"Damn. Don't you see? The truck is a death trap at this point; we've got to stay out of sight. Damn," he grumbled. *This woman is as dumb as a rock*, he thought. "What did you tell her about the other four in the car?"

"I didn't say anything about them. Honest. I swear."

He looked out the window and watched the seagulls coasting along the offshore breeze as he put his thoughts together. *What's done is done. There is no way we can stay in Sonora or go north to the border. If these people can travel as easily as they are and have the money to buy the obvious connections with the border people, we just can't risk it. They'll ask everyone, including the long-distance service, looking for answers.*

"Okay. After dark we drive south. We can't stay in Sonora, and we can't drive this truck in daylight. The burgundy color looks almost black at night. If they're coming north, we go south. What makes you think Carmen is not going to tell Rosa everything you talked about?"

"Carmen is my friend. She wouldn't tell Rosa anything. And besides, Rosa is flying to Sonora too."

"You didn't say that."

"Well …" She sighed. "That's what I meant when I said they were flying to Sonora."

"Where in Sonora?"

"I don't know."

"Well, if they knew the deal was going down near Guaymas, you can bet that's exactly where they will be. Right in our backyard."

It was a hard late drive to Mazatlan. Zack had called ahead for a room at the Playa Hotel so that they could check in late. They pulled off the beach road through the manned gate into the hotel complex at two thirty in the morning. He checked them into a seaside room and unpacked. Two more Americans would go unnoticed in this tourist sanctuary by the sea, and in her new garb, Veronica was hardly anyone to look at.

Veronica curled up on the sofa, deep in thought, but Zack was exhausted. He'd slept poorly the night before with the woman in his house, and the five hundred mile drive to Mazatlan had worn him out.

At least he felt he had as much information from Veronica as he was going to get at this point. He could hardly keep his eyes open when he crawled into one of the queen-sized beds and immediately slipped into a deep sleep.

She took him in the night like a bat. So quiet and soft was her lovemaking that he could have been dreaming the whole thing. She had completely engulfed him before he knew she was on him. Her skin was as smooth as silk and as soft as velvet. The woman, her scent, and the soft sound of the sea slipped him back into a warm, deep sleep.

It was almost noon when the sounds of the sea filtered into his consciousness and he opened his eyes. Damn, he'd overslept. Immediately he knew something was wrong. It was too quiet. A quick glance around the room told him Veronica was gone. He pulled open the closet door and saw that her clothes were gone. He walked back across the room to look in his carry bag, into which he had stuffed two packets of dollars and a fistful of pesos before leaving San Carlos. That's when he saw the envelope on the TV.

Zack,

Thank you for what you did for me. I owe you my life. The best I can do for you is leave. I only put you in danger.

I know what I'm doing, believe me. I'll be out of the country and won't be coming back. I thought over what we talked about, and this is my chance to start over.

You're a nice man, so don't look for me or get further involved in this affair. Go home and forget it all. Get on with your life. I'm sorry you got involved, but if you hadn't, I'd be dead. My being with you is far too dangerous.

Thanks for the loan and please stay out of California. Thank you from the bottom of my heart.

Love,
Veronica

He read it twice. She was right, but why stay out of California? She might be going there, or maybe Ivan was. She could easily make it in that community and would fit right in.

"I'd better see how much I loaned her," he mumbled as he picked up the carry bag.

About half the pesos and all but a thousand dollars were missing. *Easy come, easy go*, he thought as he began to put together his things. It was time to call Mickey and make his next plan. This one had fallen apart in the middle of the night.

When he told Mickey of the woman's disappearance, Mickey was furious. "Christ, Zack. How could you let her get away? I thought you were trying to make a contact there."

"It's a long story, Mickey. Apparently the Guadalajara Arabs are going to Sonora someplace in a chartered plane, and that's the last place I want to be with her. She wouldn't think of going to the police: if she did, she would be dead. She's a pretty savvy lady when it comes to those things. I had to keep her undercover all the time. What I do I know is that these Arabs are probably in Sonora now, and there may be others there as well who will be trying to cross into Arizona. I don't know that for a fact, but it's a very real possibility. Some of those guys at the drug buy sure looked the part, as I told you. The home free card didn't work. She had her own plan, and I need to move on with the Guadalajara plan right away. I need to meet this Rosa woman. She, I believe, is the key to this operation."

"Zack, this is important. Get your ass to Tucson immediately. Call me with your arrival time, and I'll set up a meeting. We can talk about all this then. We need to sit down and talk. This thing has a whole new dimension. I can't discuss it on the phone. Get here pronto, Zack."

"Where? Your office?"

"No, Zack. This is too sensitive to meet here. We'll meet in your townhouse in Tucson at the El Conquistador. You just tell me when you'll be there, and I'll be there."

When they met in Arizona the next day, and after the preliminaries were over, Mickey said, "I've got some things to show you, Zack, and we have a lot to talk about. You'll see why we couldn't do this anyplace where there might have been anyone else around."

Mickey had set up a slide projector in Zack's townhouse on the dining room table and aimed it at a bare wall as he loaded it and talked. They both sat on dining room chairs to view the slides. The only sound in the room was the soft movement of air from the air conditioners.

"Let me tell you what we have here. This, Zack, is Little Ivan. It's a nuclear artillery projectile. It's 152 millimeters wide, and it's a very sophisticated piece of weaponry."

"Holy shit!" was all Zack could say.

"Let me give you a little background so you will know just what we think we are up against." Mickey went through the entire program he had received from Walker: the history, the background, and their best guesstimates.

When he was done, all Zack could do was stare at him.

"Christ. Do you mean to tell me that the people I will be dealing with in Guadalajara are actually involved in smuggling a nuclear device into the United States?"

"It all fits. I'm afraid so. This is a top priority matter, and we need all the intelligence we can get. We've put people on the border with Mexico, but from what you say it sounds like anyone can just walk in and out anytime they want."

Zack said, "Well, somehow it appears from what you say that these Arabs have apparently come up with one of these. I don't know where it came from, but it's in Mexico for sure and probably in Guadalajara."

"Remember, whoever these people are, they can just as easily take it to Washington or Houston. We have to locate Ivan. If they have IEU or plutonium, we need to locate that also. I've been well briefed, Zack. I know we can't go to the Mexicans on this for help. Hell, we don't even know who's involved, and it sounds like its well up the ladder. From what you told me, you know that better than any of us. I don't think some of the people involved really know just what they're involved in, and I'm sure many of them don't even care.

"The Border Patrol guys on the take are doing it for the bucks and think that drugs and people are coming in anyway, so they might as well get in on it. We don't know who's involved there either, but we can probably push for a sudden rotation in the field. That should help for the short term at least. Let me show you some other pictures, Zack, and see if you can identify anybody. I know you thought some of these people at the site were Arabs. What makes you think that?"

"When I lifted the man into the Buick, his features were not right for a Mexican. They were heavy, and his build was slight.

The hair wasn't right. I can't put a finger on it, but it wasn't right. Remember, it was twilight, and the light was bad. I think he also had a beard until recently. When I thought of that in hindsight, I think the man who was standing by the Ram Charger had the same features."

"What makes you think they had beards recently?"

"Their tan and skin tone and texture were lighter on the bottom part of their faces than their foreheads and noses."

"Good observation. I'm going to show you some pictures of people and see if you can identify any of them for us."

He ran through twenty pictures of people of Arab decent with beards and computer renditions of them without beards and with short hair. He narrated each slide with presumed names and contacts to terrorist groups. Zack couldn't recognize any of them no matter how hard he tried.

"I'm sorry, Mickey. I don't think any of them fit the people I saw. But remember, the light was bad, and I didn't have a lot of time to observe. I just wanted out of there."

"I think Veronica was window dressing. She filled a role but was not involved in any management decisions and had very limited actual knowledge of what was going on. Whatever Veronica learned was probably from Nicholas's bed." Zack told Mickey about her cryptic note to stay out of California. It was now interpreted to surely be a warning. But where in California was the question. If Little Ivan was that small, it could go and be anywhere at any time.

They discussed the massive amounts of heroin they had processed through the Nicholas family and the money that apparently stayed in Mexico. By simple calculation, it had to be in excess of fifty million dollars. It seemed that the drugs were funded in Afghanistan from another source so that most of the cash could stay in Mexico.

They were moving Little Ivan to the United States, and they wanted it there before the holidays—the biggest consumer spending time of the year. A nuclear explosion at any place in the United States would stop shopping and spending in its tracks. The retail sector would be devastated. The trickle-down effect to manufacturing and other sectors would kill the American economy, regardless of where the bomb went off.

"How difficult would it be to transport?" Zack asked.

"Remember, the entire projectile is only about six inches wide. When you take off the casing and balancing material, and remove a sophisticated receiver or altimeter for arming, you now have a package that you can carry in a large briefcase or a backpack. Instead of an artillery piece, the delivery system now becomes a fanatic, and there appears to be no shortage of them. So movement is not a problem.

"We know a lot of enriched fuel has disappeared from the USSR. The inventory of waste material was terrible prior to Minatom. Everyone felt that nuclear fuel was too dangerous to fool around with, so no one was worried. The Russian bureaucracy just never took into account the fanatical suicide bomber. The suicide bomber knows he's going to evaporate anyway, so why not carry along a little HEW or plutonium for the added results? Remember, the Russians were more worried about us than anyone. They would have no reason to think this stuff was going to Arab nations, especially when they were having trouble with them themselves."

"What are the added results?"

"Well, the bang isn't any bigger, but the fallout is a hell of a lot dirtier. The 152 was designed to be pretty clean and had very little tritium fallout. But add a little nuclear garbage to any sizeable explosion like this and you have a nuclear wasteland.

"Now you see why you're here. We need to know where Little Ivan is, where it's going, and if one actually is in Mexico. Zack, we need you on the ground at all costs. We'll give you everything you need: equipment, manpower, you name it. You're the only one on the inside, Zack. We need you there, and we just can't bring in a bunch of people we really don't know. All that is going to do is push Ivan underground somewhere, and we need him up and available and not going into deep hiding."

"I don't know if I can find out much more until I get to Guadalajara. Hopefully that's where the answers will be. I think this Rosa is the key. Veronica obviously didn't know anything about Ivan. I'm sure. She thinks they are in the drug business. But it's obviously connected."

"Ivan's out there somewhere. We have to find it. If he's out there, I'll bet there's some nuclear waste out there also. Too much is missing not to show up somewhere. We can only guess that Hussein had one or two of these 152s. We can only guess that there may have been others in the Middle East. This is as close as we've come to one, and the damn thing is on our back porch!" he said in a heavy voice. "We've got to find it.

"Now, the problem with Ivan in Mexico is that Mexico isn't our enemy. Ivan just comes into the States and *bang*. Who's responsible? We don't know, and it makes it damn hard to retaliate," Mickey said as he nervously walked around the room.

Zack looked through the photos again as Mickey talked. "They can eat us up piece by piece, and there isn't a damn thing we can do about it. The people who bring the bomb in evaporate in the explosion. Everyone denies it. Our enemies all over the world cheer," Mickey said as he rubbed his forehead. He continued, "We're in a tough spot on this, Zack, and we sure as hell have to stop Ivan."

"We've talked to the president on this, Zack; he has to know. He agrees with our evaluation. We'd be looking for a needle in a haystack and probably tip everyone off and lose control. There is no way we can move around down there snooping for Ivan and not tip them off. We want them to think nothing has changed and no one knows what's going on. That's why you have to stay on top of it. It's damn important that we find Ivan before he finds us. It sounds like this drug deal is the final thing to put it all together. We need you to delay that transfer for as long as possible without being obvious."

Zack sat staring at the ceiling for a moment and then said, "Okay, equipment I can use, but there is no way I can get anyone else openly involved. Our DEA plan is a one-man situation. It may be nice to have some backup stashed away down there if I need them, and I'll need sophisticated communications for sure. I'll create a list of the things I think we'll need."

Mickey and Zack talked late into the night. Zack filled him in on his plan to get the drugs turned over to the authorities through Mickey's contact without jeopardizing himself and his plan to meet Rosa, the leader of the family unit.

"It sounds dangerous, Zack. What about the actual people you will be dealing with? Things are pretty loose down there, you know."

"I know, Mickey. I'll have to rely on your contact. That's the best we can hope for. If something changes, I'll let you know as it goes along. I'm starting to think of an idea that may appeal to the government down there. Haven't worked out all the details yet, but I think it will lead me to this Rosa woman. I think she just may be the key. We just can't tell the people down there what's really happening until we know whose side they're on and if they know what this is really all about. I'll keep you informed."

CHAPTER 10

When Zack called the attorney the next morning, his conversation was hesitant. He didn't know what to expect, regardless of Mickey's assurances. He didn't trust politicians and didn't want to get involved with another agency. Mr. Chavez was way ahead of him and assured Zack that he was a good friend of Mickey's and that he understood Zack's position. He asked that Zack come to Guadalajara as soon as possible. "All expenses will be paid, Senor Sinclair. We will be happy to have you as our guest."

Zack was comfortable in his first-class accommodations as the Aero Mexico 747 plowed through the gray smog generated by the big city. It looked like they were flying underwater as the thick haze enclosed the Boeing. *Thank god for high technology and radar,* Zack thought as the view from his window changed to solid gray. The captain announced in a casual voice that they would land in Guadalajara at 3:30 p.m. on schedule.

He followed the crowd off the airplane to the bag retrieval area with the feeling that he was constantly jockeying for position as the passengers moved in and out of line, craning their necks, looking for loved ones and familiar faces.

The line was long and slow in the customs checkpoint. Zack rolled his bag along behind him, listening to the constant din of music, babbling people and Spanish announcements that sounded like they were coming from the inside of a barrel. He was thinking of his meeting with the attorney with some apprehension when a man's quiet voice behind him said, "Senor Sinclair?"

Hesitantly, Zack turned and saw a middle-aged man with thick black hair. He wore the official government garb of black pants and a white shirt and was smiling at him, surprisingly without the ever-present dark sunglasses. The pleasant man was a little shorter than Zack's six feet, and he had the soft physical appearance of a desk jockey.

Zack glanced around, and his mind raced ahead. He said, "Yes, I'm Zack Sinclair. May I help you?" Perhaps he was being arrested and hauled off to jail, or worse, but the man's smiling face remained friendly.

The man flipped open a wallet and showed Zack his photo identification and said his name was Eduardo Chavez. "I'm not related to the world champion prize fighter either," he said as his eyes crinkled and his smile grew larger. "You'll be seeing a lot of me, so please call me Eduardo. Senor Camacho sent me to drive you into town. Please, let me take your bag for you," he said, promptly motioning for a young man to take Zack's Samsonite suitcase.

"I haven't passed through customs yet," said Zack, pointing to the line.

"I'll take care of that for you, senor," Eduardo said.

As Zack followed his bag around the long line of passengers at the customs desk, Mr. Chavez merely waved to the stiff standing chief inspector, who nodded with respect.

The drive into the city was slow and noisy, even in the attorney's big car.

"The man you will meet is Senor Camacho. He's a politician first and foremost. He has connections with the old guard and the new, including this Nicholas Bosque. Who they all are, I don't know, and I don't ask. I've outlined your efforts in getting the drugs to us, and he is very anxious to talk to you. Zack, you and I—we need to be on the level with each other. That way I can help you all I can, and you can trust me."

"You need to know, Eduardo, I don't like politicians. I go a long way back with them, and I don't trust them."

The attorney laughed and continued, "As I told you, we've made reservations for you at the Hotel Frances, senor, as it is just across the street from our headquarters. If you prefer, we can put you up somewhere else, in a more modern hotel. This one dates back to before your Pilgrims even arrived in America, you know, but it's very clean, and it's handy for us."

"No, the Frances is one of my favorite hotels, and I like the central location. It'll be just fine."

"Yes, we heard that you are very familiar with our country, and we hope that your stay in Guadalajara is pleasant and successful. I'll do everything I can to make your trip enjoyable."

The driver pulled the Chevrolet van with heavily tinted windows to the curb and parked directly in front of the hotel on Maestranza, the small one-way street that separated the hotel from the government building. The driver unloaded Zack's bag and gave it to the doorman. The manager was obviously expecting Zack and had him preregistered. He took personal charge of seeing that the bellman took Zack's bag and escorted him into the ancient French-styled glassed-in open elevator that hung in an ornate steel cage. With a groan, the huge man-sized pulleys whirled and took him to the fourth floor. Once in the room, the bellman opened the ancient French windows overlooking one of the town squares and quietly left. Zack dumped his gear but didn't unpack, as Eduardo was waiting in the lobby.

As he rode down in the elevator, he saw Eduardo talking to the hotel manager, who was nodding profusely. Eduardo was heavier than Zack's 190 pounds, and his office softness showed, but the man's charm and sincerity put him in a class of his own.

Zack walked up to them and said, "Your hotel is as lovely as ever, senor. I'm sure I'm going to enjoy my stay here."

"Mister Sinclair and I have an appointment, so we must leave, senor, but be sure to take good care of our guest," said Eduardo as he took Zack's arm.

Zack walked with Eduardo across the crowded cobblestone street and marveled at the old limestone building that was gracefully showing its age of almost three centuries. The small street was not crowded, but the one-way traffic was fierce. They trekked up the well-worn stone stairs in the cavernous stairwell to the echoes of chattering ladies pointing out details in the huge ancient murals on the walls that lined the stairwell to a group of uninterested students who were more interested in looking at each other and giggling.

On the second floor, Eduardo pushed open an unmarked door badly in need of paint that led to the attorney's office. Several of the decades-old gray steel desks had manual typewriters still clattering away even though the black face of a computer screen stared unused into the room from atop each desk.

An overworked bulky middle-aged woman in a bright floral dress barely had time to acknowledge them as she guarded the inner sanctum of the attorney general's office. It was her domain, and she manned the only wooden desk in the room.

"We're expected," Eduardo told her with authority as they walked through the heavy wooden door into a large office that was Spartan at best. It was in need of paint and very utilitarian. The hand-carved heavy wooden antique desk had three or four portfolios stacked on the left side and two large silver framed photos showing a happy family. The man behind the desk matched the one in the photo with a pleasant brunette woman and two smiling children. Two high-backed black leather chairs, well-worn and cracked with age, faced the desk and looked out huge French windows overlooking a small park surrounding a beautiful iron gazebo bandstand in the center. The Mexican flag was well displayed in the office, and the poorly painted walls were covered with framed photos of various dignitaries. The man behind the desk with his back to the French windows looked up as Eduardo entered. He stood up, smiling.

"Ah, Senor Sinclair, a real pleasure. Thank you for coming," he said with a politician's professional smile as he extended his hand.

"Please have a seat. I am Ricardo Camacho. May I get you something to drink? Perhaps a soda or coffee?"

"No, nothing for me. Thank you, senor," Zack said.

"Senor Sinclair, we are pleased that you have come to help us. We are looking forward to a successful and profitable relationship. Please call me Ricardo if you would. May I call you Zack?"

"Of course."

Ricardo extracted from a filing cabinet behind his desk a file that was four inches thick and had all the dog-ears of age. "This is the file on our friend, Rosa Sanchez Villareal. We take it out, add to it, and put it away. We should have disposed of her years ago," he said, still smiling as he shrugged, "but she's had very good protection in her godfather. He was one of the untouchables. I knew him well," he said with a knowing smile. "Now that the family head is gone, we can do something about it, but we must be very careful that we don't step on the wrong toes, if you know what I mean."

Zack gave the expected nod of acknowledgment and wondered why he was hearing this.

"Well, the last administration started to clean up the politics in Mexico," Ricardo said as he gazed around the room. "And this administration is continuing on with that process, but it's a very slow process indeed. I'm sure you have read about Narco politics in Mexico, and Central and South America. It's a way of life, and it even reaches into the United States. A man named Nicholas Hernandez Bosque headed the Nicholas family. He was an old-time mafia politician. He knew everyone and paid off all the right people. He was indeed very strong politically, well connected, and very wealthy. He came from the old school where drugs were not a part of business, but he got into it as a banker. Supply and demand, you know. He ..." Ricardo paused as if in recollection. "He ran a pretty clean operation, investing heavily in the local economy, and he owned several business properties, all the time keeping a low profile," he said almost apologetically.

Then he smiled and said, "His family was small but very powerful, had excellent credit, and could call on any number of people at any time because his word was solid gold. He had this Rosa working for him, and she's a looker too, I might add. Now that he's gone, we don't want her around. We want her and the remainder of the family taken care of. We would like the publicity of the arrests, of course, as it is politically smart at this time, and we can now possibly get away with it if we work it right. It must be done correctly. The old guard that protected Nicholas will look the other way we think if we work it right, and it will be good for the funding we receive from the United States for drug enforcement."

"Why are you telling me all this? Why not just drive up to her house and arrest her and the rest of her gang, if that's what they are, and let it go at that? What's the big deal? Just bag 'em up, throw them in jail, and forget it."

With a condescending smile, Ricardo rocked back in his big chair. "Well, it's not quite as easy as that. You see, I don't know who all the people are in her inner circle, and we don't know who she is using in her *gang*, as you call it. I was kept out of that information. We don't really know who she associates herself with. If we arrest her, then they all go out and get jobs with other families, or someone else takes over the Nicholas family, and we gain nothing. We want to get them all together at one time so we can take care of them all at once. That's where you come in."

"Wait a minute," said an excited Zack. "What do you mean that's where I come in? I'm here to make arrangements to give you some drugs I picked up in the Sonoran Desert, to get them off the street. That's the only reason I'm here. I'm DEA, remember?"

The politician went on like he hadn't heard a thing Zack had said. As he casually gazed around the room, he continued, "We feel that you have certain qualities and knowledge you can use to entice her into making a drug deal with you that will allow us to arrest her and the whole family. You would call it a 'sting' operation, I believe.

We think we have a plan we would like to talk to you about and see if you can help us."

While Ricardo was talking, he removed a second file from the cabinet and opened it. This file had Zack's picture prominently displayed in the inside of the front cover. It was an old *Phoenix Gazette* photo Zack recognized from an awards banquet several years ago. Ricardo wanted Zack to know that he knew all about him.

Grumbling, Zack said, "Before we go anywhere with your plan, as you call it, and before you even tell me what your plan is, I would like to know what's going on. I see you have a file on me, and I'd like to know what that file is and where it came from."

The attorney leaned back in his chair with a smug expression on his face; he was every bit in control. "I contacted a friend of mine in the governor's office in Phoenix, Arizona. I have many connections, you see. He faxed me the things I requested out of their file. We were interested in knowing what type of person you are and how you became involved in this drug operation and the resulting deaths. We found it rather curious that you should just pop up in this matter. A man of your caliber and background could be a dangerous person if you were working for the wrong people, you understand," he said with a smug, stern political face.

"Did you lure me down here so you could examine me relative to the drug deal and the deaths and to see if I was involved, or am I here because you want me to work with you in this sting operation you are talking about? I understood from Mr. O'Leary that you people promised me immunity and protection if I came down here on the behalf of DEA. Now you sound like I'm a suspect in your problem or working for you. Just how do I fit into this mess anyway? I don't want anything to do with it. It is not my problem. It sounds like yours."

"No, please. I'm sorry if I made you feel uncomfortable or feel like you are the subject of this investigation," he said with a condescending smile. "Believe me, that is not the case. We know that you were … ah … hunting and just happened on the drug exchange area, and we know that you were not, and are not, a part of this matter or any other drug deals. Senor O'Leary explained all that to Eduardo. We feel fortunate that it was you who was involved because we do need your help, and you are an American, and we need an American. You have a financial reputation and military training to act independently. That is exactly what we need."

"Ricardo, I'm no longer in the military. That was a long time ago. I'm a semiretired DEA agent, as you know, on special assignment. If you read my file you would know that I would really be of no use to you. I'm a semiretired financial planner as well, as you can see. I don't know the police business, and you need your police to handle this matter, not me."

"We don't need the police involved in this, Mr. Sinclair. They are unreliable; we need you," Ricardo said as he slowly leaned back in his chair, forming a little teepee with his thin hands as he stared up at the slow-moving antique ceiling fan.

Zack could feel the cold enter the room. He said, "Senor Camacho, believe me when I say I appreciate your problem, but I didn't come down here to work for you or anyone else, and I sure don't want to get involved in the drug trade. I just want to give you the drugs I took from the scene of the drug deal that went terribly wrong. I just want them off the street."

The smile disappeared from the attorney's face and was replaced by a surly, arrogant look from a man who knew he was in complete control of his surroundings. The ruthless politician in him showed through as he looked down his thin nose at Zack.

"Ah, well, Senor Sinclair, you see it's like this," he said with a smirk. "You have a little boat in San Carlos, Sonora, I believe. It could be very possible that the local authorities would get a call from the Federal Judicial Police and have it searched. I'm sure that they would probably find some of the drugs on that boat. It would be a shame to have it confiscated, I'm sure. Houses are seized as well if there are drugs found in them, as you probably know. Have you ever seen one of our jails here in Mexico, Senor Sinclair?" he said as he raised his eyebrows. "They aren't like the country clubs you run in the United States. Yes, they are really quite different." There was no pretense of a smile or congeniality. This was a ruthless politician who was going to get his way to feather his bed at everyone else's expense.

The muscles in Zack's jaws flexed as he ground his teeth together, and his hand instinctively went to the back of his neck, where he rubbed an ugly scar from when a lady in black pajamas had tried to cut his head off in a stinking hellhole in Vietnam. One of his big failings was trusting people.

He'd turned his back on the frail woman, who had claimed she was just an innocent farmer, when she cut him with the big machetelike rice knife. And here he was again, trusting a stranger and being blackmailed by a politician.

As Ricardo ranted on about all the things that could happen to an uncooperative Zack, he glanced over at Eduardo and found that Eduardo was in shock. His fingers had bitten into the leather armrests of his chair; he was ready to jump to his feet.

"So you see," he continued, "it is the very price you pay for your reputation. It's the price you must pay, Senor Sinclair. You're perfect for the job," he said as he confidently watched Zack squirm in his chair. "It would be a political nightmare if a DEA agent was involved in the drug business. It's happened before, you know."

The silence hung like lead in the room. It was broken by an anxious Eduardo, who said, "But, Ricardo, Senor Sinclair came down here to tell us where the drugs are and—"

He was cut off with an arrogant wave of a well-manicured hand.

"So you see, Senor Sinclair, your help is needed and expected, but you will not go without compensation, believe me," Ricardo said as the tone in his voice again turned friendly and the smile returned. "You will be well paid for your help."

"So you're saying I have no choice in this matter. If I don't cooperate my boat and house will be seized and I'll be sent to jail. Is that what you're saying?"

After a long delay, while the politician stared at Zack with his black eyes and rocked back in his big chair, relaxed and with his hands folded, Ricardo said in a very quiet voice, "You're very perceptive, Senor Sinclair."

Zack was stunned. He was trapped in a foreign country by another damn self-serving politician who was probably acting independently out of authority and promoting his own agenda and career, and there wasn't a damn thing he could do about it. He knew the type; Washington was full of them.

After a long silence, a sweating Zack said, "Well, to start with, you can give me a letter signed by some federal official that gives me complete immunity from arrest or prosecution of any sort as a result of anything that has arisen or may arise, and states I am working with you for the state and federal government. I also want this same thing from the states of Jalisco and Sonora or any place else this matter may take us. I also want a written guarantee from you that my house and boat will not be seized or disturbed in any way."

"Well, perhaps that's premature," Camacho said with a sly grin. "But I'm sure we can arrange that when this matter is over."

"I don't think so. If you know me as well as you say you do, then I don't think you want me as your enemy. I think you want and need my cooperation or you wouldn't be forcing me into this."

"Is that a threat, Senor Sinclair?"

Zack openly judged the distance between the two of them and delayed his answer just long enough to give the man a moment to think about what he'd said. He not too subtly moved his body in such a way that the muscles tensed into a catlike spring mode. The message was very clear: this is a dangerous man—a very dangerous man—and he was too damn close.

Very quietly Zack responded, "Of course not. It's reality. If you want my help in your scheme of things, then there are certain assurances I need before I do anything, regardless of what you say."

Ricardo had not missed Zack's calculation of space and time. Swinging around to face the assistant attorney while he continued to stare at his hands, he said, "*Hmm*, well yes, I think we can work that out. Don't you, Eduardo?"

With confusion still showing on his face, Eduardo stammered and cleared his throat, "Ah, well yes, I know you can handle that. Definitely."

Then in a light, friendly tone as if nothing had happened, Ricardo smiled and said, "Yes, well absolutely. It will be taken care of immediately. I have the authority to sign on behalf of the federal government, and the states are not a problem, I assure you."

"Depending on what we are talking about after I hear your plan, I'll need money for expenses."

"Of course. We can arrange for you to use a Visa card or cash, whichever you prefer," he said as he rolled his eyes. "But first let's discuss the plan and what we would like you to do."

"Pardon me, Senor Camacho. I don't mean to interrupt, but it's late in the day, and I would rather not hear about your plan or how I fit into it until such time as you can hand me the documentation we've talked about. Your office can put together the federal documentation and have the states fax something signed by the governor or some other person of authority of each state. I won't buy a letter from some low-ranking official; I want an official document signed and stamped by someone with authority, and the same from the federal government, with all the proper seals. If you can put that together by tomorrow morning, we can meet at noon and discuss this further. I'm sure you can see my point of view. I will cooperate in any way that I can, but I want to make sure I'm not just working my way into one of the prisons you talked about."

"Absolutely, senor. No problem. This will all be taken care of immediately," Ricardo said with a smile as he leaned back in his chair with accomplishment. "I understand that you know where the heroin in located and the subject of the drug deal that went bad involving Nicholas Hernandez Bosque. Can you tell me about it?"

"Ricardo, please hear me," Zack said, looking directly at the attorney. "You're asking me to become involved in something that may not be legal or ethical. It's most certainly dangerous, and you are now asking me about drugs that I really know nothing about. I have no idea what the drugs are. This is the first I've heard that it's heroin. I may or may not have some information for you, but what we are discussing now is certainly illegal in any country. All of this you want me to get involved in without any assurances in writing that I will be protected from arrest or prosecution.

"I want full immunity, period. Before we start, I need to make this perfectly clear, and I will not be involved without it. You will have to deal with the DEA. It's your choice and your time frame. As I said before, you can work it out and call me at the hotel when you have the documents and are ready to talk. I hope you understand my position." Zack leaned back in his chair for the first time and watched the attorney.

"Yes, of course. I'm very sorry if I seemed to be pushing on this matter. We're just anxious to get started and need your full cooperation. We're so glad you have accepted my proposition, and believe me, you will be well rewarded."

"If all goes well, Ricardo, I'll help in any way that I can. Please get the documentation together as soon as possible."

"Very well. We will call you tomorrow and let you know how things are going. Once the documents are together we can talk some more. Everything should be ready in a day or two. Again, thank you for coming down here to help us. I feel that it will be very successful," Ricardo said with a smile of dismissal as he glanced back at Eduardo.

With a quick look at a very perplexed Eduardo, Zack left the room. He wanted to get as far away from that man as he could and as quickly as possible.

He decided not to call Mickey right away with this news. He would wait to see how it worked out. The attorney was actually putting in place the very plan he had been working on himself.

CHAPTER 11

At 10:00 a.m., a messenger found Zack finishing his coffee and reading the English version of the *Mexico City News* in the dining room of the Frances Hotel. Zack opened the envelope while the deliveryman waited for a reply.

> *Zack,*
>
> *I am very sorry how this turned out. I assure you that I had nothing to do with this or any knowledge of Ricardo Camacho's plans. We must talk. I can have a car pick you up at 9:00 p.m. It will take you to my house. We can have dinner and talk there. I am looking forward to seeing you.*
>
> *Eduardo*

Zack wrote a note of acceptance and gave the messenger twenty pesos.

The Dodge Caravan arrived at the Frances at 9:20 p.m. The stocky driver only nodded as Zack got in the backseat. The drive this time of day was slow and crowded, and his apprehension didn't make the trip go any faster. Camacho had locked him in whether he liked it or not. What the man had in mind, Zack had no idea, but he sure wasn't following police procedures, and that just might suit Zack's plan.

When they finally arrived at an upscale suburb in the outskirts of the city, the car pulled onto the paved driveway of a modern home. The apparent opulence that the assistant federal attorney enjoyed seemed far above his station and pay scale in the government.

"*Bienvenidos su casa, amigo,*" said Eduardo with a big smile. "Welcome to your house." Eduardo was definitely a bright light in this whole operation. He extended his hand and said, "This is your house in Guadalajara. Please take off your coat and relax. I'll fix you a drink, and we can sit on the patio. Dinner is being prepared, and we can eat whenever you're ready," he said as they walked through the tile-floored entry to a large living room.

"We have time, Eduardo. Let's relax first. I'll have Canadian Club on the rocks with lime if possible."

"Yes, of course." With this he turned to a uniformed young lady and spoke to her in rapid Spanish, telling her to get the drinks and take them to the patio.

As they walked through the modern living room, Zack could hear other ladies chattering in the kitchen area, preparing dinner. The floors were white tile covered with several thick area rugs under modern furniture that was placed in various seating areas. Modern paintings of striking colors hung on the walls. It was all the obvious work of an expensive decorator. One wall was glass and overlooked a completely enclosed tile patio with a small bubbling fountain. Eduardo led him outside to the patio, where the only sound was the soft flow of water.

Eduardo was very polite and didn't bring up business until well after dinner. They were sitting on one of the terraces overlooking a small garden when he said, "You'll have to excuse Ricardo, Zack. He is a politician and is in a very awkward situation. As you can see, he talks like a politician. Nothing is a problem; everything is fine."

"Well, I didn't think everything was fine when he was in the process of blackmailing me into working for him. Was he really serious about that?"

"I don't think so, Zack, and I apologize for that. I really don't know. It's just that he wants you in on this matter very badly. After all, it won't work without you, and he knows that. All he talked about after he got your file from his friend in Arizona was that he wanted you on this. He kept saying, 'Did you see this guy? He's perfect.' He liked the fact that you had a financial background and were educated and intelligent, and he knew you could negotiate and felt that your military training would be of some benefit. He was also impressed for some reason that you did not have a family. He completely disregards your DEA involvement and thinks it's an asset to get you to work with him."

"I don't know what's perfect about it. I've never done police work. You have lots of police down here, and I don't see why he doesn't use them."

"The police are generally poorly trained, Zack. The Federal Judicial Police are the only ones who get any meaningful training, and for some reason he doesn't want to use them. He wants to keep this low-key so there aren't any leaks."

"Well, I can appreciate that, but why didn't he just say so instead of blackmailing me?"

"It's his way. He kills flies with a sledgehammer. A typical politician. He feels he has to grab you by the balls first. Our friend Senor O'Leary told me that you are knowledgeable of the Mexican way and speak fluent Spanish, so I know you understand many of these things. Ricardo will tell you exactly what you want to hear or do anything he feels necessary to get his way."

"How can I possibly trust someone like that?"

"I'm the one you will be working with, and you'll meet my people who will be working with you. These people are not politicians and are well trained. They work directly for me and are paid by me, not Ricardo or the attorney general's office. You can trust them. Most people don't even know they exist."

"You mean they're your employees? I thought you worked for the attorney general's office and were employed by them."

"I am, Zack, but you must understand the politics here. It's important that you understand this, as it will put things on a better basis. We can then be more honest with one another in this matter. I had no idea what he was going to do, and I still can't believe it happened. I think he was just very desperate to get you to help him. You're the perfect outsider. His police force is very ineffective, and he has grand plans for some reason.

"You see, politics here at all levels have a trickle-down effect from gifts, as you may call it, from one source or another. That means Ricardo and others, me included, get some 'bonus money' from various sources to supplement our salaries. This has always been the way to pay people in these positions. One day you get a call for a favor. It must be fulfilled; it is the way. That's how I pay my people. I get a little extra to carry my load, as they're very effective and make Ricardo look good, so more gets passed on to me.

"It's difficult for Ricardo, as he's pressured from both sides. The old guard wants to forget this matter with this redhead, Rosa, but the pressure is not great, and it's weakening. The pressure from the administration is now greater to wrap her up and clean up crime. Therefore, it has to be done in a manner that will satisfy both sides and not offend anyone. If she and her gang are removed in this fashion, then all is well.

"I'm not sure who all calls in favors for Ricardo, as he doesn't let any of us know his dealings. He's very private. I just know that he wants her out of the way so the old guard can smile and say it was a very neat job and we didn't like her anyway. The administration can show that they have cleaned up a whole mafia family of drug traffickers, and it will be good in the news in America that Mexico is working to clean up the world's drug problem."

Eduardo shook his head and took another sip of his cocktail. Then he continued while he looked at Zack. "You and I both know that as long as people keep using drugs and have the money to buy them, there'll be drug traffic. As long as there are jobs, free medical care, and welfare north of the border, people will go. But we must all make it look as good as we can. It's a big show on both sides of the border. I'll be working with you on this operation, and Ricardo will not be physically involved. He is a politician and nothing else. He will, however, be the one to call the shots on how the operation will be handled. Mickey O'Leary told me to look out for you, and I intend on doing that. Do you understand, my friend?"

"Yes, of course. I am glad you told me about Ricardo. I think I can understand him a little better now. I was worried that he may be trying to trap me into something he could use against me and that he may use me as some political stepping-stone. This deal is obviously based on blackmail. And, Eduardo, I must confess, I don't like it at all," he said, shaking his head in disgust. "I don't trust the bastard, no matter how many excuses you use. He needs to know that if I'm willing to do anything, I must be taken care of, and that I am completely immune from problems from any Mexican government, be it state or federal. I don't need to be here, you know."

Leaning back in the overstuffed patio chair, Eduardo sighed and said, "I think you and I understand one another, and that's important because you and I will be working together. We need to have understanding and trust. I'll make sure Ricardo knows how you feel, and I think I can keep him in check. I'm sure tomorrow Ricardo will have the documentation you want to satisfy your needs of immunity. In these matters, Zack, these things can be arranged without a problem. This is where the telephone rings and someone tells you what is needed and it is done. That's the way it is. You must remember that Ricardo is always looking out for Ricardo. As Ricardo says, no problem." They both laughed. "I can have my driver take you home anytime, my friend, but first let's have a nightcap. We'll keep our fingers crossed."

CHAPTER 12

Zack immediately detected a different feeling in the air the next day as he settled into one of the leather chairs in the big office. Ricardo was talkative and friendly as if the past threats didn't exist. Ricardo showed him two faxes from the governor of Sonora and the original documents from the governor of Jalisco. Both were signed for the state governments on official letterhead and witnessed and stamped several times. Eduardo witnessed the English translation Ricardo had signed on behalf of the federal government. Zack was surprised that the paperwork could be completed and in order so promptly. Ricardo was his political self and apologetic for the last meeting.

"Okay, it seems we have the documentation taken care of. Let's hear what your plan is and how and why I fit into it," Zack said.

Zack called Rosa three times the next morning from different pay phones so the calls could not be traced back to a single location. The plan was simple enough: sell it to Rosa. The problem was he was only getting an answering machine. He left a message once saying that it was important that he talk to her. Eduardo was getting frustrated, and they decided to try again in the afternoon. The plan Ricardo had outlined was having trouble getting off the ground, and that was not a good omen.

Rosa answered on the third ring with a soft, husky voice. The voice matched what Veronica had told him about her sensuality, and

Zack tried to match it with the photos of her he'd seen in Ricardo's office.

"Rosa Sanchez? My name is Robert Anderson. I'm a financial consultant from Denver, Colorado, and I'm in town to talk with you. I have some clients with merchandise that they want to sell you. Apparently you know about it, as it was once owned by your former boss, who I understand passed away recently. They would like to do business with you because you're familiar with the merchandise and it's in Mexico at the present time."

"Who the hell are you? Calling me up and giving me that crap," she yelled.

Zack jerked the telephone away from his ear, remembering her temper, and said, "Look, lady, calm down. I don't know what you're so excited about. I'm just working for my clients, and they paid me to come to Guadalajara and see you. It's as simple as that. Do you want to talk about this or not? I can just go back to the States and tell my clients that you don't want to do business. That's not a problem. So if you want me to do that, just say so, and I'm out of here."

After a long silence, a calmed Rosa cleared her throat and responded. "Yes, of course. I'm sorry I yelled at you, I've had a very disturbing day, and I'm tired. I could meet you tonight. I know a place that is quiet, and we could talk without being interrupted."

"No, I'm sorry. I'm not going to meet with you where you suggest. I'll meet you at the new Hyatt hotel in the restaurant at ten o'clock tomorrow morning. It shouldn't be too crowded. You get a booth, and I'll come and sit with you. I know what you look like and can find you. If I see anyone else around, I'll presume they're the police or people of yours, and I'll just return to the States. I was told to stay away from both and to talk to you and only to you. Do you understand?"

"Yes, of course. I'll be there at 10:00 a.m. How will I know you?"

"Don't worry about that. I'll know you, and I'll come and sit with you. You'll know me when I get there. I'll see you in the morning." He hung up the telephone before she could respond.

Eduardo smiled as he took the little black Sony earphones off his head and rolled up the wires. "That was her, my friend. It looks like you're in business. I wish I could be there to listen in and watch. We'll have someone in the restaurant, however, just in case. I don't want you to worry about the meeting. You'll be well covered, believe me."

In a small French restaurant in downtown Guadalajara, they sat in a private dining room in the back, out of sight and away from the other diners. The opulent room was decorated in a green and red silk wall covering with dark tongue-and-grove wood paneling on the bottom half of the walls that matched the serving sideboards. The chandeliers needed cleaning but added a feeling of opulence.

This night was a celebration of sorts. At least it was a celebration for Eduardo and Ricardo. Ricardo was ecstatic. He talked like the job was all over. His simple plan had so many variables in it that it wasn't a plan at all, only a faint outline of one. Either he knew more than anyone else or he was completely out of touch with the reality of the situation. Zack was getting more apprehensive all the time, but they were happy because at last something was happening. It was moving forward.

"Remember, my friend," said Eduardo. "There will be others in the restaurant who will be watching all the time. They will not hear what you are talking about, however. We don't dare wire you tomorrow because she will probably frisk you as best she can without being too obvious, and she would find a wire. She's a smart woman, and our transmitters are a little old-fashioned and too bulky to pass even a casual search."

Ricardo butted in like he was in command of the situation and said, "Remember, you negotiate the price. Maybe you can do it tomorrow, maybe not. Do the best you can, and whatever it is, we'll make the arrangements for the transfer for you. You just collect the money, and we divide it up, and you get a nice commission." He beamed. "And we'll make the distributions. We trust you with the numbers. So you work it out, okay?"

A surprised Zack looked over at Eduardo and after hesitating said, "Yes, I understand. I'm just worried about dealing with this woman at all. Aren't you afraid that Rosa has people within your organization who will know I'm a fake? She certainly has connections with the police, so why not your staff? If she knows what we have planned, then I'm dead for sure."

"Yes, I'm sure she does have people in my organization who will sell her information for a few pesos. The difference is that my staff doesn't know that this is happening. The only people who know about this are Eduardo, you, and me. Eduardo has two undercover officers that work very closely with him. They are Victoria Morales and Jorge Martinez, and both are very competent. They are never in the office because we don't want them compromised by a secretary or a janitor. I've only met them on one occasion two years ago, and they only deal with Eduardo. You'll meet them in time, but for now Eduardo prefers that you don't know them so that you won't recognize them. You will not be coming back to my office again either," he said, smiling.

"That's fine, except I plan on scouting the area thoroughly before I go in there to see this Rosa. I don't want to meet one of her brainless goons and get myself killed."

Eduardo said, "We understand. We will also be checking out the area and the people. We'll try and have that place wrapped up tight before you get there. Don't be too obvious when you look around. We don't want you to get too involved," he emphasized. "We'll cover it, and if there's a problem, one of our people will come up and tell you. We'll do our best to take care of you, because we feel that you'll be the key to pulling this off. You're our best option," he said with an intent look of appraisal.

"I guess I'm the key because I am the only person who can find the heroin to make the deal with. I'm just not real fond of the position I'm in."

"Don't worry, my friend," said Eduardo. "I'll be right outside in a van in contact with our people inside at all times. If they say to come in, I'll be there."

"We're going to keep Victoria in the background tomorrow. She'll be in the restaurant just in case, but of course, you won't know her. She'll look entirely different than what she normally does, so no one will recognize her later either."

Wondering what that was supposed to mean, Zack said, "You mean you're keeping her disguised?"

"I think I may want to use her as your wife sometime later on as this matter progresses. I think it would be wise to have her close to you. She is very competent, and it would be better protection for you and easier for her to contact us in a hurry, as she'll always have her cellular phone. She can reach us at any time, and she knows her way around the city. Ricardo's staff doesn't even know she or Jorge exist. I want to keep it that way. Once they're compromised, it becomes difficult, and their use is limited."

With dinner and wine finished, everything that needed saying was said.

Eduardo lifted his water glass to toast and said, "To tomorrow, gentlemen."

Zack called Mickey early in the morning to catch him at home before he left for the office.

Mickey picked up on the second ring.

"Hello," he said with a groggy voice as he sat up in bed, clearing his throat and rubbing his eyes. He didn't like these early morning calls, as they were usually bad news, and his wife's low groan confirmed his feelings.

"Hey, Mickey. Rise and shine, pal. The day is half over, and you're still in the bag," Zack said with a chuckle.

"Why the hell are you calling me at this un-Christly hour, Zack? It's the middle of the night here."

"Come on Mickey. It's already five o'clock. Most people are hard at it already," he joked. "A lot has happened, and I need to fill you in on where I'm going from here and my personal thoughts. I'm working up a personal plan here, as the people I'm working for are completely out of touch with reality in this instance, and I don't trust the AG. He sounds too sure of himself and far too aggressive in this case. He is completely without finesse of any kind, and I think he's a little dangerous. They have no experience and have no clue as to what is involved. That's why I'm filling you in. Perhaps you have a suggestion or two.

"I faxed you the so-called agreements from a 'web shop' last night to your personal fax at the house so they wouldn't be around the office. I just hope they honor their agreement, and if they don't, get someone to kick ass down here. He isn't impressed with my DEA connection and thinks it's an asset for him to discredit the DEA if they could claim I was involved in the drug business. He likes the political sound of it. He feels like he has me and the DEA by the balls now and is going to exploit it."

Zack gave Mickey the plan they had worked out, the changes he had made to it without telling Eduardo, and his reasoning for the changes.

"I think you have a handle on it, Zack. I know you're going to have to play it by ear, and from what you say you could be getting in a little deeper than you planned or wanted. Just keep in mind the big goal here, and you know what that is. Don't worry. We will keep your ass covered here, but be careful. This thing can come unraveled at any time, it seems."

CHAPTER 13

Zack got an early start, taking a cab to the Sanborn's restaurant across the street from the Hotel Hyatt. He ordered coffee and watched the front of the hotel carefully for anyone hanging around who seemed out of place, but he wasn't a trained policeman and didn't think he would know the good guys from the bad guys in a big city unless it was damn obvious.

He could spot the obvious people who didn't fit, but everyone he saw looked like they belonged there. He hoped Eduardo would be in a van nearby like he said, but he didn't see a van. Zack continued to read through the *Mexico City Times*, but his attention was not on the paper or his coffee. He was worried about his meeting with Rosa. He wasn't trained for this kind of espionage.

Just before ten o'clock, Zack left Sanborn's with the newspaper under his arm and a valise in hand. He strolled around the parking lot on his way to the hotel, casually observing everything from behind his dark-tinted sunglasses. Everything looked normal enough, and the only van in sight was a beat-up hunk of iron that was parked in the rear of the building with a plumbing sign on it and pipe racks on the roof. If it was occupied, he couldn't tell.

He entered the lobby, checked his watch, and walked directly across the polished white marble floor to the lobby telephones. He picked up a pay phone near the front desk, where he could observe the lobby and the entrance to the restaurant. He casually acted like he was talking to someone as he looked around the lobby. The big reception counter was busy, and tourists and businessmen came and went with purpose, but there were no loiterers.

Zack entered the restaurant, and the hostess walked up and said in perfect English, "Where would you like to sit, sir?"

He requested a table in the back of the restaurant and quickly spotted a red-haired woman sitting alone in a back booth. He could feel her looking him over when he came in, but he didn't look in her direction or respond. Sipping her coffee, she went about her observation of the others in the restaurant. He took a seat in the brightly lit room with his back against the wall so he could see the woman without being obvious, and ordered coffee.

Zack checked his watch and looked toward the entrance as if waiting for someone. Then he shook his head and proceeded to read the paper. He slowly peered over the top of the newspaper to observe his quarry and was astonished at the woman's beauty. He had only seen the fuzzy candid photos of her in Ricardo's office and was totally unprepared for the woman who sat in the restaurant, impeccably dressed in a green outfit in the latest fashion.

Her obviously well-cared-for body was set off by a swirl of red hair that ended in a French twist on the back of her head, framing a sun-shy flawless face. He quickly scanned the room before ducking behind the newspaper to see if there was another redhead. This couldn't be the high-tempered woman he'd heard about.

But she was the only woman in the room with red hair, and she was obviously impatiently waiting for someone. Zack noticed that others in the room were glancing at the stunning beauty as well.

Rosa continued to watch everyone who came into the restaurant with very quick eyes. There were three other Americans in the restaurant, and none of them acknowledged her presence. *Perhaps Mr. Anderson isn't coming,* she thought. *Damn. I'd like to know what's going on. I've been spending money hand over fist trying to catch up with these people, and then I get a phone call out of the blue. Wouldn't you know it? Maybe it was all a waste of money.*

Rosa finished her third cup of coffee and then checked her diamond Rolex. He was late if he was coming, and perhaps he wasn't even going to show. *Maybe this is some kind of a setup now that Nicholas is gone. I'll wait fifteen more minutes, and if he doesn't arrive, I'll just wait at home and see if he calls again.*

"Rosa Sanchez?"

Rosa almost jumped out of her skin. She hadn't seen the man approach from the side, but it was the same voice, and she knew it. It was the American who had been sitting at the table in the back. She looked him over from head to toe and liked what she saw. "Yes? I'm Rosa Sanchez."

"I'm Rob Anderson. I talked to you on the telephone yesterday. May I have a seat?"

Rosa was surprised at the businesslike attitude and dress of the American. "Of course. I'm sorry Please have a seat. Would you like some coffee or anything?"

"No, I just finished breakfast. Thank you," he said as he sat down in the big booth. "It seems I have some clients who may be acquaintances of yours. They wish to continue doing business with you in some fashion or another. They've contacted me relative to talking to you about the purchase of certain merchandise that they have warehoused here in Mexico. I presume that you know what they're talking about. I want you to know that I'm not a part of their group, and neither do I represent anything other than what I tell you. I can only guarantee delivery for the correct price. Nothing more! My job is to discuss terms we can all agree on."

"Mr. Anderson, or whatever your name is, I think it's time that I come and sit on your side of the booth for a while. I would not like to have our conversation recorded in any way, and I would like to touch you to reassure myself, and I'm sure you would like to do the same thing. It's important to both of us, if we are negotiating in good faith."

Those jade-green eyes could burn a hole in you, he thought. Her beautiful mouth was the only thing on her face that was smiling. It was all for show, for the others in the restaurant.

"Yes, by all means," he said as he scooted over deeper into the booth. Eduardo was right; he had prepped Zack well.

Rosa came around the booth and sat next to him with a seductive smile that didn't reach her eyes. Acting like they were old friends or lovers, she put her arm around the back of his neck and hugged him to her in a typical Mexican *abrazo* of greeting. As she did this, she put her hand behind his jacket collar and felt his neck. Then she ran her hand down his back and felt all the way to his waist. Then she ran her other hand inside his jacket. He could feel that her hands were soft with long delicate fingers as she ran them inside his jacket and along his body while pretending to kiss him on the cheek. It was more of a caress than a search. She ran her hand into his crotch and down both of his thighs. Then she waited for Zack to do the same thing.

While she was holding him, he shot his hand under her suit jacket and ran it across her stomach and full bosom and down her sides, feeling her jacket as he went. She wore a tight skirt, and when they had both finished, she leaned back against the plush cushion in the booth, turned in the seat, and smiled at him in a very soft, knowing way as she lowered her eyes. Rosa then slid her skirt up to midthigh, slowly spreading her legs apart, and said, "Would you check the rest of me too? I would feel better if you were comfortable with the fact that I'm not wired either." Her eyes said she was enjoying this.

Zack was afraid to look around the restaurant to see if anyone was looking. His embarrassment had to show, as he could feel the hot flush on his face.

He slid his hand under her skirt after glancing around the room to make sure no one was watching, and the only response from Rosa was a warm smile. The fact that she didn't get excited about him putting his hand under her skirt was proof enough to him that there wasn't anything there that didn't belong there. He cleared his throat and, with his embarrassment showing, looked at her directly and said, "I think that'll do for now."

"You have a hard body, Mr. Anderson. I like that in a man."

"Ah … Well, thank you," he stammered. "You're put together rather well yourself."

Rosa made no attempt to leave his side of the booth and go back to her own side. She intended to keep this conversation very low and personal. She was all business now.

"I would like to see these clients of yours face-to-face, Mr. Anderson," she started.

"Wait. Please don't call me Mr. Anderson. Call me Rob, if you would. And may I call you Rosa?"

Taken aback, Rosa said, "Yes, of course. Now, about these SOBs you call clients."

"Please, Rosa. I don't know what problems there may exist between you and my clients, and I don't want to get into an argument about something I don't know anything about. I just want to keep this as businesslike as we can. Is that okay with you?"

Rosa turned in her seat, put her elbows on the table, and took another sip of coffee. "Yes, it's fine. Tell me first about your clients. Who are they? Maybe they're the ones I think they are. What are their names?"

"The names, I am sure, are immaterial, as I think you will agree as we progress. The two Americans speak with an eastern accent. One is about thirty years old, blond, of medium build, about five feet ten, and 180 pounds," he went on as he described a good friend of his so that he wouldn't forget what he had told her. He went on and described in detail the other American, using another friend as the model. "One man was a Mexican, but I only saw him once." With this said, he went ahead and described as best he could the driver of the Buick automobile that was now in the bottom of some rancher's stock tank.

Rosa got more agitated as he provided the details describing the Mexican. He knew he had hit pay dirt of some kind. He didn't know what it was, but he would soon find out. She was damn near ready to burst at the seams by the time he finished.

"Rosa, are you all right? You look like maybe you don't feel well. Would you rather meet another time?" Zack said in an attempt to throw her off guard even more.

Rosa realized then that her mouth was open in surprise. The Mexican he described sounded a lot like Chuy, that Tijuana guy. *Are they all in on a scam?*

"No, no I'm fine," stammered Rosa. "I'm just upset about the people you're talking about. I don't know if I want to do business with the people you represent," she said, trying to regain control of the negotiations.

"Hey, that's no problem at all," he said. "If they're those kind of guys, you probably shouldn't do business with them anyway. We don't have to put anything together if you don't want to. Hell, I'm paid. I did my job and found you and talked to you. It's immaterial to me if you put a deal together with these guys or not. I'm good to go. I just had breakfast with a beautiful lady. I'll go back to the States. No problem," he said with a smile.

"No!" Rosa said a little too loudly as she glanced around the room. "I didn't mean it that way. I just meant that maybe they're bad people. Tell me about the girl."

Zack looked blank. "Girl? What girl? I didn't see a girl."

Now it was Rosa's turn to be dumbfounded. "They weren't with a blond girl called Goldie? Didn't they bring her to your office? You didn't see her, or they didn't talk about her as another partner? They're working together; I know they are. They have to be," she said as she started to wind up again.

"I've never seen her and never heard of her. Who's she supposed to be?"

"You don't know her?"

"No. I've never heard of her, and my clients have never mentioned any Goldie person, or any female for that matter. Should they have?"

"Well, I was informed that maybe she was with this group of clients you have."

"You must know more about them than I do then, because I don't know anything about a woman."

"What about the Arab? Wasn't he there?"

"What Arab? I didn't meet an Arab, and they didn't mention one. What's a blond and an Arab got to do with this?"

Rosa just stared at him like she didn't hear or believe him.

Zack could see that the woman was really confused now; this could be the time to give her a little space. As he started to move to get up from the table, he said, "Would you excuse me for a moment? I would like some iced tea. Would you like anything?"

"No thank you!" she murmured as she stared at her coffee cup.

As Zack left the table, he casually looked around the restaurant. No one seemed to give him a glance as he made his way to the front to order some iced tea and tell the waiter he had changed tables to talk to a friend.

Zack went to the men's room to kill time and washed his hands. There were three or four other men in the room, which made him a little nervous until he looked in the mirror and saw Eduardo staring back at him. Zack didn't acknowledge Eduardo's presence and returned to the restaurant and Rosa.

The booth was empty. Damn, she'd left. Maybe he was too hard on her too fast. *I blew it*, he thought as he looked around the restaurant. His iced tea was on the table, so he sat and waited.

Ten minutes passed and he had signaled for the bill when Rosa walked up to the table and slid in alongside him. She smiled and said, "Do you think we should search each other again?"

Zack smiled back and said, "I'd love to. Perhaps we could do it a little slower this time. I'm better prepared."

"Well, perhaps it isn't necessary after all," she replied, turning away and picking up a cool coffee cup as she signaled the waiter.

Trying to bring things back into line, he said, "Too bad. I was looking forward to it this time. Tell me how you plan on proceeding with the negotiations and how you will verify it so that I can pass this information on to my clients."

"I don't know how I can verify it with you, Rob. I'll have to think about it. You could be anybody, and I wouldn't know for sure, would I?"

"No, I guess not. You'll just have to trust me on that, I guess. Just like I'll have to trust you on a number of other things as this thing gets put together. How much time will you need?"

"It will take time, of course, but I'll confirm this with a number of people over the next few days and let you know."

"Well, all right. Let's discuss the price of the merchandise my clients want to sell you. They've told me they want $1.4 million US in cash."

Zack thought Rosa was going to pass out. Her face was pale, and she openly struggled to catch her breath.

"One point four million dollars?" she stammered, trying to maintain control and keep her voice down. "Are you mad, for Christ's sake?"

"Rosa, please. I'm not sure what the merchandise is, and I don't care. I'm here just to work out a sale with you. If you think that amount is too high, say so, and I'll take them any counteroffer you want."

"This merchandise, as you call it, belonged to me to start with. I don't want to pay anything to get it back, period."

"You know what they say, Rosa. Possession is nine-tenths of the law, and apparently they have the merchandise."

"Hell, they stole it from me to start with. It never was theirs."

"I understood that it was owned by a Nicholas Bosque, who is now deceased, and they fell heir to the property somehow. I didn't know you ever owned the property or ever had an interest in it. Please correct me if I'm wrong."

"Well, it did belong to Nicholas, at least to a group in which I was second in charge. Therefore I was entitled to it by succession. It should go to no one else."

"Rosa, they have the merchandise. They feel they're the rightful owners. There is no sense in arguing about who owns it. They have it, and we can't change that."

"One point four million is ridiculous. I couldn't even raise that much."

Zack took another sip of iced tea to delay responding as long as he could. Then he moved on with the plan. "Rosa, why don't you take in a partner? Let them put up the money, and you put the deal together for a piece of the action. I could help you if you want, and you wouldn't have to come up with anything. I can guarantee the delivery as long as you can deliver the cash. I understand the merchandise is worth considerably more than the $1.4 million they're asking. They can get more money from a lot of different buyers, they say."

He could see in Rosa's eyes that he had planted the right seed. Somehow Ricardo had known she would go for this. She brightened considerably and said, "You know, Rob, I'm beginning to like you. Perhaps you have an idea that could work. It'll take me some time, though, to think this idea through, and I'll need proof that the merchandise exists and is deliverable. Can you arrange that?"

"I can, but it will take some time, as I have no idea where or what it is, and someone will have to come down here to convince me as well as you and your partners. What about the price?"

"Well, with a partner, it's different. If the merchandise is as I know it, then the value is there. I just need to be convinced it's the same."

"How about I go and call my clients and tell them what's happening, and you go and find a partner with deep pockets so you can put your end together. I should be ready to talk to you again tomorrow afternoon. Let's say dinner. I think I would like that," Zack said with a smile as he looked her over, indicating that he liked Rosa's company.

"I'm not sure I can put together a partnership by then, but I think I know where to start looking. Perhaps I can, but let's plan tomorrow evening for dinner. When will I hear from you next?"

"I'll call you at about three o'clock tomorrow afternoon, and we can make arrangements. You can tell me who your partners are, if you like, but I don't want to have any dealings with them whatsoever. I deal only with you. That will help hold you into the transaction as well. You'll become an indispensable party. Is that okay with you?"

"Yes, I like that. You think well, Rob. We'll get along just fine," she replied, looking him over with an appraising gaze. "Call me tomorrow and I'll let you know how things are going."

CHAPTER 14

Eduardo was ecstatic. Things were working out better than they could imagine. Ricardo's idea of the partner he thought was brilliant, and now they could catch an extra big fish in their net on this operation.

"Who knows where it may lead," Eduardo said to Zack as he got up from his executive chair in his small office in the state building and then wandered around the room in deep thought. "Let's talk to Ricardo right away. I'll set up a meeting. We'll have to keep you out of sight from here on in. Someone may be looking for you right now. You can't trust or believe Rosa, no matter what she says. Remember that. I think you have her in a position now, so she feels your guard is down and that you are interested in her. That's great. She may be a little vulnerable herself right now because of everything that's happened."

"Somehow, Eduardo, I doubt that woman is ever vulnerable. I think she's always in control."

Later that day, Zack was on the street outside his hotel with Eduardo, waiting for their ride at the appointed time for the evening meeting Eduardo had set up with Ricardo.

The driver was the same one who had picked Zack up in the afternoon, and he was an obvious professional, maneuvering Eduardo and Zack through the heavy traffic like the car was greased. The heavily tinted windows made it impossible to see who was in the car, and the quick moves and numerous turns made it impossible for anyone to follow in the heavy city traffic. They arrived at what Eduardo called a "safe house" in the small town of Tonala outside of Guadalajara. The enclosed yard quickly enveloped the car as the big steel electric door rolled closed.

"Zack, amigo," said Ricardo with a big smile on his face as he approached Zack with his arms spread, ready to hug him. "Eduardo tells me that things are going well."

"Well, I think things went pretty well for the first meeting. We'll know for sure when I talk to her next," said Zack. "The problem is going to be producing some of the heroin. They're going to want to sample the quality we're going to deliver. I have no idea how to go about this without getting the drugs in person and delivering a sample. I don't know if the stash is still there or if its good quality, and I sure don't want to be transporting it around the country if I can help it. If we turn it over to the authorities, we're without a deal and won't be able to put it together. We need to weigh it and get some samples so we're ready for them when it comes time for the trade."

"No problem," said Ricardo. "It sounds good to me."

There it is again, thought Zack. *It's never a problem with Ricardo.*

"Ricardo, if it's no problem, how do you plan on solving it?"

"We'll think of something, amigo," he said with a dismissive gesture. "I think your suggestion may be a good one. How long will it take you to get a sample and get the entire amount weighed?"

Zack was irritated that the work was again passed back to him. It was obvious that Ricardo was going to be very little help.

"Well, I'll have to make a trip. I don't want anyone to know when I'm going and when I'm coming back. I'll give you a call in ten days or so and say that I am here with the sample. I'm concerned about traveling with a sample in the car or in my luggage, so I would like some kind of a letter to cover that square in case that I'm stopped and it's found."

"Perhaps it's time you meet Victoria," said Eduardo. "Then if you want, she could travel with you and would be there in case you needed her."

"It sounds like she will be your eyes and ears, and I'll just be the gofer. I don't want her or anyone else controlling where and when I go. All of a sudden I could find myself being of no value to anyone and just everyone's enemy. Perhaps I shouldn't have gotten involved in the first place. It looks like it's getting complicated, and I sure don't want any trouble over this. It's your problem, not mine."

"Look at it this way, Zack: you'll get 20 percent of $1.4 million. That isn't too shabby by anyone's standards. A good piece of change, as you Americans say. And you do a good deed to boot, so quit worrying about it. We'll work it out. Let's have dinner and we can talk about it some more," said Ricardo.

This was the first time Zack had heard that he was getting a commission on this job and 20 percent of $1.4 million was exorbitant. *That is too much for the politician to part with, regardless of the stakes. His agenda is getting dangerous. He won't just throw out over a quarter of a million dollars without a plan. He has to have a plan,* Zack thought.

The dining room was old and elegant, with antique hardwood furniture standing on a heavy planked and pegged floor that showed traffic marks of over a century. A large stone fireplace occupied the far end of the room; it was accentuated by a dusty wrought iron chandelier and old tapestries on the walls. The massive fireplace was cluttered with several different heavy antique cooking pots and utensils, symbolizing a bygone era of old Mexico.

Appetizers consisting of smoked marlin and tuna and a variety of cheeses and olives were served in the enclosed patio of the colonial home, under the protective canopy of a huge tree. Zack knew better than to ask who the house belonged to, as there was no indication that anyone was living there at the time. Numerous doors opened off the second floor balcony surrounding the patio, indicating there were many rooms for many people.

Ricardo looked at his watch and abruptly got up and made his excuses. He said he had a prior engagement. Eduardo could take over from here, he said, as his mind was obviously elsewhere. He left without further comment.

"What's going on, Eduardo?"

"You'll see shortly, Zack. Relax and enjoy the evening."

About an hour of small talk passed without any hint of business when suddenly two people entered.

Eduardo stood and said, "Zack, I would like you to meet Victoria Morales and Jorge Martinez. These are the people I've been telling you about, the people who no one knows exist."

They all laughed at some obvious inside joke.

Jorge was handsome, in his midthirties, and three inches shorter than Zack. He had the body of a weight trainer. His black windblown hair was thick, and the color matched his eyes. He moved his two hundred plus pounds around with the ease of an athlete.

Victoria was younger. Her slick black hair was pulled into a tight ponytail. She had large expressive eyes and generous lips that shined with bright red lipstick that set off her perfect teeth. Her figure was curvaceous and well kept. She was a real natural beauty. Her five foot five frame was all woman.

"*Con mucho gusto*" (With much pleasure), said Zack in the familiar greeting. "I've heard a little about you, and it seems that Senor Chavez is quite proud of you both."

"Thank you. You are too kind," said a smiling Jorge as he engulfed Zack's hand in his large fist.

The look on Victoria's face disclosed the fact she had heard she might be traveling and living with Zack. She was obviously sizing him up. Her pretty face was happy and expressive as she walked toward him, extending her hand. "I'm glad to meet you, Zack. May we call you that?"

Zack took the opportunity to spark things up and said to Victoria, "Look, regardless of what they told you, I'm really not all that bad. And yes, by all means, call me Zack."

Everyone laughed as Victoria blushed and said, "Was I really that obvious?"

"You were, but that's okay."

A short time later, an elderly lady who was apparently one of the chefs called to them that dinner was ready, so Zack followed the others into the dining room, where a heavy hand-carved wooden table was set for dinner. The china was heavy white pottery, hand painted with blue flowers and obviously very old with occasional chips that added to its character of antiquity.

Victoria sat next to Zack, and their conversation soon relaxed into a discussion of what she did when she wasn't working for Eduardo. She was an accomplished craftsman in disguises and had attended many schools of makeup to learn the art of altering her facial features with silicone masks and attachments. The greatest teachers were in Hollywood, she told him, and the next best were the circus and carnival people.

"Do you recall seeing me at the Hyatt Hotel?"

"No, I didn't see you there, and I wouldn't have missed you. Now that's for sure," he said with a grin. "Oh, don't tell me you were in disguise. Where were you?"

"I was the old lady sitting in the lobby at the entrance to the restaurant. I could see you all the time from there, and it was easy to carry an automatic and radio under my coat."

"Well, I think I may have seen you, but I'm not sure. I tried to look everyone over I thought could be a threat. I think I'll have to be more observant, little old ladies or not."

"Thank you. That's a compliment. The image I was trying to achieve was exactly that, and as far as you're concerned, it worked. The idea is that no one is supposed to see me; I just fit in."

"One thing," said Zack. "If we work together, don't dress like that when we're alone. And also, when you are in disguise, give me some kind of a signal so I'll know it's you."

"That I can do."

"One thing that's been bothering me, Victoria, is something that Rosa said. I don't know what it is. Perhaps you do."

"What is it, Zack?"

"She asked me about a blond woman called Goldie and also about an Arab. She didn't give me a name, but I presume it was a man. Who are these people, and how do they fit in?"

"Goldie is, or was, Nicholas's girlfriend. She worked with Rosa for a while. What she did, I don't know, but they traveled a lot together. She is a looker like Rosa, and when the two of them walked into a room, you could hear the eyeballs snap. They were quite a pair. We've been looking for her since Nicholas's death and haven't found her. We've talked to the maid at the house and even had someone check at her mother's house near Mazatlan. Nothing, zip, nada. She's just disappeared. I'm surprised Rosa would ask. If anyone would know where she was, it would be her."

"What's the story on the Arab?"

"I don't know anything about that, Zack. I do know that heroin comes in from Afghanistan and then moved to the States. Nicholas was a facilitator for this. He had the Afghanistan connections and was seen with Arabs at different times. We think he also moved them into the United States. He had a lot of connections on both sides of the border. As you Americans say, money talks and bullshit walks, and he had the money. No one was concerned about him moving Arabs to the United States until recently. People are always going to and from the United States without crossing through the border control."

"Is it really that easy?"

"Well, if you're playing the coyote game, hauling wetbacks by the truckload is one thing, but if you do like Nicholas and have the right people paid off, you know exactly where to go and when to cross. Hell, they probably serve meals as well." She smiled. "I would guess that when the drugs go north, the Arabs go with them. Why make two crossings when you only have to make one?"

"My god, if you know all that, why didn't you shut him down?"

Her pretty face stared at him for a while like he really didn't understand any of this. Then she finally said, "Well, Zack, I guess they're finally getting around to that, aren't they?"

The next day seemed to drag by slowly, with things happening that Zack had no control over. Victoria called three times, bringing Zack up to speed on what she had learned about Goldie. She had disappeared. Veronica had been right when she told Zack she knew how to disappear; she'd done it. The Arab still remained a mystery.

At three o'clock in the afternoon, Zack called Rosa to see if the meeting was on. Dinner was agreed upon for eight o'clock. She offered to pick him up at his hotel, but Zack declined, saying that he would meet her at a public restaurant in the city. They selected Sanborn's, a busy restaurant in downtown, as the place. It was brightly lit and always crowded. He could walk there from his hotel, but he would arrive by taxi from another hotel in order to appear as if he was staying somewhere else.

Eduardo was happy that things were moving along rapidly, and Zack said, "Don't get too excited. We don't know what we're dealing with yet, and I don't know if we have a deal or not. Let's wait until this meeting is over. Then we can decide if things are moving along or not."

"Never mind, my friend. Things are moving along, I assure you. Rosa is a person of action, and if you're meeting with her, she has a plan. We'll have our people in place again, so you'll be well covered."

"Victoria will be there again?"

"Oh yes, she'll be with you most of the time. As a matter of fact, she followed you to breakfast and on your walk in the park today."

"Christ, I'd better be a little more observant," Zack said with surprise. "I'm not used to this cloak-and-dagger stuff. What did she look like?"

"Who knows? She changes like a chameleon. She's very good at what she does. I think she likes keeping track of you. One more thing, Zack. She told me what you said about the Arab matter. This is very important. It's important that we have some idea of where these people are and how many there are."

"Why don't you just drag Rosa in and ask her?"

"We thought of that, but she'd lie to us, and we'd blow our whole operation. This matter is too big to blow."

"I'll do what I can, Eduardo. I'm not making any promises, but I understand the problem."

At five o'clock, Zack took a taxi to the Holiday Inn off the beltway, or Periférico, and ordered an iced tea in the lobby restaurant. As he sipped at the iced tea, he looked around to see if anyone looked suspicious or seemed interested in him. When he was convinced he was alone, he walked through the large brightly lit lobby to hail a taxi to Sanborn's so he would arrive just before eight o'clock. He wanted to arrive on time to see how prompt Rosa was going to be.

Rosa was a knockout, wearing a black sheath dress with a matching jacket and gold high heels. Her pulled-up red hair glistened in the brilliant lighting. She was dressed for the evening. She was sitting in a back booth in the crowded restaurant, keeping an eye on the entrance. As Zack walked to the booth, toward the lady with the big smile, he noticed that other casual diners hadn't failed to see the impact Rosa was making.

"Good evening, Rosa. You're looking very beautiful tonight. Sanborn's will never be the same."

"Ah, Rob, thank you. Please come and sit with me," she said in a husky voice. She was in a good mood; her stare was happy and very friendly.

Zack slid into the booth, and she immediately put her hand inside his jacket, caressing his body like a desperate lover while looking for a wire or transmitter. Zack put his cheek to hers in the familiar greeting, put his hand under her jacket, and quickly felt her firm body and bust.

"God, I like this part," he whispered in her ear. "Should we do it again?"

"Yes, we could, but I don't think this is the place," she said as she glanced around the restaurant and saw people staring at them. "Perhaps we could go someplace else later?"

"Perhaps we could," said Zack, following through. "Under the circumstances, I'm a little more than reluctant, as we both have a situation that is a little delicate, and we certainly have grounds for a lot of distrust."

"I know, but that will pass. I think you and I are going to be partners, so we will have to trust one another to a certain extent. You like how I look?"

"Hell, I think you're gorgeous tonight. You're a very attractive woman."

"You don't think my dress is too revealing?" she said with a coquettish look.

"Well, perhaps a little for Sanborn's, but not for me."

"I'm glad you like it. I wore it for you," she said with a knowing smile.

The waitress arrived for their order, and all conversation stopped until it was placed. They both ordered a salmon salad. Zack had his usual iced tea, and Rosa settled for coffee.

In an attempt to change the subject before it got any farther off track, Zack said, "Tell me about this partnership you're trying to work out."

"I talked to a man who is going to finance our transaction. He's concerned about the value and wants some assurance of the merchandise's existence and quality."

"That's understandable. I was thinking that I could get a sample from my clients that your friend could examine to convince him that it is as advertised. Do you think this would be satisfactory?"

"Yes, I think so. Also he wants to meet you face-to-face and talk to you about it, and your clients."

"I thought I made that clear, Rosa. I would rather you deal with your financier and I deal with you. He isn't going to learn anything from me, because I don't know anything except what I've told you. I don't want to have anything to do with him apart from knowing his name so that my people will know he's real and has the clout to get the job done. That's all that's important."

"Well, I suppose if you don't want to meet him, it's all right, but someone will defiantly want to talk to you to confirm that you're real and that I'm not just making this all up. We can arrange that, I'm sure. Let's eat our dinner, and we can talk about what we're going to do tonight."

"Who is this guy, Rosa?"

"His name is Ruben Marquez; he's been in the business a long time. He's a banker like Nicholas. I presume you know that Nicholas was a banker of sorts?"

"Well yes, it was mentioned, but I'm not sure just what kind of a banker he really was. That's immaterial now. It's you and me that have to put this together. Let's eat and get out of here. We can surely find a better place to spend the evening," he said as he looked around the restaurant.

"Now that sounds good to me," she said with a sexy smile.

After finishing her mediocre salad, Rosa suggested they go somewhere and dance. "I know just the place to go. Do you like disco music?"

"You mean all that noise and no music?" He was afraid she would suggest the Crystal Disco, and he didn't feel he was ready to get into her lair just yet.

"Well, I guess you're right. If you want slow music to dance to, the discos are not the places to go. What kind of music do you want?"

"If I have a beautiful lady with me, I want to be able to hold her while I dance with her and be able to talk to her and feel her body next to mine."

She stared at Zack for a long while as a seductive smile slowly crept across her face. She cooed in her husky voice, "Well, you are a romantic, aren't you? I think I know just the place; it's a small dance floor in a hotel bar. You can give the group leader twenty dollars, and he will play what you want all night long. How does that sound?"

"Perfect. Let's go."

The small old midtown hotel showed its age. The black and white checkerboard tiles of the lobby floor were cracked with age and hadn't seen a mop in years. The ancient hotel clerk matched the decor of the lobby, as he sat behind a heavy spindled mahogany cage in his rumpled white shirt. He barely nodded at Zack and Rosa as they crossed the lobby, refusing to look up from his six-inch black-and-white television. Music led them into the small dark bar.

Zack escorted Rosa in through the doorway and stopped to let his eyes adjust to the dark room. He could barely make out the high booths that lined the walls in the dim light from the miniscule bandstand. Four bored men in shirtsleeves hammered out a revolutionary tune in offbeat time, ignoring their surroundings. It was obvious that this was a place for lovers who could rent hotel rooms by the hour if they wished.

As Rosa slid into the booth, she looked at Zack and said in a soft, sensuous voice, "Sit with me, Rob. It will be much nicer that way."

As he moved in close to her, he said, "Is it time to search you again?"

No sooner did he say that then Rosa put her hand on his cheek, pulled him to her, and kissed him full on the mouth. Her full lips were soft and warm, and the lipstick she wore had a heady taste and smell. She smelled of Shalimar perfume, and her breath was heavy on him. Her right hand slid under his jacket and went round his back. She pulled him even closer. He could feel her strong, hard body, and her soft full breasts pressed against his chest.

Zack slid his hand inside her jacket and onto her firm stomach and felt her flex. She let out a small groan of pleasure. He slowly but deliberately moved his hand up the soft, smooth material to one of her braless breasts and caressed it softly. He moved his thumb across a nipple several times and felt pleasure as it hardened under his touch as she gave a little sigh of enjoyment.

He could feel that he was starting to get aroused. He could feel the heat down to the core of his body. Damn. With this woman, where would it lead? She was the manhandler. Rosa slowly took her lips away from Zack's and lightly ran her tongue over his warm lips. "Now this is more like it," she said in a low, heavy voice. Heat and passion were obvious in her eyes.

Zack looked up to see a waitress standing casually by the booth, chewing gum, ignoring them, and waiting patiently for their order. She was obvious about completely ignoring them but didn't miss Zack's hand still inside Rosa's jacket. Rosa ordered a pina colada, and Zack ordered a Tecate black beer in the can, with limes.

The waitress returned with the drinks and a small unlit candle and waited for payment. She explained that there were no tabs here and they could light the candle if they wanted too. Zack didn't see any others lit and decided lighting the candle was not the norm. His eyes had adjusted to the dark now, and he saw couples completely oblivious to their surroundings occupying several of the booths.

Rosa talked to the waitress about the music and asked her to have the leader come to the table when he could. The man was given twenty dollars and a round of beers for the four-man group, and he agreed to play all the slow music Zack wanted.

Zack and Rosa made their way to the minuscule dance floor when the music started; it was an oldie from the '50s. Two other couples hung onto each other, barely moving with the music, completely ignoring everything. Rosa moved right into Zack. He slid his arm up under her jacket and around her waist and pulled her in close. She wasted no time putting both arms around his neck, pulling him to her, and kissing him on the mouth. She slid her warm tongue slowly through his lips, caressing them as she went. Zack was warming to the close contact and slowly lowered his hand until he could feel the rise of her buttocks and pulled her even closer. She moved into him unhesitatingly and slowly moved her hips against him.

They were no longer dancing; they were making love on the dance floor. Her mouth was inches away now, and he could feel her excited, heavy breath on his face as she watched him. She was literally undressing him with her eyes and devouring him. He couldn't believe the sensations those expressive eyes portrayed. The music was forgotten except for the slow beat.

Their bodies, held tightly together, seemed to take on lives of their own in the slow music, slowly caressing each other in a sensuous, intimate motion so that each could feel every part of its partner's body. The mood only got headier and more passionate as the night wore on until Rosa said, "I can't take much more of this, Roberto. I'm hot and sticky. Either we get a room right here or I have to go home. I've felt you hard against me all night, and I'm sure you must be very uncomfortable by now too."

"I'm sorry if I made you uncomfortable, Rosa. I was enjoying every minute of it. It felt like our bodies were one the whole evening. I don't know when I've ever felt like this, and it's difficult to remember that we've just met and are here for business. Perhaps when this is all over we can take up where we left off this evening. I think I'd like that very much. I can't get enough of the closeness of your body and hope you were enjoying this perhaps almost as much as I."

"No. Please don't get me wrong. I'm saying I am enjoying this too much, and either we are going to have to become lovers starting right now and get a room, or I'm going to have to go home. I can't take this passion without more. Roberto, I really don't know how to say this, but I want you to know that I want you very much indeed, and I want you now."

"Let's wait until we have finished our work then, so we can keep things in proper perspective. I won't be able to keep from touching you and feeling you, but let's try to keep it at that level for now. I can lose my head here, but I've got to keep it straight for the job."

"Okay, but let's see each other as much as possible during this Rob. I think I need you. Please? Let's see where it goes," she said with a glistening face.

"I'll get us a taxi, Rosa, and see you home. I'll call you tomorrow and see if the plan we outlined is satisfactory with your new partner," he murmured in her ear as he continued to hold her close.

As the taxi drove through the dark neighborhood, Zack was surprised at the size and quality of Rosa's house. The section of town, he didn't know, but it was definitely upscale, and her house was modern and expensive. Rosa pulled a remote out of her purse, and a large gate opened. Their parting kiss was hot, lingering, and passionate. "You can stay over if you like, Roberto. I cook a hell of a breakfast."

"Another time for sure," he said.

"Goodnight, my love," she said.

"Goodnight, Rosa. I'm looking forward to seeing more of you," he said as he walked her up to the big door of her house.

"You sure you don't want to come in?"

"I'd love to, but this is moving awful fast for me. It's been a long time for me. Hell, I don't know what I'm doing here. I don't even know what this merchandise is I'm selling to you, and I sure don't know a Goldie or any Arabs. Perhaps I should just go back to Colorado and tell them I couldn't find you. I hate being left out in the dark like this."

Rosa's deep-throated laugh was encouraging. "Rob, you are naïve, aren't you? You mean to tell me you don't know what you're selling or what's going on?"

"I don't have the foggiest idea, Rosa. The whole thing sounded like a nice all-expense-paid holiday. Hell, I don't care what it is, except now I have the feeling that perhaps I need to know more about it."

As Rosa slowly pushed the door open with a high-heeled shoe on the foot of one of her elegant legs, she looked longingly at Zack and said, "Pay the cabbie and come on in, Rob. Take your tie off, and I'll tell you just what you're involved in. Like I said, I cook a hell of a breakfast."

When Zack called to report in to Eduardo, he found he was wasting his time; they knew all about his evening and were ecstatic at the progress Zack was making.

Victoria came on the line and said, "Well, lover boy, you don't waste any time, do you? You were something else last night. I think Rosa was really enjoying herself."

"Well, perhaps she was just faking it. That's a possibility, you know."

"No, Zack, she wasn't faking it," she said with a chuckle. "You forget I'm a woman. I know what she was feeling because I watched her, and you are a very handsome man, if you didn't already know it."

"Thank you. You're very kind. I'll continue to do my best for the cause," said Zack. "It's a lot harder than I thought it would be."

"Yes, I'm sure you are overworked." She chuckled with sarcasm.

"You know, I really don't like people spying on me all the time. Pretty soon I'm going to have a neurosis attack or whatever the hell happens when someone is being watched all the time.

"Well, at any rate I think I found out a few things. This Nicholas guy has been banking drugs for Arabs for more than two years. His contacts have been mostly in Sonora, but now some cartel called *Grupo Beto* from Tijuana has moved in and is the main buyer. They still cross in Sonora, and there seems to be some kind of a turf war going on. I guess this is what we read about in the papers every day. The Arabs cross with the drugs most of the time, but apparently they come and go as they want. The *Beto* outfit or the Sonoran handlers see to it all."

Zack slumped back in the heavy upholstered chair in his hotel suite while he gazed out on the massive greenery of the interior of the hotel grounds, trying to collect his thoughts before he continued. This job was getting to him. The pool area was crowded with young people in their swimsuits. The girls were catching as many rays of sunlight as they could in their skimpy suits. He hadn't thought of it much before, but they reminded him that the lovely Rosa was getting to him. It had been too damn long since he'd been with a woman, and he was afraid his emotions would cloud his efforts. He hadn't felt this much emotion since his wife, and he had thought he would never be emotional about a woman again, but Rosa awoke desires he had thought were gone forever. He knew it couldn't possibly go anywhere, but he wanted her, and there was no doubt about it. *She only knows that they are in the drug financing business and the facilitating of getting people into the United States. She doesn't have a clue as to what's really going on. We've got a nuclear device out there, and the people involved don't even know about it.*

"You still there, Zack?"

"Yes. I'm sorry, Eduardo. I was just thinking of something. They have several Border Patrol people on the payroll on both sides that facilitate their crossing. These people are very well organized and connected. It's a lot more difficult since the Trade Towers fell, but it just takes more money, and money they have. They just raise the price of the drugs and let the American users pay for it. The Arabs think it's very funny."

Zack stood up and walked around his room, pulling his gaze away from the window in frustration, and said, "It appears that the drugs we're dealing with were the last of a series of sales. The Arabs apparently have some kind of project they have been financing in Mexico, but I don't know what it is, and apparently Rosa doesn't either. All I know is that it's a damn expensive project, and they're very secretive about it. You folks know anything about it?"

"No, I've heard nothing of a big project, Zack. But yes, it's a damn dirty business and a tough one to stop, but you did great. This has got to be top secret to this family. We'll work on the project matter and see what we can find and let you know if we learn anything."

After hanging up with Eduardo, Zack called Mickey with the latest report including his escapade with Rosa. He emphasized the fact that he didn't think she knew what was really going on except for the sale of the drugs. She knew there was a project of some kind but didn't know what it was other than they wanted to be in the United States during the holidays. She said they always have some kind of a project so she wasn't very impressed.

Mickey sat in the nervous silence that had fallen over the room like a black cloud. He stared across the big mahogany desk at Walker. The man just shook his head, deep in thought as he heard Mickey's report, and sank back in his big chair.

"So what you're telling me, Mickey, is that Sinclair has bought us some time by all that happened in Sonora. Is that about right?

Nothing will or can happen until the drugs get sold to whoever the bastards are. They need the money to finance this Little Ivan project."

"Yes sir, that seems to be the case, but the operation is far from over from what he says, and it gets more convoluted at every turn."

"How is he getting this information, and can we rely on it?"

"Well, sir," he stammered, looking around the room, wondering how to break the news. "He's sleeping with the enemy."

"Damn! That guy is something else," Walker muttered with a smile. "Let's review what we think we know at this point. We sure can't let this out of the bag. We give him the entire backup he needs and then some. At least we can pass on names to the Border Patrol. It sounds like our guy Mitchell and his pal aren't going to be showing up for work. They may have some pals who need to be looked into as well. We have to be damn careful how that info gets to them to keep us out of the loop, but I can handle that.

Walker leaned back in his chair and looked at the ceiling in contemplation. *Damn, this operation is really getting involved. At least it seems we have a handle on it for the time being.* "Okay," he said, swinging forward and putting his elbows on his desk. "We now believe they have a nuclear warhead somewhere in Mexico and that they're planning on smuggling it into the United States. We aren't sure where it is, but the loss of the heroin that Sinclair controls has held up the purchase and the delivery. It appears we are on hold for the time being.

"We can find out just how much of a bang this damn thing can make, but wherever it goes off, it's going to cause one hell of a calamity and a hell of a lot of damage. And to make it worse, we don't know who the enemy is. We knew it was just a matter of time before something like this would happened, and now its on it's way," he said as he put his head in his hands and leaned on the desk. "We can't let this thing get across the border regardless. Damn. This will be one hell of a deadly crossing, Mickey," he said, slowly shaking his head. "The public will go absolutely wild, and the markets will crash, The holidays would be the perfect timing. Boy, what a mess that will cause," he said as he leaned back in his chair and gazed at the ceiling, again deep in thought.

It was quiet in the ornate office for several minutes as Walker continued to stare at the ceiling and drum his fingers on his big chair. He finally continued, leaning forward again, "We're only speculating that it comes from the Arabs from what we've learned about the origination of that cell phone call to Mexico, and god only knows, but if they're calling each other brothers, there's a good chance it's the Muslim Brotherhood. It's the only thing that makes sense, and they're the group that spawns some of these terrorist offshoots. They apparently have the cooperation of certain Russian individuals who we think are in it for the money. Is that about it?"

"Yes sir. Except Zack has a long way to go according to his plan. He still has to make the drug sale to appease everyone, including the attorney general, who by the way he doesn't trust. He somehow has to get involved enough that he can be in the same place as the bomb so he can perhaps terminate this operation. If anyone can do it, he can."

"Okay! From what you say, it sounds like he has a plan in place, and it also sounds like it changes with some regularity. One thing I've heard about Sinclair is that he thinks outside the box, and that's the best thing we have going for us. I realize we can't put anyone in place at this point, but we're going to have to in the near future, so we need to pick the people now and get them ready to travel. Sort through them and get me names and their skills. We can clear them and get them ready to move. We know we can't have a bunch of people down there. Hell, they'd stick out like a burnt hole in a blanket, and it could drive this operation underground and out of sight. "

With that, Walker stood up, walked around his desk, extended his hand to Mickey, looked him in the eye, and said, "Damn fine work, Mickey. We've got the right guy for the job. Stay real tight with him, Mickey. We need that guy, we need Little Ivan, and we need to be ready to move—and move fast."

CHAPTER 15

Not wanting to appear anxious, Zack waited until late afternoon before calling Rosa.

"Rosa, how are you today? I had a great evening with you last night" he said in a cheerful voice.

"I fell asleep before you left, my love. You should have stayed for breakfast. I haven't done those things on the dance floor since I was a young girl, and the rest of the evening was divine. I haven't slept that well in years and oh the dreams. Could we get together tonight and pick up where we left off?"

"I'm sorry, Rosa. I can't," he lied as he looked out the window at the greenery surrounding the pool area. "I have work I have to do, and it can't be put off. Did you talk to your partner about our meeting?"

"Yes, he definitely wants to meet with you to make sure I'm not putting him on. I believe he thinks I may be pulling a scam on him. He wants us to meet with one of his people tomorrow at a motel he owns. We'll talk to the man so you can tell him what the deal is and explain about the sample."

"I don't know how the trade will be made. That's not my decision. All I can say is that it will have to be something we will all agree on and that will allow the trade to be made without my people being there. I'm afraid I'll be the one making the trade along whatever lines we can agree to. From what you've told me, I don't want it in my possession at any time, so something will have to be worked out. I don't want to be involved with your partner or even know who he is. You told me his name, but that doesn't mean a damn thing to me, and I don't want to know any more," he said.

"Please, Rob, you have no idea how important this is to me. I'll do anything to make it work, but you must meet with them. They want to make sure you're real."

"When and where?" he said as he shook his head in frustration.

"Tomorrow at 6:00 p.m. we meet with them at the motel. I'll have my driver pick you up, and we'll go together."

"Where is this place?"

"It's here in the city. The motel doesn't have a name. They use it for different things, and it's more of a place to take your girlfriend."

"It sounds like one of those motels that have the covered carports so no one knows who's there."

"That's exactly what it is. I'll pick you up at your hotel at five thirty tomorrow afternoon, and we'll go from there. Where are you staying?"

"I think its best that you pick me up somewhere else, Rosa. I don't want those guys following you and finding out where I'm staying. You can pick me up at Sanborn's restaurant across from the Hyatt, okay?"

"Five thirty, we'll be there. Perhaps we can have dinner after that. It shouldn't take too long."

As soon as Zack hung up the phone with Rosa, he called Eduardo to give him the details of the proposed meeting. "Eduardo, I need your help. I have to have another hotel room in the name of Robert Anderson from Denver. It has to be backdated a week, and someone has to cover it to see if anyone tries to get in. Things are getting a little tight right now, so let me tell you what's happening tomorrow."

Zack relayed the whole story to Eduardo. He promised that Zack would be followed and that the motel would be secured. Zack didn't really believe all that but had little choice. He hadn't seen a lot of coordination of efforts yet, but perhaps he was a little paranoid working in a new situation. He couldn't wear a wire and knew he would be "hanging out" alone.

Ruben Marquez sat in his plush office in downtown Guadalajara with the telephone jammed to his ear. He leaned back in the high back chair that dwarfed his small frame. His girth almost matched his height. He stroked his shiny bald head habitually as he talked and rocked gently in the oversized executive chair, his feet only occasionally touching the floor.

He slammed the white phone down and swiveled around to face the three men he had called in. They were an odd group. Their wrinkled sport coats and mismatched slacks looked like they had been slept in. The rail-thin man rarely talked. The corpulent one was a lecher, but Juan, the smallest man, could hold them together. He was the coordinator of the team. He stood up to his full five-foot-three-inch height and wandered around the big office in deep thought. Then he said, "We don't need this bitch once we have the gringo. He's the one who has the stuff. I have a deal put together with the man, and if the three of you are satisfied that this is the same guy I told you about or if it smells bad, waste her. We don't need her, and that should get the gringo in line. He's new at this. If you feel there's any trouble, then we will hold him until the trade. Then we don't care what happens to him. This is a good deal but a much better deal without the redhead. Do we understand one another?"

"Yes, boss," the thin man muttered. "Waste 'em."

"No, asshole. Don't waste *them*. We need the gringo. You hurt him and you're dog meat. I said waste the redhead once you're convinced we have a deal. Do I make myself clear?"

"Yes, boss."

"Then get out of here and get over to the motel to wait for them. And remember, don't hurt the gringo; maybe later, but not now. Understand?" he shouted in an angry voice, driving home his point while shaking his finger as he wandered around his big desk and resettled in his chair.

"Can we enjoy the redhead a little first?" said the fat man.

"Get out of here. This is business. Enjoy the *putas* on your own time," he said, shaking his head.

The black Oldsmobile pulled up at Sanborn's at 5:20 p.m. The back window buzzed down. Rosa's beautiful face lit up with a smile, and she said, "Get in. We're on our way."

Zack got into the big air-conditioned car and slid across the black leather seat to sit next to Rosa. He was surprised to find another man in the front seat with the driver.

"This is Rudolpho," she said, indicating the small man in the right front seat. "He'll be going with us. The driver is Burt."

Burt merely looked into the rearview mirror and nodded. Rudolpho turned in the seat and, barely able to see over the seat back, gave Zack his best smile, which seemed to almost crack his stone face. Zack thought, *My god, this is not a face that smiles much, and his dead weasel-like eyes have the look of being owned by a psychotic. What the hell have we got here?*

Under his breath, Zack said, "Why do we need the extra people, Rosa? I thought we were going alone."

Rosa reached over, squeezed his hand, and said, "Knowing Ruben, I'm sure he will have more than one person to see us, and I thought it would be a good idea to take Rudolpho along. Don't worry. Everything will be just fine. You don't have anything that won't pass a search, do you? I'm sure they'll search us."

"No, I'm fine. Now you say you expect more than one person? I thought they would only have one person there to talk to us."

"Well, I know Ruben, and I'm sure there will be more than one person, as we're not particularly friends. He's just that kind of a guy, and I'm sure he expects us to bring someone as well. Don't worry, my love. Everything will work out fine," she said under her breath as she breathed heavily on his neck.

Victoria sat in the kitchen of the safe house, listening to Eduardo's report of Zack's phone call. Eduardo was nervous but tried to act like it was an everyday event as he walked around the small area.

"Damn it, Eduardo, you know we can't cover that place," said Victoria. "If it's the place I'm thinking of, it's on the road to Tlacapaci, next to those industrial buildings. There isn't anywhere we can get close to that place, and we sure as hell can't rent a room. We don't even know if they rent rooms, for god's sake. We don't even know what room they'll use. We can seal off the perimeter, but that's all after the fact. If something goes wrong, there is no way in hell we can help Zack out. Christ, he's on his own, and Ruben Marquez is one mean son of a bitch. We've let him go in there with a roomful of crazies."

"Relax, Victoria. We'll get some people there and keep an eye on things. Jorge will call us as soon as they know the location for sure. They're keeping track of the car now, and we have two people ready to check in as soon as we know which motel it is. I know it isn't the best scenario in the world, but we'll pull it together. We just need ten or fifteen minutes after we know where they are before we're in position."

"I don't like it at all. I know this is necessary, but it's too dangerous. Who's keeping an eye on Ruben's bunch of hoodlums?"

"Ricardo assured me that it's taken care of."

"Sure, Ricardo always says it's taken care of. No problem, remember?"

The Oldsmobile pulled into the parking area of a tired old two-story cement block motel; heavy canvas curtains hung over all the carports, ensuring privacy. The no-name motel was not unaccustomed to people coming and going at all hours of the day or night, so the Oldsmobile crawling down the crumbling concrete driveway went unnoticed. The only attempt at greenery was a single sparsely leafed oleander bush at the entrance to the gray building with the peeling paint, and the bush was almost dead from lack of water. All the windows were covered tightly with a variety of curtains and tinfoil that hung at various angles; most of the window coverings were water stained from rainwater that had leaked in through the cheap, cracked windows.

Rosa said, "Right here, Burt. Keep your phone on, and I'll call you on the cell as soon as we want to get picked up. Don't wander too far away, and stay with the car. This is not the time to stop for a beer."

"Yes, ma'am. I'll be nearby."

"Okay, let's go," Rosa said as she, Zack, and the odd one she called Rudolpho got out of the car. It was shortly before sunset, and the hot sun had already dropped behind the motel.

"We want to be out of here before dark," said a worried Zack. "This isn't the kind of neighborhood we want to be caught in after dark."

"This shouldn't take long, Rob," Rosa said as she led the way up rusty iron stairs leading to the second floor. She wore a short-sleeve blue shirt, designer jeans that said she was all woman, and low wedged shoes. The odd one had dirty sneakers, well-worn jeans, and a faded black shirt with some band logo of a seminude woman playing a guitar. They made quite a pair. Rosa knocked on a stained yellow door with peeling paint; the only fairly clean spot on it was where the room number, 15, had fallen off. He could see the water-stained curtains sagging on a broken rod through the dirty window, and he could feel the stored-up heat pouring off the cement building in the late afternoon.

The door opened, and a short, stocky stone-faced man in a tan sport coat popped his head out and around the door and said, "Hola, Rosa. Come on in."

Rosa went first and was followed by a nervous Rudolpho as Zack quickly looked around outside. He saw nothing and no one he might recognize as help before he entered the dimly lit room. He closed the door and locked the chain so he would know if someone tried to get in.

"Hello, Juan," said Rosa without a smile, casting her gaze around the dingy room.

"Hello, Rosa," said the pudgy Juan with a sneer as he ogled her body.

Zack looked around the scruffy room that smelled of cigarette smoke, sweat, and hot stale air. It was obviously used for short-term liaisons. He saw that Juan was the only one there. The dark red tile floor was chipped and broken, and the grout had washed out of the joints in numerous places. The dirty off-white walls were adorned with black velvet paintings of nudes that had been popular in the '60s; the paintings were screwed into the walls for security at various angles throughout the room. The overstuffed mismatched furniture was heavily worn and stained. A dirty sliding glass door led outside to a windblown balcony that was void of furniture. Another closed door, apparently to the bathroom, was off to their left.

Juan seemed much too casual to be alone after seeing Rudolpho walk in. As a matter of fact, he seemed cocksure of himself.

"I need to search all of you for weapons and wires, so spread your arms and legs." He didn't take his eyes off Rudolpho the whole time he was talking.

"Bullshit, Juan. You don't need to search us any more than we need to search you. Ruben and I have a deal. You're here to convince yourself that we can deliver, and nothing more. You can talk to this man here," she said, pointing at Zack. "All you have to do is report to Ruben and nothing else. The day I spread my legs for you will be a cold day in hell."

"Well, all right, if that's the way you feel about it," he said as he turned and walked across the room toward the dirty sliding glass doors that opened onto the narrow balcony. In midstride, he quickly turned around, and with his right hand pointed a Colt Model 1911 .45 automatic at the three of them.

He was really serious now. "Now just stand right there," he said as two more men entered the room behind Juan from the bathroom. The one behind Juan and directly in front of Zack was thin to the point of being emaciated. He was more than six feet tall, and his narrow face had an ashen gray, almost dead quality to it. The narrow slits that hid his eyes disguised what he was looking at, and his gash for a mouth was a darker gray than the rest of his face. His black hair was thin and slicked down with a heavy coat of oil. He looked like a standing cadaver. Zack knew this was the dangerous one, the one to watch. This man knew death and was comfortable with it.

The other man sported a trophy-sized gut that hung over his pants, hiding his belt, and his shirt stretched in front, pulling the buttons apart and exposing a dirty undershirt. His bulging bloodshot eyes peered out from a sweaty, flushed face, and his forehead spanned halfway across the top of his head. He was nervous and emitted a small *"eh, eh, eh"* noise as he lecherously stared at Rosa like she was something to eat. He was too busy looking at her bust to see what everyone else was doing. He was just a fat hanger-on—no threat and slow both in body and mind.

An interesting combination, these two. They both wore suit jackets, and in this heat it meant they were both armed. This would not be a casual meeting.

"Hold 'em up real high now so I don't get too nervous," said Juan with a grin. "First, I'm going to search you, and then we're going to have a little talk."

This was trouble. There was no way out of this that Zack could see, and it was becoming more obvious that the possibility of getting out of there alive was dwindling. He had a bad feeling about it, the kind he had learned to pay attention to. The gun! Watch the man with the gun and then the skinny one.

Juan was three feet from Zack, slightly to his right. Rosa stood between Zack and Rudolpho, who was nervously holding his hands straight up in the air and about to explode. He was lifting his feet up and down like he was walking in place and groaning as he did so. Rosa was busy cursing Juan out while the others laughed at Rudolpho.

Juan was close, too close—an amateur thug. He was dangerous only because he had the gun, and it was cocked with the hammer full back. He was smiling and pointing it at Rudolpho. That was where he perceived the threat.

Zack held his hands up shoulder high and said, "Easy, man. Easy."

Then the cadaver spoke. *"Termina.* Finish it," the thin man said.

Oh shit. Oh dear, thought Zack. *Here it is.*

Juan had been pointing the gun at Rudolpho and was swinging it back toward Rosa when Zack moved.

His right hand moved so fast that no one really saw it until he grabbed the barrel of the automatic and pushed it away. His left hand grabbed Juan's right wrist and pulled while he pushed on the gun barrel, bending his wrist and twisting the barrel into Juan's belly. At the same time Zack stepped into him. The first round from the already cocked gun crashed like a cannon as Zack was bending the arm and moving into the man. The spent shell ejected into Zack's right cheek.

Zack could see the blow coming, but there wasn't anything he could do about it. He could not let go of the man's arm, as he had control of it and the gun's direction. Juan's left fist was aimed at Zack's face, and Zack knew he had to take the hit. He tucked his head down hard, and Juan's fist slammed into the top of his head, bringing with it a cascade of bright lights. Juan howled in pain.

Zack shoved his right foot behind Juan's left leg and threw all of his weight into him. The two of them started to fall to the floor with Zack bending Juan's wrist almost double. The movement caused Juan's hand to open slightly, so Zack squeezed it shut and assisted in the next shot that went off with a silenced thud; the bullet buried itself in Juan's chest just as they hit the floor. Juan's howl of pain from when he'd slugged Zack ended in a grunt as the air rushed from his lungs.

Zack rolled to his left off Juan, taking the gun with him. As he looked up, he could see fat boy reaching inside his coat for a gun he had stashed somewhere in his belt at his back. His face was frozen in horror. Zack rolled on his back and pulled back on the slide, ejecting the spent shell and clearing the chamber while bringing the gun up to the thin man, who had just gotten his gun out of his shoulder holster and was swinging it toward Zack. He hadn't changed his expression since he had walked into the room. He was the iceman, but things just weren't going his way.

Rolling onto his back, Zack pointed the gun over his head, aimed at the center of the thin man's chest, and squeezed the trigger in a double tap. At this distance, even shooting upside down, he couldn't miss. The big gun roared in the small room, and the heavy slugs tore the thin man off the floor and hammered him into an overstuffed chair, sending both him and the chair rolling.

Zack swung the gun toward the fat man, who was having trouble getting his gun free from his overloaded belt. The man's expression had changed from horror to deadly fear, as he knew he was about to die. Zack could hear the big man's bowels let loose just before he pulled the trigger, and the slug slammed the fat man into the corner, where he slid in slow motion to the floor, wearing an astonished look.

Juan was still lying on Zack's leg, so Zack kicked himself free, looked around the room, and saw Rosa standing in the same position with her mouth open. Her eyes were as big as saucers, and she was hyperventilating. Rudolpho had disappeared completely. *Damn him. Where the hell did he go?*

Zack quickly checked all three men. They were obviously dead. Then he grabbed Rosa, who was bent over as if someone had knocked the wind out of her. She was staring with vacant eyes at Juan on the floor. Zack shook her hard. "Rosa, get with it. Where the hell is Rudolpho?"

Rosa turned her glassy eyes to where Rudolpho had been standing and said, "I don't know. He was right here."

Zack saw the chain still hanging on the door catch, so he had to be in the room somewhere. Just then Zack saw a foot sticking out from behind a badly scarred and chipped heavy wooden coffee table in front of the ragged overstuffed couch. Carefully, Zack looked over the table, and there was Rudolpho, faceup, looking surprised with a big hole smack in the middle of his chest. The first round that had gone off when Zack was pushing the gun away from Rosa and fighting for control of it must have hit the little man in the chest and thrown him over the table.

Rosa still stood transfixed, staring at the bleeding Juan on the dirty floor as Zack hurried to the two sliding glass doors, quietly but quickly opened one, and looked out on the little balcony. It was enclosed on each side with a solid block wall, and a rusting iron railing connected the two side walls enclosing the balcony. It was about ten feet from the ground, which opened on a patio for another room.

Zack wiped the gun off, put it back in Juan's hand, and pressed the man's dead hand around the butt of the gun for fingerprints. Then he let the gun slide to the floor. He shook the dazed Rosa again to get her attention.

"Give me your shoes. Hurry."

"What, what do you want my shoes for?" she mumbled absently as she started to come around.

"Rosa, we have to get out of here and get out fast. The only way is out the back. You'll break your legs trying to run in those high heels. Now give them to me." With that, he bent over, lifted her foot, and pulled off a shoe while she leaned on his back, complaining. He stuffed both shoes into his shirtfront and rebuttoned it. Then he grabbed the still mesmerized Rosa by the right wrist and dragged her to the balcony. "You do exactly as I tell you."

She continued to stare at Zack blankly and said, "Why?"

"Rosa, it's important. Your life depends on it. Now keep very quiet and follow directions exactly, or you could end up like your friends back there."

With a visible shudder, Rosa weakly mumbled, "Okay."

Zack crawled over the sun-hot railing and told Rosa to do the same. Over her continued whispered objections, he lowered her as far as he could by holding her wrist and then dropped her into the pea gravel below. Then he dropped down alongside her. She was just starting to complain when he jerked her to her feet and glanced toward the lower motel room to see if anyone was watching. If the room was occupied, the occupants weren't showing themselves. With the shooting going on overhead, they'd be crazy to stick their heads out. The small enclosed yard was surrounded by a redwood stake fence about six feet high. Zack shoved a complaining Rosa over the top, and she toppled into the unknown with a grunt.

Zack hit the ground alongside a confused Rosa. She rubbed the bottom of her feet and groaned about them being scratched.

"Don't worry about that right now, Rosa. They'll be a whole lot worse before we're out of here."

Looking around, he saw that they were in a long alleyway with the motel's board fence on one side and a high thick oleander hedge on the other. He charged through the poisonous oleanders and found that on the other side of the hedge they were behind a fenced industrial complex. To the left was a riverbed of some kind that ran under a major thoroughfare with stores and commercial outlets beyond. To his right, there was more industry. There was about four feet of a gravel alleyway between the cyclone fence of the industrial park and the oleander hedge.

He went back after Rosa and, despite her objections, dragged her through the hedge and ran for the riverbed. He continued to drag her while she complained loudly.

"For Christ's sake, Rosa, shut up and run. You're running for your life right now, so act as if you mean it. If you stay here, you are either dead or in jail. Now move."

Rosa was now on the move, and Zack could hear her grunt and groan with pain as her bare feet pounded the rock-strewn alley between the cyclone fence and the oleander hedge as he continued to drag her along. So far no one had challenged them, and there were no shouts of alarm from behind them. They had to get into that riverbed and out of sight fast.

After a quick look around, without hesitation he pulled Rosa, stumbling and falling, down the steep dirt slope into the almost dry drainage way, which was cluttered with every imaginable piece of debris cast off by the big city. The dry riverbed was about seventy-five feet wide, and fifty yards to their right was an overpass that supported a major roadway. They had to make it there at least before they could stop and rest; they would be hard to see in the dark shadows. The area under the overpass was pitch-black.

"Rosa, we have to make the overpass before we stop, so just keep pumping those beautiful legs of yours," he encouraged her. "It'll be easier running down here, as the ground is softer, so just hang in there."

As he pulled Rosa by her left wrist, they dashed into the heavy black shadow of the overpass. The thundering traffic noise of the cars pounding across the concrete bridge made it sound like they were in a rail yard. The place smelled of urine and feces, and an occasional whiff of something dead reached them as the cooling evening air moved through the black tunnel.

After stopping briefly, Zack said, "Okay, let's move it." He grabbed her wrist again and started to jog at a slower pace.

They were running under the overpass when fifty feet ahead of them on the right side, a black figure appeared out of the dark shadows, silhouetted against the dim light at the end of the overpass tunnel. The figure deliberately moved to block their path.

Rosa saw the man and pulled back on Zack's hand, grunting in protest. There were two of them now. Zack growled, "Keep moving," and gave the hesitant Rosa a jerk.

He knew about these misfit thugs of the underworld who lived in these underpasses and sewers; they were diseased, malnourished, and dangerous. Many were subhuman people who killed anything and everything that came into their domain for anything they could get. *I wish I'd kept the gun,* he thought as he sprinted toward the two men, who had now multiplied into a gauntlet of three and were now making a soft wailing sound.

When they were about twenty feet away, Zack pointed back over his shoulder with his right hand and yelled in his best Spanish, "Run! It's coming! Run for your life!"

They were black silhouettes against the fading light, but he knew where they were standing, and his shout of alarm caused them to stop their wailing for a moment. They looked down the dark underpass behind Zack in the direction he was pointing as Rosa caught on and took up the chant as well. They rapidly closed the gap between themselves and the black figures.

Zack was still pointing back over his shoulder and yelling as he ran up to the first man. He was really sizing the man up as to how and where he was standing. He could make out his black outline against the far end of the tunnel. The first man was looking down the wash behind Zack. Then he slowly turned and looked directly

DEADLY CROSSING

at the rapidly approaching pair. Zack and Rosa were three feet away, and the man reached out to grab Zack.

Zack brought his tightly clenched right fist forward from behind his body where he had been pointing. Using all the power he could muster, he hit the first man square in the middle of the face. The force of the blow sent a shock wave through his shoulder. He could feel the man's face break like glass. The unexpected blow had knocked the thug off his feet, catapulting him into the next man, and they both went down in a grunting heap. The third man was about eight feet ahead of them now, and Zack had lost some momentum delivering the blow that had taken the first two out.

Zack was dragging the reluctant Rosa when the third man stepped in front of Zack, blocking his path. Zack saw the man's right hand come out from his side, and Zack heard the unmistakable *snick* as a blade snapped out of a switchblade knife. With only twenty yards to go to get out from under the overpass, they couldn't stop, but this man was determined.

Zack let go of Rosa's wrist and rushed into the man, who looked surprised that his show of the knife didn't stop the charging pair. The man started to step back when Zack held his left arm out to fend off the knife blow while jabbing with his open right hand. It was so dark, it was hard to tell just where the knife was.

The heel of his hand flashed in under the man's chin, hitting his Adam's apple. It sounded like crushing an empty beer can as the stiff cartilage of the larynx and trachea crushed under the blow. The man wheezed and fell back, but the knife was already on its way. Zack tried blocking the knife in the dark and thought he'd made it when he felt a sharp sting in his right side. Their momentum carried them past the three men, and Zack turned around, grabbing Rosa by the arm and yelling, "Run or you're dead!"

Zack hadn't seen any other sewer dwellers but knew this would move her along, and it did. Bursting into the fading twilight of the open wash, Zack looked around for an escape route only to find that the sides were ten-foot-high concrete walls supporting the maze of streets above the wash. They were trapped, and they couldn't go back. He could not deal with the three men again and could feel his side bleeding. The concrete walls of the drainage channel went as far through the commercial complex as he could see in the fading light. There was no way out.

CHAPTER 16

What a place to die. A stinking sewer drainage channel, Zack thought as his lifestyle and memories started to flash through his mind like a high-speed video. The pattern he recognized, as it had happened to him many times in the past when things seemed hopeless, but somehow he always managed to pull through. Nothing was hopeless. Just think it through and work it out and do it fast.

On the far side of the wash, he spotted a large lump of waste material jammed by floodwaters against the wall. He hurried over to examine it. In the middle of the debris was a fifty-five-gallon drum lying on its side, and he tipped it up on its end. The distance from the drum to the top of the concrete wall was about six feet, and a ten-foot cyclone fence ran about two feet from the edge of the cavernous canal wall. He put a heavy wooden box in front of the now upright drum.

He turned to Rosa and said, "Get over here quickly, Rosa. It's time to go. I'll help you up on the drum, and you do exactly as I tell you. No questions. We don't have time for that."

As he helped Rosa up onto the drum, he said, "Face the wall and put your hands on the it. Lean in close to the wall. Do not lean back or look back. I want your feet far apart on the edge of the barrel. I'll move them for you. Don't worry. You'll be okay. I'm going to crawl up onto the barrel and put my head between your legs and lift you. You stay close to the wall and move your hands up the wall as you go. Understand?"

"Yes. Please hurry. Please."

Zack struggled on top of the barrel, as there wasn't a lot of room to maneuver, but he finally got his head between her legs and Rosa on his shoulders and then stood up slowly.

"That's great, Rosa. I want you to bend your knees. I'm going to put your feet in my hands."

Zack maneuvered Rosa's feet into his hands and held them tightly against his lower chest. "Okay, Rosa, stand up very slowly. Stay close to the wall and run your hands up to the top.

"I can reach the top now, Rob."

"Great. Hold on and I'm going to boost you up. I want you to keep your legs very straight. Just make them rigid. I don't want them to bend at all. When you go up, grab the fence as soon as you can."

Rosa didn't weigh as much as some of the iron he worked with when he worked out, so lifting her up was not a problem except that he felt a tear in his side where he had been stabbed.

"I've got it. I've got it."

"Pull yourself up now, Rosa," he said as she lifted her left leg to the ledge while Zack pushed higher on her right foot. *Thank God. She's out,* he thought.

Zack backed off into the wash as he heard moaning noises and commotion from under that dark overpass. It sounded like they were coming. He gauged his distance. He was right-handed, so he needed to hit and vault off the barrel with his left foot. He judged the distance to the box to make sure his right foot would hit that, taking him to the barrel with his left without losing speed.

The ground was soft and loose, but he gained the speed he needed. His momentum carried him well up the wall, and he easily reached the top and, using that momentum, pulled himself up to grab the fence. This time he knew something tore badly in his side. It was no longer a sting. It was a burn.

"Rosa, work your way down to the end of the fence to that big vacant lot. Hold on to the fence at all times. There isn't a lot of room up here, so let's go."

After Rosa put on her shoes, they worked their way along, clinging to the fence on the narrow drainage way wall, and headed toward the lights of the nearby stores.

Zack moved slowly, holding his side. He knew he was bleeding a lot. He said to a limping Rosa, "Get on the cell phone and call Burt. Tell him where we are and that we need to get out of here and fast."

A frightened Rosa held Zack's arm, trying to help him as they made their way to the first street just as the big Oldsmobile bounced over the curb and headed for them across the unpaved lot. Rosa looked over at Zack and gasped as they neared the lights of a Pemex gas station.

She said, "Rob, you're bleeding and bleeding bad."

Zack looked down and saw his shirt was soaked on the right side, as well as his pants. Blood oozed out from between his fingers, and he could feel it running down his leg. He knew his sock was soaked as well, as each step had a mushy feeling. "I'm hurt pretty bad, Rosa. I've got a real bleeder in there. We have to get me to a hospital right away to get me fixed up." The adrenaline rush was wearing off now, and a heavy weariness started to envelop him.

Rosa helped him into the backseat of the car as Burt looked around with alarm at Zack's blood-soaked clothes. He then looked back into the open lot and said, "Where's Rudolpho?"

"He's not coming, Burt," said Zack. "Let's go."

Burt didn't say any more and accelerated the car down the street, constantly looking in the rearview mirror. Zack took off his shirt and twisted it into a ropelike shape with the sleeves on each end. He grabbed a box of Kleenex off the floor, took a two-inch wad out, and jammed it over his wound.

"Hold this in place, Rosa, and help me wrap this around my waist so it's tight."

Rosa was a big help getting the tight bandage in place. When he was finally satisfied, he leaned back against the seat of the sedan with a sigh and closed his eyes.

Rosa rummaged through the massive handbag she had left in the car, all the time cursing Ruben, and came up with some towelettes, which she used to clean her dirty scratched-up feet.

"That son of a bitch was going to have us killed," she said. "Those bastards were there to shoot us. What happened to Rudolpho?"

"Rudolpho's dead, Rosa. Juan killed him, and you'll have to forget about him. Yes indeed, you sure have a nice partner, Rosa. You sure know how to pick 'em."

"Don't worry, Rob. I'll get you to a doctor. I know one who will take care of you, and no one will know about it."

"Don't take me to your doctor, Rosa. Your friends know them all too. Just take me to a hospital."

"Damn, Rob. Holy mother of god. You saved my life back there."

"If you think about it, Rosa, I saved your life two or three times today," he said, trying to subtly obligate her. "You owe me, so just take me to a hospital, okay? What are you going to do about your partner?"

"I don't know. I think now he will do everything he can to hunt us all down."

"Why don't you turn the tables on him? Call him up and chew him out for trying such a stunt. Let him know that you're better and stronger than him and aren't going to take any crap from him. Tell him that if he doesn't get in line, you just may wipe *him* out. Be aggressive. Remember, he doesn't know what happened over there. He may not even be aware that there was a shoot-out, so call him before he finds out. Show him you're in control and get right on his case, but do it right away and use the cell phone so he can't trace the call."

Rosa just sat deep in thought for a minute and stared at Zack with questioning eyes. "Rob, you're just full of surprises. That's a good idea." With that, she pulled out her cell phone and punched in some numbers.

The conversation only lasted a few minutes, but Zack was too tired to pay attention.

Ruben's face looked like a bright red tomato as he slammed down the phone and yelled for one of his lieutenants. He punched in the number of the motel manager and shouted, "Manuel, what the hell is going on over there?"

"I can't talk right now, sir. There's police all over the damn place. Your guys made a mess of it. There's four bodies up there, and the place is a mess. I'll call you later," he said as he hung up abruptly, leaving a shocked Ruben sitting in his office with the dead phone still at his ear.

Holy balls, it's true, he thought as he groped for one of his heart pills. *Rosa took them out, and they were my best men. How could that be? I didn't think she had the men or the smarts, damn her. Who the hell do the four bodies belong to?*

"Get over there and see what you can find out," he said to the nervous man standing in front of the desk, shifting from one foot to the other. "See who the hell is dead over there, and get back to me. Talk to your friends in the station and see if they know what happened. We know that she showed up with the gringo and the little man. If she's alive, she's a better woman than I gave her credit for, but she'll get hers. It's just a matter of time," he mumbled under his breath. "We'll find a better time, but we'll finish this job first. Now get going," he shouted as he paced the room.

Ricardo picked up the telephone in his office. It must be the lookouts checking in. They should be in place by now, as they had called about fifteen minutes ago and said that Zack and Rosa and Nicholas's little shooter had gone into the motel. It couldn't be more perfect.

Leaning back in his chair, feeling all was under control, he said, "How's it going?"

Almost yelling, Jorge said, "Christ, all hell broke loose. We heard a lot of shooting and went over and kicked the door in, as it was locked from the inside. The American and the woman were gone. How they got out, I don't know, but they must have gone over the balcony. We got four stiffs over here. I'm not sure who they are, but it's a mess, so get this place sealed off so we can check it out. We need an excuse for being here so fast. Hell, we weren't even to our room yet."

Ricardo's jaw dropped open, and he bolted upright in his chair, almost tipping it over. "Wait, what did you say?"

"I said we have four bodies all shot to hell, and the American and the woman are long gone. They couldn't have been in there five minutes before all hell broke loose. What happened, I don't know, as we haven't had a chance to look it over yet and we need help from the office to keep the local cops out of here. Make a federal case out of it, anything, just send help, because the locals are gathering. I told the first patrol car guy to have his men clear the area and let no one in, but I need help."

"Okay. We're on our way," he said as he slammed down the phone and yelled at Eduardo down the hall.

Eduardo burst into the room wearing a frightened expression, and Ricardo said, "Get a car, Eduardo. We're going to the motel. We've got four bodies over there. Everything apparently went to hell. Holy balls of fire, let's move."

"Zack?"

"No, apparently he got out of there, but I don't know how. We need to know what happened."

"Ricardo, everyone told you we couldn't handle that place, and we're lucky, just maybe, that we don't have a dead American on our hands who was working for this department. The political fallout would put us all out of business. You know the administration would love to put family in here."

"Let's go."

"No, you go, Ricardo. Zack doesn't have anyone to call but us if he needs help. I plan on being here if and when he does call and to give him that help. We let him down, and the least we can do is to get him in if we have to. Anyone can look over the scene. You go. It'll look good in the papers," Eduardo said with a little sarcasm and a lot of concern.

Eduardo used his cell phone and called the safe house. He was using it as a command post for Zack now, and it would keep him out of the office and keep better control of the operation. Ricardo was just too loose on these things. Victoria answered the phone. He filled her in and told her to stay available to pick up Zack if necessary.

Zack leaned back in the seat of the sedan as it rapidly moved through traffic, collecting his thoughts and slowly bringing his mind and body under control. "Rosa, I've been thinking about a hospital. I think it would be smart to just drop me off at the emergency room and you folks take off. If you go in there with me, it will raise all kinds of flags, and I think we could have some real trouble with the police. They know who you are, so just drop me off. I think that's best. We can't possibly answer their questions of why I just happen to be with you. It's too damn complicated. Just drop me off. I can handle it from there."

Rosa sat there thinking and then said, "Perhaps you're right, Rob, but I'm not going to leave you alone if you can't make it. I'll take you in and take my chances."

She leaned into him as the Oldsmobile pulled into the emergency entrance of the big Social Security Hospital.

Rosa helped Zack out of the car and said, "Are you sure you can make it, Rob? I'll stay with you if you want. Just tell me."

"I'm a lot stronger after my rest," he lied, struggling to stand up and to keep from falling over. "Just help me to the door. Then you guys get out of here. If you come in, we can never answer their questions."

She kissed him quickly and walked back to the car as Zack leaned against the swinging doors and staggered into the hospital. He looked out through the glass door as it closed and saw the black car accelerate out of the emergency driveway.

He made his way through the busy emergency waiting room. It was a small room filled with plastic chairs of all kinds from a variety of beer companies. The floor was as clean as chipped concrete could be, and the white walls were spotless. He didn't look any worse than a lot of the people there and definitely not as bad as some he noticed as he glanced around the room. No one was interested in him; they all had their own problems and stared ahead, not focusing on anything. He was relying on this as he sized up the people sitting on the plastic chairs.

"Pardon me. Where's a telephone?" Zack asked in Spanish. "I have an emergency."

"So does everyone else," said the tired, overworked nurse as she barely glanced at Zack.

"I need to use the telephone right away, and I'll pay for it. It's a local call, so I can use the pay phone. Just tell me where it is."

"There aren't any pay phones here. You'll just have to wait your turn."

"My turn for what? I need a phone."

"Look, do you want to see a doctor? If you do, then sit down and wait your turn. If you want a telephone, go down the street to a restaurant. They have a phone," she said, pointing up the street.

"Thank you very much," said Zack as he walked away from the window. He knew he couldn't make it down the street to a restaurant. He couldn't walk another hundred feet.

The nurse went immediately back to work and forgot him. While she was processing another patient and wasn't looking, he slipped through the swinging doors to the doctors' offices in the emergency area, acting like he knew exactly where he was going. No one stopped to question him, as they were too busy. Zack continued down the hall until he spotted a telephone on a cluttered desk in an open office. He walked in and shut the door.

Eduardo picked up on the first ring.

Without any preliminaries, Zack said, "I'm not sure that I can trust you assholes anymore, Eduardo, but I'm asking you as a friend. If you want out of this, let me know, and I'll fade into the woodwork."

"Zack, oh my god, I'm happy it's you. Are you okay? Where are you? What can I do?"

"I'd say more, but I'm too damn weak and need to get to a hospital where I'm not going to be shot. I need blood, antibiotics, and sewn up. Can you handle that? If not, just say so, Eduardo. I'm damn upset at this point."

"Where are you?"

Zack was too weak to argue. "I'm in the emergency ward at the Social Security Hospital."

He could hear Eduardo yelling in the background to someone, and when he came back on the phone, he said, "Okay, we have a doctor in that hospital. He's not on duty right now, but he will be as soon as we track him down. We'll have an ambulance pick you up, so stay in the emergency room area. The doctor or someone else will get you within fifteen minutes. That I promise. If I have to dress like a nurse myself, I'll get you. How bad are you, Zack?"

"Well, I'm not a doctor, but I bled like a stuck pig for quite a while. I need some help, amigo, and I need it now."

"Go sit in the waiting room. I'll be there."

"Senor Sinclair? Senor Sinclair?" The voice drifted in from some far-off place. It sounded like it was coming off a lake. It seemed to fit into the disjointed dream he was having, but it was too insistent, and it was now shaking him.

Zack pulled himself up from the heavy dream and pried his eyes open; they felt like they were glued together. He tried to focus and looked directly into a pair of black eyes about a foot from his own. The man's facial features were too fuzzy to make out, but he wore a white doctor's coat, and a doctor's ever-present stethoscope hung around his neck. The man seemed to have a concerned look on his face.

"Yes?" Zack croaked through a parched throat.

"Let me help you. Do you think you can walk a little bit?" the man said, reaching for Zack's arm.

"If you help me, I think I can. I feel pretty shaky and am having trouble waking up. Give me a hand, please."

The doctor helped Zack into a wheelchair and pushed him down the same hall Zack had used to find the telephone. His side was sore again. He looked down and could see that his wound had bled through his Kleenex bandage. If the doctor hadn't woken him, he would have bled out in that jungle they called a waiting room. They reached an alcove, and the doctor wheeled him to a side door that had a burned-out *salida*, or exit sign, over it.

They emerged outside in the cool evening, and a parked ambulance sprang into action. The gurney was rolled out, and many hands lifted Zack onto it. They slid it into the ambulance and started to roll the instant the doors closed. The lights came on in the back, and the doctor mumbled something to a nurse who was busy strapping Zack's right arm to a board and inserting a line for plasma. The doctor put something into a hypodermic needle and gave Zack a shot in the upper arm.

The doctor said, "This will make you a little sleepy, so just relax. It's a little morphine."

As the ambulance moved through traffic with sirens blaring, Zack started to relax and noticed a familiar, pleasant scent that fought its way through the rest of the pungent odors in the ambulance. "Victoria, is that you?" he mumbled.

"Yes, Zack, I'm here. How did you know that? I'm in the front of the ambulance, and you can't see me. How did you know I was here?"

"Ask me some other time," he said as he chuckled and dozed off.

Ruben picked the phone up on the first ring. "*Si?*" he said.

"You're right, boss. They're all dead. My guy at the scene, you know the fat one with the scar, he told me it looked very professional. All four of them were shot in the middle of the chest; they didn't stand a chance. I don't know how many guys there were, but they wasted all four of them. Rosa's guy was that little guy we thought did Joey. Remember him? He was shot too."

"I remember. I wonder how she got other men in there. We only saw the three of them go in. Did he say how many shooters there were?"

"No. That's a funny thing. He told me it looked like Juan did the whole thing himself. He said Juan's gun was the only one fired, and the empties on the floor were the same caliber as Juan's cannon, and the number of empty cases matched the number of holes in people. Damn fishy, boss. Do you think she could have gotten to Juan and paid him off?"

"Not possible, not possible," he mumbled. "You think he did that and then shot himself? Not possible. I'll see you when you get back."

Ruben knew a day might come when someone offered his men more money than they were being paid. That was always a possibility. But why now when things were so well put together? What could have gone wrong, and who in the hell shot Juan?

Zack woke to find himself in a bright, colorful room with large French doors that opened onto a patio where he could hear softly running water. The open doors let in a soft breeze that gently moved the gauze drapes. *This is no hospital*, he told himself. Just then he heard a rustle of fabric, and a woman in her late fifties, with coal-black hair and eyes, and wearing a starched white nurses uniform walked into view.

In excellent English, she said, "How do you feel? You've had a real nice nap."

"Where am I, and what time is it?"

"You're at a federal safe house that is used for a variety of purposes. I am here to take care of you until you're on your feet. I have instructions to call Eduardo as soon as you wake up, so I'll go and do that now. I'll be back shortly. Can I bring you anything to eat or drink?"

"Yes, I'm dying of thirst. Bring an iced tea with a lemon if you have it, or just a glass of water. What time is it?"

"It's three o'clock in the afternoon. You were brought in here last evening. I was brought on the job when the doctor left at seven this morning." She left the room just as determined as she seemed to be to do everything else.

Zack had just closed his eyes when an excited Eduardo rushed into the room and said, "Zack, how are you doing? I just heard that you were awake, and I came right over. I'm glad to see you're doing so well, and the good news is that you have no complications. The muscles were sewn back up, and the skin was taped and glued shut, and your abdomen was not punctured, so everything should go along just fine."

"Just fine, Eduardo? Where the hell were you guys when I needed you? I'm in a shooting gallery with a bunch of thugs, and you folks are out enjoying the evening. I thought you were going to have me covered at all times. Oh sure, I know, no problem, but I think it's time you folks start looking for another guy for this job. As soon as I can get up, I'm out of here. Speaking of out of here, when can I leave?"

"The doctor says you can go in a couple of days, but you have to take it easy. Look, Zack, I know things didn't go as we all expected, but at least you're all right, and that's what's important."

"What's important is that you didn't deliver on your end of the deal. I was left hanging out there in the unknown, and the only person I had on my side was a psychotic that went down with the first round, and that was by accident. What happened to you?"

Victoria had come into the room while Zack was unloading on Eduardo. She just stood inside the doorway with a worried look on her face, saying nothing, while Zack continued to chew on Eduardo.

"Look, Zack, we need you," Eduardo finally admitted. "Please tell us what happened in there."

"First tell me who those people were."

"The three men of Ruben Marquez's have records as long as your arm and were his top henchmen. He only sent the best. We've wanted to put them away for years, but Marquez had too much pull for us to do much about it."

As best he could, Zack told them in detail what happened from the time he was picked up by Rosa until the doctor woke him up in the hospital. When he finished, Eduardo and Victoria just stared at each other, not saying a word.

Eduardo slowly shook his head and looked at Zack in amazement. With a smile on his face, he said, "You mean there was no one else there but the three of you, and all the shooting was done by you?"

"That's exactly what I'm telling you. We were all dead if I didn't do something. The skinny guy said *termina,* and I knew what the hell that meant, and Juan was ready to do it. They got their orders from someone. I don't think they were there to talk about the deal at all. They were there to get rid of us. What the hell is going on? I thought they needed us to complete the deal."

"That changes things dramatically," said Victoria, speaking up for the first time as she walked over to the bed. "We'll have to figure out what to do now. Rosa can't move without the money, and she obviously doesn't have it."

"I think that may have taken care of itself," said Zack, and he filled them in on the conversation Rosa had with Marquez when she was cussing Ruben out on her cell phone from the car.

Eduardo said, "Get some rest, my friend, and we'll talk about it later."

"Did you get a room for me in the name of Smith?"

"Yes, it's taken care of. You checked in the same day you arrived in town and are staying at the Holiday Inn downtown."

"I may have to use that room before I leave town, so you'd better get me a key and have someone say they've seen me around there from time to time. I'm sure Rosa is probably checking on me, as she is a little dubious as to whom I am after the mess in the motel. I think she'll be asking a lot of questions, and that Marquez guy will probably be looking for me as well."

Victoria came over and put her hand on Zack's forehead just as he was closing his eyes. He just couldn't hold them open any longer. The shot the nurse had given him was pulling him down.

She said, "Zack, you are an amazing guy. I'll stop in and see you later. I'm very happy you're all right."

"There is more to this than meets the eye, Victoria. I hope you realize this."

"We're working on that right now, Zack. Believe me," she said dismissively as she walked out of the room and quietly closed the door.

Eduardo arrived at ten o'clock in the morning and was all apologies again, but Zack cut him off by saying, "Eduardo, I'm through with you people. I'm out, finished, *termino*, whatever, but I'm through," he said, still playing the DEA card. "I've been thinking this over, and this is a one-man show, and I'm the show."

"Zack, please, I understand. Truly I do," he said desperately. "Ricardo was putting together the cover for you at the motel with local people, and they were slow in getting in place. He knows he can't be on the outside and still try to call the procedure. He's given me complete control of the operation now, and Ricardo will structure the transfer only. You and I will approve everything from here on in, and what you say goes. I know we treated you poorly at the motel, and I am truly sorry. Victoria and Jorge could not be in on the motel scene because we didn't want them recognized in the future. Victoria insists on being with you all the time now."

Eduardo leaned down close to Zack's ear and whispered, "When we are alone, I will tell you what we think and what we are doing about it. This is on the level, Zack. Rely on it. You need some rest now and to take some time off," he said as he stood up, looking Zack straight in the eye. "We can arrange to have you flown to the States or San Carlos, whichever you prefer, and you can recuperate while things settle down."

"I'll think I'll go back to the States as soon as possible, which won't be soon enough. I'll let you know my decision on my continued contribution to this matter before I leave. I really thought I could help and was doing some good by getting the drugs off the street, but this is a war zone down here. I'll need some expense money, as I'll have to move into my new hotel room when I leave here."

"Zack, you can have anything you want. Believe me."

Zack had thought long and hard about what he was going to tell Eduardo and Victoria. He needed them, but he couldn't tell them the real reason he was staying on the job. He had to continue with the DEA cover-up as long as he could.

When Zack finally got into his new hotel room, he called Mickey. There had been no way he could call him from the safe house hospital bed. There were too many eyes and ears there. He told him as completely as possible everything that had happened.

"What the hell is going on down there, Zack?" Mickey's alarmed voice conveyed the concern he had for his friend.

"Mickey, you won't believe how devious these drug people are and how little concern they have for human life. There's absolutely no value when the greed and drugs kick in. This is a whole different dimension. These people are crazy, and I have to keep that in mind when I'm dealing with them. The woman Rosa is defiantly on my side at this time, I think. I know that's a presumption, but I feel it's valid."

"How bad you hurt, pal? Sounds like you need to get out of there for a while, if you think this operation can simmer a little longer. From what you've said, it sounds like it isn't going anywhere until you show with the drugs and the sale is made. Is that about it?"

"I think so, Mickey. They're so focused on the drug issue and the money at this point that there isn't anything even mentioned beyond the sale. I think things are on hold for now. This could help us with our goal. What's our friend Walker got to say about this?"

"We put together a team to get in place when you need them but not before. He knows they would be a burden and may blow the whole thing at this time and run it underground. It's obvious that timing and relationships are critical at this point. They've been handpicked and are ready to move on a moment's notice."

They talked for some time and planned a sit-down meeting when Zack arrived in the United States. They both knew Zack had a lot to do yet.

Zack called Rosa at 7:00 p.m. She answered on the fourth ring, and her lilting voice disturbed Zack because she still didn't sound as bad as everyone said she was. *She sure hasn't acted crazy yet*, he thought.

"Hi, Rosa. How are you doing?"

"Rob, where are you?"

"I'm back at my hotel. I had to lay low for a few days so I could be taken care of without staying in the hospital. I didn't trust the security there. It wouldn't be difficult for someone to call and ask if a wounded gringo was there. I would have been a sitting duck. So I made a deal with a doctor to send me to a private home where they took care of me. They didn't have a telephone, so I couldn't call you until now. How are you doing?"

"I'm fine, but I must see you."

"Trouble for a change?"

"No, no, nothing like that. I just need to see you. I've made some serious decisions in my life, and I would like to share them with you. Can we meet somewhere?"

"No, I'm afraid not. I'm having a tough enough time just getting around. Say nothing of going out anywhere. If I fall or strain myself, I'll tear out all the stitches."

"Please, can I come over and see you at your hotel."

"Well, okay. But make it early and come alone. I don't want anymore of these thugs around. I'm at the Holiday Inn, room 235. It's in the back, and if you drive you can park right outside the door. Make damn sure you're not followed. All I need is for some of those crazy bastards to show up."

"Yes, I know where you are. I've been trying to call you and was getting worried about you."

Suspicions confirmed, thought Zack, "Well, come on over. I'm pretty much restricted to bed, so I won't be much company. I'm pretty beat, so I'll be going to bed early, okay?"

"That's fine, Rob. I'll be there within the hour."

True to her word, there was a knock on the door at 7:45 p.m. Zack looked through the security peephole in the door and saw that Rosa was alone. He waited and watched her for a moment to see if she would look around suspiciously or signal someone. When she continued to knock and appeared to be alone, he opened the door on the chain.

"Hi. It's you. I hope you're alone."

"Yes, of course I am. Please let me in."

Zack closed the door, released the chain, and opened it wide for Rosa. He was in a white terry cloth hotel bathrobe, slippers, and a pair of short pajamas, every bit the patient.

"Come on in, Rosa. How are you? I was worried about you and didn't know what happened after the big event."

Rosa put her arms around Zack's neck as her coat fell open. She pulled herself close to him and kissed him hungrily on the mouth. The soft polyester dress she wore easily revealed that she probably didn't have anything on underneath it as she moved against Zack's body. Her warm body was firm and inviting.

"Easy, Rosa. You'll pull me apart. I'm only held together by thread and glue, you know. It'll take a few days before things start to heal up. Right now I'm pretty fragile." Zack's eyes scanned her beauty and stopped when he saw her blue sneaker boat shoes. He looked at her with a grin and said, "Your shoes go with your outfit real well, Rosa. You may start a new fashion trend."

Rosa laughed and said, "My feet are sore as hell, Rob. I hope I didn't hurt you when I squeezed you. It's just that I've really missed you a lot. I'm surprised I feel this way. Let me help you to the bed." She held Zack's arm and led him to the bed, where she plumped up the pillows and stuffed and stacked them so he could sit up.

"Thanks, Rosa. Now tell me, what has happened with you and your good friend Ruben?"

"Rob, Ruben apologized all over himself and said he didn't know anything about what happened. He said anything those men did, they did it on their own and he didn't have anything to do with it."

"Sure, sure."

"Rob, you are truly a genius. I did just like you told me to, and Ruben is all friendly and helpful. He is anxious to get this project underway, and as soon as possible. He wants to get it done before the end of the year, even during the holidays, believe it or not."

"Forget about getting it done in the next couple of weeks. I plan on taking off as much time as necessary to get back on my feet and make sure my body has healed up," he said, tapping his stomach. "We can't get a lot of cooperation from anyone during the holidays in the States, say nothing about Mexico, where everything shuts down. No, I don't see this happening much before February at the earliest, and that will give your friend Ruben time to get the money together. Just what are you going to get out of this anyway, Rosa? It sounds to me like you're a middleman, like me, and the bucks just aren't that good, are they?"

"That's what I want to talk to you about," she said with a big smile.

"What do you have on your mind, Rosa?"

"I think I may have my house sold. I put it on the market the day after we met with Ruben's men, and I think it's sold."

"What's that supposed to mean?"

"I'm sorry. I don't know where to start, Rob. I've done a lot of things in my day, and a lot of those things I'm not very proud of. As a matter of fact, when I think about some of them, I'm ashamed of myself. I didn't think about it until Juan pointed that gun at me and was going to kill me, and I knew right then that I was going to die. They always say your life flashes before your eyes just before you die, and mine did, but it lasted a lot longer than that, and I didn't like what I saw. When I saw Juan lying on the floor in a pool of blood with that hole in his chest and the others half blown away on the floor, I knew just how close I had come to dying, and I was frightened."

Rosa sat on the bed, got really close to Zack, put her hands on his cheeks, and looked him directly in the eyes as he lay back on the pillows. "I saw myself lying on the floor, bleeding all over the place, and I was really scared. I didn't think I would ever see that day, but Tuesday was the day, and if it hadn't been for you, my dear, I wouldn't be here today. I don't want it to end like that for me. It seems that's where all the people I've been working with end up sooner or later. The horror of running under that overpass was just too much. I didn't know people, or whatever they are, lived like that, and there I was right in the middle of it.

"Without you, my love, I wouldn't have come out of that black stinking hole, and I have nightmares thinking about what would have happened to me. Just thinking about it sends shivers up and down my spine. I just can't live like that anymore."

"Well," said Zack, totally surprised, "what's that got to do with your house being sold?"

"I decided that I am going to sell my house and a couple of businesses I have and get out of this town. I have a little condo in Manzanillo on the beach in another name that no one knows about, except you right now," she said, smiling. "And I'm just going to sneak off and enjoy the rest of my life. When this thing with Ruben finishes, I'll get 20 percent of the profits for just putting it together, and with the house and the business sold, I'll be in good shape. Not rich, but we can live a good life and travel and do things. What do you think of that?"

"Well, I'm a little surprised that you've seen the light. I hope it all works out for you. You'll certainly be better for it. Good luck."

Zack just stared at her, thinking about what this project was really all about and how it had gotten started and what was probably in store for her. It wasn't Manzanillo on the beach; that was for sure. If the government got what it wanted, she would be in prison forever. *Fate sure deals some strange and ugly hands,* he thought.

"What do you think of my idea?" she said with wide, expectant eyes.

"Sounds wonderful, Rosa. I hope it all works out for you," he said.

"Rob, I want you with me. Wherever I go or whatever I do, I want you there. We can go anyplace you want."

She was pleading now, and Zack wasn't ready for that. Zack thought, *Can this woman really be telling the truth this time? I'm working on a sting operation to put her in jail, and she wants me to move in with her. Is this just another ploy to put me off guard, or is it for real? A woman who*

*thinks she's in love with me and a government agency that can't keep both
oars in the water at the same time. What the hell have I gotten myself into?*

"Rosa, this is obviously pretty sudden. I don't even think that
I actually know you yet, and I'm sure not ready to move in with
anyone. Let's just see how this thing plays out, and we'll take one
day at a time, okay?"

"Okay, Rob, but let's work on it. Please?" she pleaded.

Rosa laid her head on Zack's chest and began telling him all
about her numerous conversations with Ruben and how concerned
and solicitous he was of her well-being. She unbuttoned his pajamas
and kissed his chest, slowly caressing his stomach, which was largely
covered by a huge bandage. Her hands were cool and soft to the touch.

At 9:00 a.m., a knock at the door jarred Zack out of a heavy drug-
induced sleep littered with strange dreams brought on by the pain
medication he had taken before going to bed. The drug had done
its thing for the pain, but he'd spent the night plowing through one
abstract dream after another, leaving him as tired in the morning as
he had been when he went to bed.

He dragged himself from bed without thinking, and then with
alarm he wondered who would be there. *No one knows I'm here except
Eduardo's group and now Rosa.* He peeked through the peephole and
saw two nurses in starched white uniforms. He could only see one
clearly and saw it was the middle-aged nurse who had taken such
good care of him in the private safe house. So he opened the door.

"Good morning, senor," she said.

"A good morning to you, ma'am," said Zack.

The second nurse came inside with a big smile on her face and,
sure enough, damned if it wasn't Victoria.

"Well … to what do I owe this great pleasure? Having two lovely
nurses coming to my room … Surely I'm not expected to die or
anything like that, am I?"

The older nurse mumbled and told Zack to get back in bed; she
wanted to check his bandage.

Victoria said, "We thought it might be a good idea to have a nurse here under the circumstances, as things could get a little out of hand. We're not sure just what Rosa may do, and we're still concerned about her. Ruben, we're worried about, but we don't think he knows who you are or where you are or what you look like. Remember, the only men of his who saw you are all dead. He may not even be looking for you. We just know that things are quite volatile out there right now, and we want to be ready, especially after that motel fiasco. We saw Rosa here last night, and apparently you survived that, so we won't worry about her too much."

Zack decided he would not discuss the Rosa thing with Victoria or any of them; he wasn't sure just who was on his side at this point. He had a gut feeling that Victoria and Eduardo were genuinely trustworthy and trying to help, but he wouldn't really know until the chips were down.

As Victoria was letting the nurse out the door, they had a muted conversation. Victoria came back into the room and said, "We leave you alone for just a couple hours, and look what happens. You let another woman in your room. I'm not going to let you out of my sight from here on in. How about breakfast?"

"Sounds great. Let's look at the room service menu. I'm not going anywhere. What's happening out there in the world of intrigue and danger?"

"Interestingly enough, things seem to be quiet, probably a little too quiet."

"Look, I made a mistake getting involved in the first place. I thought I would be doing a good deed and it would be intriguing and interesting. I even thought I could use a little excitement, but I didn't know that everywhere I turned someone would be trying to kill me; and for what?"

"You can rely on Eduardo and me, Zack; that I can promise you. We both feel bad about the other day at the motel, and we won't let it happen again, I promise. I plan on being with you at all times, for one thing, and Eduardo is keeping an eye on things as well. Eduardo and I need to talk to you when we're all together and when you're up to it. The problem is he can't be here right now, and you need to know what's going on. Right now you just sit tight and get well. We have men outside watching the hotel and the area. They'll call me on my cell if anything looks suspicious. Before this is over with, you'll get tired of seeing me around, I'm sure."

"Don't count on it. I like your company. But what happens at night when you go home and I'm left here to fend off the bad guys?"

"I'll stay if you want," she said with a gleam in her eye.

"No, that's not necessary. Really it isn't. And I'll lock the door."

"Someone will be outside at all times, so don't worry about it. Now let's order,"

she said, scanning the room service menu.

After breakfast, Victoria made a call on her cell and said she had something important to talk about.

"There is something else you need to know. Eduardo told me to talk to you about it. He wanted to be here, but he can't, and he knows you're going to the States." She paused deep in thought.

"Well, get on with it," he said.

"I don't know how to say this … but Eduardo and I don't trust Ricardo. You were right. Things aren't going just right. It just doesn't pass the smell test."

"What makes you think that?"

"Well, for one thing, I overheard Jorge talking to him on the extension phone in the safe house about what we were doing."

"That's bad?"

"It's absolutely forbidden. Nothing, and I mean *nothing*, is said to anyone before it goes through Eduardo, and he's the one who does the talking. Jorge isn't even supposed to know Ricardo, let alone be talking to him secretly on the phone."

"So you don't trust Jorge either?"

"That's right. Eduardo and I are worried that there is more to this than a sting operation. We don't know what, but we're taking steps to find out. We don't want to be compromised."

Incredulous, Zack shook his head and said, "Like what?"

"Zack, the only reason I'm telling you is that we know we can trust you. You have nothing to gain by any of this, and you've already smelled a rat." She hesitated for a long time and then said, "We tapped his phone lines."

"What? My god. What happens if you're caught?"

"We just deny it, of course. Eduardo did it himself with equipment Ricardo knows nothing about."

"You tapped his office phone?"

"We tapped the phones in his office, his house in town, and his country house. We wired his office too."

"Boy, you're really serious about this. That takes a lot of people to keep it running. How do you do it?"

"Don't ask. We have them. They aren't from our department, and they have the same suspicions we do. Everything he says and every telephone call he makes is taped."

"Just what do you think you're going to find out?"

"We don't know, but now we know he talks to Jorge, so we've cut Jorge out of the loop, as you would say. I think Jorge may suspect, but Eduardo has him busy tailing Marquez or his men."

"How long do you think he'll buy it?"

"Not long. He's already complaining to Ricardo, but Ricardo can't go to Eduardo without tipping off his contact with Jorge. The interesting part is that Ricardo is talking to Ruben as well and giving him instructions."

"I can't believe this," he said. "What do you mean giving him instructions?"

"Well, remember the big plan where you were to suggest to Rosa to get a partner?"

"Yes, of course."

"Well, Ricardo and Ruben apparently already had that set up. Ruben and Nicholas worked together for a number of years, so he was a natural. Ruben cleverly timed a call to Rosa right after your meeting to tell her how sorry he was about Nicholas, and things just naturally fell into place."

"So somehow Ricardo is involved in this deal. That doesn't surprise me for some reason. I never did trust him, and he knew right away that the drugs were heroin. It must be the money. He wants this sale to go through, and that's why he's not involving the police in this operation. He's got his own little army—me."

"It looks that way, Zack. We'll learn more with the information we get from the tapes. You get out of here and go to the States. Eduardo is arranging a ticket for Robert Smith to Denver with a connection in Tucson. You just get off there."

"What about a visa for Robert Smith?"

"That's taken care of. Zack, I'll miss you. I want you to know that. I would like very much for you to come back, but I'll understand if you don't.

Victoria came in early the next morning in her nurse uniform and helped him pack his bag. She looked at him softly and said quietly, "I'll miss you, Zack. Have a happy holiday and get better. I'll be waiting for your return." Her hug and lingering kiss were definitely more than a fond farewell, and Zack found that he liked it. He really liked it.

Eduardo drove him to the airport personally in his own car after picking up Zack's other clothes at the Hotel Frances.

"Zack, I hope you stay with us on this thing. We need you, as you have a good feel for what's happening now. This is going to turn out to be more than a low-level drug operation, and we have a very limited number of people we can rely on. Victoria said she filled you in on what we know, and we'll keep you informed as we learn things. We won't be able to talk over the phone because we don't know how far this has spread.

"When you return, I promise you that Victoria and I will be the only ones that know about it. We'll keep you completely under wraps until such time that you have to make the trade. Then we will do everything we can to ensure your safety. Zack, I can assure you that I'll always be there for you. If I can't, I'll tell you that, and you can quit right there on the spot. Victoria, I know, would like to be with you all the time and she'll be there too. Think about it, Zack, and call me anytime to talk about it. We need you."

They shook hands as friends. Zack would miss Eduardo and Victoria. He told Eduardo he would let him know his decision when he made it, but this job was really getting out of hand. What the hell was he going to tell Mickey? They had to come up with a plan—and now.

CHAPTER 17

Zack's call to Eduardo three weeks later was short, but he told him that he would be in Guadalajara sometime in the second week of January. He had told Eduardo he didn't want anyone knowing where he was going or when he was arriving. He actually called Eduardo on his new satellite phone after he was already in Mexico, rolling down Highway 19 to Guaymas and San Carlos. He hadn't wanted anyone catching up to him or following him into the hills, where, hopefully, the heroin was still stashed.

It was a cool day when Zack left the quiet little town of San Carlos an hour before first light. He planned to arrive in the edge of the hill country as early as possible so that he would be in and out before anyone else came into the desert. His cover again would be bird hunting.

The early morning air was beginning to warm in the desert as the sun first cracked over the eastern horizon. Zack spotted the stock tank he had parked near the last time. He drove off the road and pulled under the same mesquite tree where he had parked before. He took his time getting his old vest on and loading the over-and-under 12 gauge. He had a small Sony Cyber-shot digital camera packed in the game pouch in the back of his vest along with two extra 4 GB memory drives and other equipment he felt he would need. He was very quiet in his preparations as he listened for any unusual sounds in the early morning.

He reluctantly headed for the big dirt stock tank and slowly walked up its side. He was fearful of what he might see on the other side, but there were no new tire tracks of trucks or heavy equipment, so hopefully the occupants were still there. It had been over a month, and the crabs and fish had probably picked them over pretty well by now. Visions of seeing the driver's face with most of the flesh gone and an open toothy grin staring at him haunted him as he crested the tank and reluctantly slowed his pace.

The tank was smooth with slime, and there was no sight of the Buick that rested on the bottom with its rotting, half-digested cargo. Zack hadn't realized he had been holding his breath and quietly exhaled.

Backtracking the way he came out the last time as best he could remember, he pretended to be hunting for birds, but the ones he flushed out he didn't shoot at so as not to make any noise.

He continued walking in the soft sandy wash until he saw the open face of the cave among others on the cliff side. He continued walking past the cave, looking for tracks or signs that others may have been around since he was there on his hurried departure. He noticed that the broken branch he had strategically placed near the cave entrance was still in place, undisturbed. He continued on down the wash until he found a little hillock where he could see the cave and the surrounding area, and crawled under a small mesquite tree.

Fifteen minutes of silence and glassing with his binoculars passed, and he didn't see or hear anything that didn't belong in the desert. It was time.

The cave was much as he left it. Deep in the mouth of the cave, swallowed in its heavy shadows, he was virtually invisible to anyone outside. He quickly removed the debris he'd so carefully placed in the hole, remembering his set pattern. It was undisturbed, so he carefully set it aside to use again. Before he took out the aluminum Prenz suitcase, he donned his throwaway plastic gloves.

Zack laid out a small plastic tarp and lined up the white packets in even lines on it with an open tape measure, and photographed them several times from different angles, with and without flash. He checked them all on the view screen in the back of the camera, and they looked good. He cut into two bags, one from the original group he'd found in the aluminum case and one from the group taken from the valise in the back of the Ram. They could be different, so he took three samples from each, labeled them, and put each sample in a small Ziploc sandwich bag. He had one for Eduardo, one for Rosa, and a spare.

He taped the two small plastic bags he'd cut into with plastic tape and returned the suitcase to its hiding place. Everything was replaced as he had found it, and he carefully removed all tracks as he backed out of the cave and replaced his broken branch exactly the way he wanted it. When the cave met his satisfaction, he made tracks for the pickup.

Three days later, he had arrived in Guadalajara without incident and called Eduardo. "Eduardo, my friend. I'm in town and checked in at the Hyatt Hotel. I need you to get a room under the same name as before, Robert Smith from Denver, at the Holiday Inn. I have the sample and some photos. I'll give you the memory drive so you can copy it. I need the original back as soon as possible. Get the samples tested as soon as possible so we can see what we have. When can we get together?"

"Zack, it's nice hearing from you. I'm glad you're here. I'll take care of the room immediately and have Victoria come over and get the samples and memory drive. I have an important meeting all afternoon and will not be able to come over, but we'll meet for dinner tonight, and I'll have the photos and the results of the tests. I'll have Victoria pick you up and take you to the same house we went to when you were here before. It'll be quiet there, and we can talk. Can she get you at eight o'clock this evening?"

"Yes, of course. That'll be fine. Please have my key for the Holiday Inn, as I'll need to put some things in the closet and in the bathroom. I'm better prepared this time."

"I'll have it for you. Don't worry. How are you feeling, Zack? Are you all healed up and fit again?"

"Well, let's say I am healed up to a certain extent. I don't do any sit-ups, that's for sure. I'm still a little sore and try not to flex my stomach muscles. I'm careful, but it feels pretty good, and it gets better every day. Eduardo ... I'd like to meet with just the three of us—you, Victoria, and me. Is that okay with you?"

"Of course; that's fine. Why just the three of us? Is there something I should know about?"

"Tonight, Eduardo. All in good time."

A very friendly, smiling Victoria came into the small third-floor suite that overlooked the pool area of the Hyatt.

"I missed you, Zack," she said as she put her arms around him and then kissed him. "It's good to see you again." They stared into each other's eyes until an embarrassed Victoria pulled away and said, "How are you feeling?"

"I'm fine. No problem, as Ricardo would say. I just don't do any quick moves that require me to flex my stomach muscles rapidly. I've learned to slow down for a little while. I have this memory flash drive for you to take to Eduardo to get photos printed and to make a copy for yourself. I need the original back. I also have two samples we need tested. They could be different products, so I labeled them. I need to know exactly the purity so I know what I'm talking about when I pass the other samples and information on.

"It's very important that I get it tonight so we can move ahead. I'll explain more when we are all together. I'm very reluctant to work with Ricardo. I still don't know why he didn't hire a couple of freelance cowboys. He doesn't need me."

"Don't kid yourself. He needs you. You're smart enough to think on your feet and do what is necessary to accomplish the task. Most of these cowboys, as you call them, can't think from one day to the next. They wake up to a new world each day and have to be retrained. They would just walk out and get killed before they even started.

The people we are up against are smart and damn tricky. Yes, Zack, he needs you. Remember, you're the key to Rosa. No local cowboy, as you call him, could possible get to her or even talk her language. She's way too smart and sophisticated for that. She's just too much woman for most of these guys. You're an American, good-looking, obviously educated, and you aren't intimidated by her. Oh yes, he needs you. I'll pick you up for dinner and take you out to the house. I'm sure we'll have the photos and the lab information by then."

Later that evening, Eduardo shook Zack's hand enthusiastically and put his arms around him in a big hug. He said, "I'm really happy to see you, Zack. I'm happy you're well and ready to finish up this operation. I know you want to get it over with as soon as possible. We all do," he said with a big smile. "Come into the sitting room and we'll have a drink and lay out the plan and see what you think about it."

Zack thought he'd hear the plan first before he shared his real activity in this matter. He needed their help.

The first part of the plan was simple enough. Eduardo and Zack would go get the drugs, and Eduardo would deliver them to Ricardo, who would hold them in safekeeping for the transfer and sale, which he apparently would control. There had to be a very important connection between this particular shipment of heroin and the Arabs. If this sale was the key to Little Ivan, he wanted to know it and delay it as long as possible without raising suspicions. He was reluctant to turn the heroin over to Ricardo under any circumstances and said so. They would then have no control over what happened, but Eduardo told him it was best this way and he could keep tabs on it.

"Zack, the purity is as close to 100 percent as you can get. It's safe for you to brag about it being 99 percent pure. It will hold up. You don't see this kind of quality in the wholesale market here, or in the United States. Both of the samples are the same, and its excellent quality and should bring a premium on the wholesale market," Eduardo said with a smile. "We're in business."

Mickey and Zack had several long detailed conversations regarding procedure. The delay of the payoff had to continue in order to give the CIA time to continue to investigate and get into position. It was time for Zack to bring Eduardo and Victoria into the real mission. They couldn't be left in the dark forever, and he needed their help and their connections. The eavesdropping on the attorney general was invaluable. They just needed to fine-tune their thoughts so they knew what they were looking for.

"That's great, Eduardo. Let me tell you just what business I think we're really in. Have a seat," he said, waiving him to a chair. "This is going to take a while."

Zack watched Eduardo and Victoria closely as he unfolded the story that he and Mickey had agreed on. Zack needed both of them, as they were the only ones who had a connection with Ricardo. It was obvious they didn't trust Ricardo at this point, and when Zack finished, he was sure they would distrust and disrespect him a lot more.

There was disbelief at first. They didn't think any of the drug people would be openly involved in moving terrorists into the United States. To think of anyone moving a nuclear device into Mexico or the United States was unbelievable. They were convinced that Nicholas, Ruben, and possibly Ricardo were just in it for the money. They didn't have any terrorist motives; they were sure.

"Well, perhaps they don't have any terrorist motives, but they sure as hell are involved. Perhaps without knowledge of what's going on or the end result, but they're involved."

Zack explained his CIA background, without the details, and explained that he was officially working for the CIA at this point. The DEA matter was just a cover-up. He told them there would be a few more agents in Guadalajara; they would never be seen but would be available to assist in any way possible. They needed to locate the Arabs that were in Mexico for the exchange. If nothing else, they presumed the Arabs would certainly be at the pickup point, and the CIA wanted those men badly.

Eduardo would have the immigration police check every hotel in Guadalajara and the surrounding communities. Passports would be checked. Everyone would be profiled. It was an impossible job that would take more people than immigration could possibly put together. They would try to photograph people as they went. None of the agents would know why they were searching, but a phony drug runner was the reason for the high alert. He was dangerous and presumed armed. They wouldn't know they were actually hunting Arabs.

Zack and Eduardo went over questions and answers to the point that Eduardo and Victoria knew the entire situation. "The drugs look great, Eduardo. I'll make an appointment with Rosa and get her the sample so she can get it checked out by her partner, and we can set up the exchange. The photos are fine, and the volume is obvious. I'll work on her some more and see if I can learn anything more about the Arabs. The problem is I don't think she knows a hell of a lot. We'll try to delay the delivery as long as possible. Maybe we'll get a break and get a lead on the real people involved."

Victoria had been mostly quiet during his narration and now spoke up. "Now I see how you survived the motel mess. I thought I was the one fooling everyone with my makeup and disguises. But you, you're the original. Do you have any more surprises for us?"

"I'm afraid not, Victoria. I'm just the same guy with a different background. That's all."

Eduardo and Zack sat on the patio, talking well into the night, working out the logistics in picking up and delivering the suitcase. They worked toward an exchange date of February 15. Zack was trying to put the date off as far as reasonably possible to give him more time to learn the whereabouts of Ivan.

The government, or whoever was now running this sting, insisted on it being on a boat and at sea, and they would work out the details and let Eduardo know.

"The idea of a dead drop sea pickup is fine, as it lends itself to a lot of secrecy and privacy," said Zack, "but it also creates a whole lot of problems. I think it will be very hard, if not impossible, for you to cover this transaction when you can't get close to the boat without being seen or picked up on radar. How are they going to do that? The only possibility, it seems to me, is when they reach port, wherever in hell that's gonna be, and there is no way to know where that is until they move."

"I've been told that it is worked out and that the whole thing will be secure. I'll give you the details when I know them, Zack. Believe me. The arrest will take place either on the water immediately after the pickup or when the boat reaches port. It will be watched at all times."

"Oh, I believe you all right. It's just that I know there's the chance that there will be some holes in their planning, and I'm the guy on the front burner, remember? Not you folks."

"We'll get it worked out. After what you told me tonight, we will be very vigilant on this matter. Believe me. I just find it so hard to believe that Ricardo, for all his little schemes, would be involved in terrorism."

Rosa was very happy that Zack was in town with the photos and samples. She came to his room immediately after he called her on the telephone.

"Rob, my love," she said as he opened the door. She was silhouetted in the doorway, wearing a black polyester pantsuit that clung to her like water. It accentuated her red hair and was set off by a heavy gold necklace. "Why didn't you call me? I would have picked you up at the airport. Oh, tell me how you are. Tell me everything. Oh, I've missed you so. Why didn't you call?" She kissed him all over his face. "Please tell me how you are," she continued to babble.

"Rosa, it's nice to see you too," he said, trying to extract himself from her strong arms as he was being smothered in kisses. "Come in. Let me shut the door, and we can talk. I have some things to show you."

With happy eyes, Rosa hurried into the room, chatting all the time like a magpie. The animated Rosa had a lot to say, mostly just about what she had been doing and how things were going for her.

Her loneliness showed through the continuous babble. She couldn't say enough and couldn't say it fast enough, so Zack got up, went over to her, took her in his arms, and held her. "Hush, Rosa, hush. You can tell me all these things later. My goodness, you've told me everything you've been doing since I left."

"I've missed you. You feel so good," she said as she snuggled into his body and pressed against him. "God, how I've missed you." Her body moved against Zack's in slow passionate movements, and she said, "Rob, I need you. I really do. I want you right now." She moved him toward the king-sized bed. "Oh, how I need you."

Rosa called first thing in the morning and sounded as happy as someone who had just won the lottery. "Rob, the samples are terrific. I knew this was supposed to be good, but this is outstanding. It's cheap at this price, and Ruben is very anxious to get his hands on the merchandise. I'm so happy you told me about the extra merchandise so I could make a little private deal with Ruben. I'm very happy, Rob. Thank you. I love you for it. When can we get this done? I want to get it finished as soon as possible now."

"I'm happy that the merchandise is so good. You should get a bigger commission from Ruben."

"I did well enough on the extra kilos. I'll come out okay, and we can leave as soon as this is over. I can hardly wait. My people will get their money after the sale to the Beto Group, and I'll be finished."

"Well, I'm happy for you, Rosa. I hope it all works out for you somehow. I really do," he said sincerely.

Zack felt like a rat, being involved in this deceitful government's sting operation, and thought of their ultimate goal of trapping her, Ruben, and the other gang members in one big grab. She would not only be facing charges of drugs smuggling but probably aiding and abetting terrorists, even though she didn't know she was doing it. He felt genuinely sorry that Rosa might not reach her retirement destination after all. This was a messy game he was involved in, and he didn't like it. *I wish I never got involved,* he thought. He hadn't failed to catch the "We can leave right away" comment.

"If we have a deal, Rosa, I'll contact my clients and try to put it together as soon as possible, but I think they're working toward a mid-February deadline. I'm not sure of the details, but as soon as I know I'll call you and let you know. If everything is a go, I'll head back to the States as soon as possible and get it started on that end and let them arrange the transfer."

"I hate so see you go so soon, Rob, but I want this finished as soon as possible too. This was supposed to be done in November, and now we're talking February. They'll be furious. Oh well. There's not much we can do about that. Thank you so much for being here and helping me. When this is over, I'm through and long gone."

Zack felt like Judas as he hung up the phone and wondered if there was a way to get out of this slimy business right now and let the governments follow up on it for themselves. That was wishful thinking, and he knew it. He could no longer walk away from it. He had Ivan to think about. He could only wade in deeper.

Early the next morning, a quiet Victoria called Zack in his room while he was finishing his coffee after the room service breakfast. Zack told her about his conversation with Rosa the day before and told her, "We are a go, and we just need to coordinate our actions to get it done." It was just a matter of time now.

"Can we meet someplace for lunch, Zack?" Victoria's voice was low and husky. "Eduardo is out of town on a matter, and you and I need to discuss some things. We can plan lunch in your suite at the Hyatt. No one knows you're there but us. Say one thirty this afternoon?"

"That's fine with me. I can't leave this damn room very often anyway, so I won't be spotted by some of your crazy shooters out there. I'll be looking forward to it, Victoria."

Later that afternoon, they lounged in the soft hotel balcony chairs, gazing out at the lush landscape with the busy pool in the center of the complex. They finished their tuna salad and a soft chilled Riesling as Victoria filled him in on the plan.

"So you and Eduardo will pick up the heroin. He'll bring it to Guadalajara and deliver it to Ricardo, who'll make the arrangements for the pickup and exchange. Ricardo says Ruben insists on a pickup at sea so he can control the time it's done. He is fearful of being set up in the city. Ruben will control the when. Ricardo will somehow control the where. He is telling Ruben that it's your plan, and Ricardo will somehow get the information regarding the where. You are the only one who will know where you put the container. You see, it's your deal after all, and Ricardo is just passing on the information to his confidant Ruben. We know that's all bull and Ricardo is orchestrating the whole thing to suit his wishes.

"The drugs will be dropped in a sealed container and suspended approximately forty feet under the surface. It'll be held in place by an anchor and held up by a buoy. It'll only be found by a GPS with the correct waypoint entered into it, and Eduardo can get that for you."

"How are they going to make the payoff to Rosa?" he said with an incredulous voice.

"The plan is that you and Rosa are to go out on the boat to retrieve the bag. Once the bag is onboard, the federal police and the navy will step in and make the arrest. You'll be arrested with the others, and after you're taken to jail, I will come and bail you out as your wife, so you'd better be nice to me," she said with a smile. "You'll meet with Eduardo and me, and hopefully we'll have the Arabs in jail during the pickup. How does that sound?"

"That's probably the most ridiculous plan I've ever heard in my life. Rosa and I will both go down with the anchor once they get their hands on the heroin."

Victoria laughed and said, "I know it sounds crazy, but if you think about it, some of it makes sense. There'll be no drugs for anyone to see until they get to the place where it will be suspended by a buoy. You pull it up, and there it is. You get paid off, and then somehow the feds snap everyone up."

"Ricardo is saying the navy can do it, but it makes a lot more sense to pick everyone up when the boat reaches port, wherever that may be. The navy sure as hell can't hang around out there forever. Ruben may wait a month. That makes no sense at all."

"Where are they going to get the boat?"

"Ruben has a big fast fishing boat in Puerto Vallarta. He'll use it. From our telephone taps on Ricardo, we know Ruben is already aware of the pickup and that he will use his boat. Ricardo is playing both sides of the street here. We know we can't trust him. Ricardo wants to make sure that Ruben is on it with as many of his gang and Rosa's gang as possible. He says it's for mutual protection. It sounds like he's double-crossing Ruben as well."

"Well, I can assure you I won't be on that boat, and I don't think I want Rosa on that boat either. It's suicide. I'll make my own plan."

"Ricardo wants his plan followed exactly, Zack. What the hell are you thinking about?"

"No problem, as Ricardo would say. Tell him we are going along as planned; everything is a go. Ruben just needs to tell us when," he said with a straight face.

Victoria stared at Zack for a long time only to be looking into a straight poker face.

The next day, Eduardo and Zack sat in Zack's hotel room, sipping on mint iced tea, rehashing the Ricardo plan. Eduardo agreed it was foolish for Zack to be onboard the pickup boat.

"Look, Zack, I know the plan doesn't sound like the best arrangement, but presumably the people in Mexico City are calling the shots. Ricardo says he has talked to them and talked to them, but they insist they are to be involved and set the plan of action; whether that's true or not, I have no idea. Victoria says you are working on an alternate plan. Please tell me what you are planning. We don't want this to upset the Ricardo plan," he said with a worried voice.

"Eduardo, I will let you know as soon as I can. I just need to work out the details alone. That's all. If and when the navy sets out this cache, you get the coordinates and try to keep them from Ricardo. You and I will make a dry run on it and make sure it's really in place. I don't want the bad guys to find out there's nothing there. Remember, we have to be around for the sale to the Beto Group. That's where the Arabs get their money, and that's when things are going to get interesting. We have to survive that pickup."

"I know, Zack. I agree with you. Now, when are we going to Sonora?"

A happy Rosa answered on the second ring and responded without the slightest hint that anything was wrong. "Rob, how are you? Ruben said he would call me back, but I haven't heard from him. I think everything is okay for the middle of February."

"Rosa, let me know as soon as he calls because I need to know before I go back to the States. I'll wait to hear from you."

"Of course, my dear. Can we get together later this afternoon?"

"I'm sorry, Rosa. I have a lot to do today. I'll be in my room all day trying to get some book work done that a client of mine needs," he lied as he leaned back, putting his feet up on the desk. "It's a project I've been working on for some time, and I'm behind on it, but I'll be here waiting for your call."

Later that afternoon, a worried Zack sat on the small veranda overlooking the lush hotel gardens in the center of the huge complex. He was lolling in the temperate air, completely relaxed, when the telephone jarred him from his reverie. Mentally, he was miles away when the telephone rang, and it took two rings to bring him back to the present.

"Rob, I just talked to Ruben, and he says February is okay with him. He would rather do it sooner, but if you can't, that's all right with him."

"Rosa, my dear, we'll get it done just as soon as they get it put together and not before. You have to have patience. Has Ruben mentioned anything more about his men trying to shoot us? That didn't make any sense at all. They don't have a deal or the stuff without us."

"No, he hasn't, and I haven't brought it up. I just don't trust him. He acts like this whole thing is all his idea and that you and I are only along for the ride."

Zack stifled a deep breath, as Ruben's mindset just confirmed Zack's worst fears. They were just along for the ride.

"It'll work out, Rosa. Just be patient. I'll call my people in the States and get it moving as soon as possible."

Zack called Mickey's team at the Hilton to see if they had learned anything with their investigation.

"Rob Anderson here. How is your holiday?"

"We've been in every damn disco in the city; my god, what meat houses. The Crystal is the only one our friends seem to be visiting. We can't get close to them at all. Mickey sent Jamal to us, and when he tried to friendly up to them, they froze him out. He left before they got downright hostile with him. We have nothing, absolutely nothing. We've had men on them 24-7 and nothing. They eat and party. That's it. They have lots of money, and they spend it on the girls like they are making up for lost time. I don't think any of their actions fall within the parameters of their religion, and they sure aren't waiting for the seventy-two virgins either. Really nice guys," he reported sarcastically.

"I guess we may as well get on with the schedule. That's going to be the only way we can smoke them into action. How many Mexican operatives do you have?"

"Three here, but the border of Sonora is flooded."

"You'll probably need them all. I'll call Eduardo and get on with the pickup."

They changed into hunting clothes after leaving the Guaymas Airport and arrived unnoticed at their destination in the late afternoon. Eduardo was dressed like a hunter, but he was city boy through and through.

When they pulled off the dusty road near the big water tank and parked the Ram Charger, Zack knew they would only have an hour of daylight, but Zack wanted to get this over with.

After fifteen minutes of watching with binoculars, Zack said, "Okay, Eduardo, let's move on. Keep your eyes and ears open. You never know who may show up and when.

"Now you know why I didn't want anyone with me the last time. The fewer people who know about this place the better. This time we could have a lot of company. I trust you, but there are too many possibilities of a leak, and that we couldn't handle. I'm sure the goods wouldn't even be here if word leaked out, and I'd probably be dead."

"You're sure no one knew when you were leaving or where you were going?"

"Absolutely! Veronica purchased the ticket under a false name. No one knows I'm here but her."

"Thank you, Zack, for your careful patience. I would not have stopped to search my back trail. I can see it's important, but I'm too much a man of the city, I guess."

The branches and twigs he set up as visual traps were still in their proper places. The big aluminum case was exactly as Zack had left it. No one had touched the case. They opened it for Eduardo's curiosity, and he let out a soft low whistle. All he said was, "Wow!"

"You carry it, Eduardo. I'm through with it. Besides, its heavy, and you need the exercise." Zack chuckled. "I'll walk well ahead of you, and you follow with the bag. That way we're separated if something should go wrong, and we will be in a better position. I'll go up the hill where we stopped coming out, have a look, and then signal you to go ahead. I want to make sure we get out of here in one piece. Let's go," he said as he trudged down the sandy wash.

Eduardo dropped Zack off at the Armeda Hotel in Guaymas. He was as anxious as Zack to get the case in the hands of someone else. He planned to start back to Guadalajara immediately. He would drive for a few hours and then stop for the night.

"Call me on my cell phone when you folks get it together, Eduardo. When the merchandise is in place, you and I will check it out. I don't want you to talk to anyone about our plans because I don't want anyone setting us up. I'll wait until I hear from you, my friend. Don't tell Ricardo or anyone other than Victoria where I am. Don't tell anyone when I arrive in Guadalajara. I don't want Ricardo or his friend Ruben finding me."

"Don't worry, Zack. I know it can be dangerous, and we'll keep you under wraps."

CHAPTER 18

Mickey and Zack sat at the kitchen table in Zack's townhouse, drinking ice tea and rehashing Zack's report.

"So what do you think, Mickey?"

"I'm in agreement with you, Zack. It seems like Ricardo has an ulterior motive in what he has planned. It makes no sense at all that he would want everyone on that boat at the same time. The arrest makes no sense. I'm surprised that this Marquez guy and Rosa haven't figured that out. I think they're just too anxious to get the job done and everyone paid off. You've been successful in delaying this so far, and as a result I think they're very anxious to move forward regardless."

"I've leased a thirty-nine-foot Mediterranean out of Mazatlan for a month. It's just like my boat. It's a fast boat but maybe not as fast as Rubin's. It really makes no difference, as I plan on only being an observer. No one knows about it at this point, of course, and I don't plan on anyone knowing it until it happens. There're just too damn many people involved.

I have a job for your man Emerson. He's supposed to be the communications guy. I want him to go to Puerto Vallarta and get on Ruben's boat and booby-trap his VHS radios the night before we go to sea. I don't know how many he has, but I want them all booby-trapped except for the CB radio. I don't want any long-distance signals going out from that boat. What we need is for him to put a

- 164 -

receiver in each radio that I can send a signal to that will short out the radio severely. I don't want it fixable onboard. You think he can do that?"

"Emerson's a real pro, Zack. I'll talk to him and get him what he'll need, and I'll get him to Puerto Vallarta pronto to wait for the signal to move. This is his first time in the field, and he's anxious to go."

Zack returned to Guadalajara on Delta Air to prepare for the pickup. He needed to make sure that the drugs were where they were supposed to be. As soon as he reached his hotel room, he called Eduardo. "I'm back, Eduardo, and ready at any time."

"I'm ready to take our little trip when you are," Eduardo said with a cheerful voice. "I have the coordinates for you to enter into your Global Positioning System or GPS or whatever you call that thing. I think it's supposed to lead us to where we're going, thanks to high technology and your satellites."

"First I have to get a boat to use, and then I'll call you back. We'll spend the weekend fishing. Where is the closest port to our destination?"

"Well, it will closer to the Baja side, but it's north of Vallarta and south of Mazatlan. It's well off of Cabo San Lucas in Baja, and I think it's pretty much out of sight of land. I can meet you any place you say."

"We'll plan on Mazatlan. We don't want to be seen around Vallarta."

Eduardo came aboard the thirty-nine-foot Mediterranean called *The Maria* at the marina dock in Mazatlan four days later and gave Zack the usual big hug. "It's good to see you, Zack. I hope you know how to run this thing. I never was too fond of the sea, and I'm afraid I am not too good of a sailor. Which side do I puke over?"

"If you get sick on this boat, my friend, I'll just throw you overboard and come back when you are feeling better."

"I only get sick once in awhile. Of course, I've only been out on a boat six or eight times and got sick all but one time. I think I'll be fine this time because I have this little patch behind my ear that the doctor gave me," he said, pointing to a half-inch patch of tape stuck to the skin behind his left ear that would slowly release a tranquilizer into the mastoid.

"Eduardo, let's have the coordinates we need," Zack said when they cleared the harbor of Mazatlan.

"Yes, here they are" he said, handing Zack a wrinkled piece of paper that had been jammed down in his pants pocket. "I hope you understand them. I don't have the faintest idea what they mean. All I know is that it is somewhere east of Cabo, off the tip of Baja, about ten miles off an island of sorts."

"Oh, I understand them all right. What's important is whether or not the GPS understands them. That's what does all the work. We're just along for the ride. Modern technology makes it easy."

Early the next morning, they rigged for fishing, put out the outriggers, and trailed four lines of artificial lures without hooks. They looked every bit the fishermen as they headed for the waypoint punched into the GPS.

They were nearing the place where the navy had supposedly suspended the case. It was supposed to be in about two hundred feet of water, lying on the bottom of the ocean floor. There were two floats attached to it, both at about thirty to forty feet below the surface. Zack kept an eye on the radar and watched for any traffic within their range, and Eduardo sat on the bridge and scanned the horizon with binoculars. They intently watched the sonar for its telltale blip and slowed the boat to six knots so they wouldn't miss the contact.

There it was—two large blips on the sonar, right where they should be. Zack magnified the blips, and they were definitely tied together. Zack punched in the *man overboard* button, and the GPS imprinted a circle on the screen where a man was supposed to have gone overboard. The electronic brain marked the spot on the plotter so that they could turn back and cross the exact spot again.

The radar was clear when they returned, so Zack wiggled and stretched his way into his wet suit and strapped on his weights and the buoyancy compensator that also held a small thirty-eight cubic foot air tank. They continued on past the mark. A nervous Eduardo continued to look through the binoculars and watched the radar closely for any changes. Eduardo knew that if they were caught, he would have a tough time explaining why he was picking up the drugs without authorization from his office. He would be finished in politics in Mexico and probably blackballed from any good job, if not dead.

"I'm going to go down and tie this line on the float, and we're going to haul it up. After we've checked out that the case really exists out here, we'll drop it back to the bottom and go home. All you have to do is to drive in a straight line and come back for me in twenty minutes. You know how to reset the autopilot now, so quit worrying. When you get close, I'll pop up to the surface. If you see something, keep on going. The autopilot will bring you back to the man overboard mark, and I'll be waiting. Trust me. I won't be going anywhere," Zack said with a smile.

Zack checked that his buoyancy compensator was secure and operating. The extra mouthpiece from his regulator, the octopus, was securely attached, as well as the gauges and night-light. He punched the regulator, and it blasted out a burst of air. He knew he could be floating out here for a long time if Eduardo saw traffic in the area. He sat on the swim platform on the back of *The Maria* in the clear light of dawn and cleaned his mask. When all was ready, he watched Eduardo and waited for him to give the signal that they were crossing over the spot marked on the plotter. Eduardo waived his hand, and Zack jumped off the rear platform, well clear of the big props, and into the clear blue water of the Emerald Sea.

He checked his compass and began a search pattern of enlarging circles as he swam around his imaginary starting point. Before he made a complete circle, he saw the two barrels caught in his light. They were about fifteen feet away. It was difficult to tell their color, as colors washed out at that depth, but they looked like the big yellow chemical barrels used in Mexico. He attached his line to the twin nylon lines that eerily disappeared into the dark below and hopefully attached to what they were looking for—the key to the sting operation, the key to the Arabs, and the key to Ivan.

When he broke the surface, the four-foot swells made it difficult to see the boat except when he was on top of the waves. In the bottom of the trough, it was impossible to see or be seen. Jesus, the boat was slowly bearing right down on him and was only about thirty feet away as he crested a wave and frantically started to swim out of the big boat's path.

He heard Eduardo put the big engines in neutral and heard the change in sound as the big screws grew silent. The low bubbling drone of the underwater exhausts was the only sound to be heard. Zack swam around to the back of the boat, and after releasing the tank catch, he pushed his air tank up on the swim platform. The towline was still spooling out from his belt as Eduardo helped him onto the platform and took the tank.

"I was worried about you, Zack. Are you okay?"

"Piece of cake, Eduardo. We didn't miss it by fifteen feet. Quit worrying. This scuba diving is safe if you use your head. No problem," he said with a wave of his hand, and they both laughed at Ricardo's expense.

Zack walked into the rear cockpit through the transom door, and Eduardo said, "Let's haul this thing up and see what we've caught."

"First let's check the radar and have a good look around before we start hauling anything onboard. We just don't know who may be watching this particular spot on the ocean."

When they both were satisfied, they began hauling in the white nylon rope they had attached to the float lines. The two big floats helped for the first thirty feet, but once they were on top of the water, the load became heavier as they hauled in the unknown cargo hand over hand. The saltwater and nylon line was tough on their gloved hands, but this was faster than any other method they could quickly think of for handling the two hundred feet of line.

"I see something, Zack. It looks shiny. We're almost there."

"Just pull it up to the surface, and I'll check it out on the swim platform so we don't have to drag it onboard. The damn weight they have on this is too heavy to fool with," said Zack.

Zack managed to get the aluminum case onto the platform and looked it over carefully. It was the same one all right. It was vacuum-packed in clear heavy plastic bags. *They made sure it would stay dry,* he thought. He could make out the size and shape, and it wasn't necessary to take it apart.

Zack dropped the case and its heavy anchor, and they played out the line as it went down so that it would not get fouled up and become too short. If it did that, they would never get it back again. They checked the GPS and made a slight adjustment to get them within the original parameters of the GPS setting. They had only drifted a few yards during their retrieval. They disconnected their line from the floats and dropped it on the bottom. They made another pass with the sonar to make sure it was stationary and still fit within the original coordinates. Now for the long trip back to the city.

When they returned to Guadalajara, Zack got on the phone to Rosa as soon as he got to his room. "Rosa, my dear, I'm in town and ready to go. How soon do you think you and I can meet so I can tell you the plan?"

"Rob, I thought you forgot about your Rosa. I was very worried about you. Why didn't you call me? I missed you terribly. Can I come over to see you tonight?"

"How about you and I having a nice dinner tonight, and I can fill you in on what's going on so you can meet with your people and we can get started?"

"That would be terrific. Ruben has been calling me every day, asking when it was going to happen, and all I could tell him was that it was still on schedule and to be ready. I thought you would call me. I was beginning to believe you weren't going to call at all. I thought something happened to you. I've missed you. Oh how I've missed you. I have so much to tell you. I can hardly wait. Oh my god, I look a mess," she said away from the phone. "I need to do my hair and my nails and everything. Why couldn't you have called me and let me know when you were coming? I would have liked to be prepared. Oh my, Rob, I'm so glad to hear from you."

"Rosa, you will look beautiful no matter what, so don't worry about it. What time would you like to go out? You pick the place and make the reservations. You know where to go much better than I do. We'll just have a nice evening together. I'm looking forward to seeing you again. I'm happy you didn't forget about me."

"Roberto, how could I forget you? I've missed you so much. I'll call Ruben right now and get ready. Are you staying at the same place? I'll send my car for you, and we can have a drink here before we go out."

"Yes, Rosa, I'm at the Holiday Inn. Pick me up at seven o'clock. Would that be okay?"

"That'll be perfect. I'll be so happy to see you," she said in an excited, sexy, throaty voice.

"It's that Rosa broad," said the sexy little secretary sarcastically as she flounced through Ruben's office door in her tight miniskirt and her ever-present undersized blouse. She spent more time looking in the mirror, doing her nails, and combing her long shiny black hair than she did doing anything else in the office, but Ruben didn't care. Her secretarial job was only a sideline for her. She could answer the phone and make a few calls for him, and he was happy. He just wanted her around as a play toy. The miniskirt and low-cut blouse exposing ample cleavage said it all.

"Hello, Rosa. Have you heard from your friend yet?" Ruben said, smiling at the coquettish girl who sat on the edge of his big desk as he slid his hand up her skirt.

"Yes, he's in town, as he said he would be, and he's ready to make the exchange. I'll meet with him, get all the particulars, and call you. Are you ready to go?"

"Yes, yes, of course," he said impatiently. "Just call me and let me know when and where we can meet."

"I'll call tomorrow, Ruben. I'll be busy until then."

The busty little secretary sat on the uncluttered desk so Ruben could see up her skirt. She wasn't even wearing a thong, and she wanted him to know that she was here and that bitch Rosa was only speculation.

"Call the boys in, sweetheart," he said as he stroked her thigh with a big smile on his face.

He wanted everyone involved. There wasn't going to be any screwup this time. This was going to be a really big score. He might even be able to eliminate Rosa and the gringo at the same time and keep it all. He had to plan carefully and get all his men onboard for the exchange. The damn gringo was calling the shots on the exchange, and Rubin didn't like that, but he couldn't do anything about it.

All he needed were the coordinates to punch in his GPS. When the load was in, he would decide how to handle the gringo and Rosa. He'd waited a long time for a score like this, and Rosa sure didn't know what she had. If it checked out like the samples he had, he was going to make a killing on this one. The boys in Chicago were champing at the bit already. *All I have to do is get it to Tucson, and they'll take it from there*, he thought with a big grin.

When Zack finished talking to Rosa, he immediately called Eduardo. "Eduardo, I'm on for tonight with Rosa. I'm starting to have bad feelings about this sting operation you've got going. I really feel that this woman is getting out of the rackets entirely and that she's genuinely trying to change her ways. Maybe you could cut her a little slack on this thing if you could. She still holds the key to finding the Arabs, you know."

"Zack, my friend, you are just too soft in the heart. She's been a bad woman for years, and she's done a lot of things you don't even know about. She deserves to go to jail. Don't worry about it. We'll find the Arabs. Believe me. Now here's the plan for the pickup.

Ricardo wants to get as many people on that boat as possible. Rubin's boat is fifty-two feet, and he can get a lot on there. The more people on there, the better and the happier Ricardo will be. Try to have Rosa get as many of her people and as many Arabs on the boat as possible. The more people on the boat, the more secure you will all be. No one would risk turning it into a shooting gallery. Then we'll arrest them all at one time."

"I'll see what I can do, Eduardo. No promises but I'll try."

The big Oldsmobile was waiting for him at the Holiday Inn when he came out the front door at seven o'clock. Burt was all smiles and said, "Good evening, Senor Smith. It's nice to see you again. Was your trip to the States a good one?"

Zack almost passed out. He hadn't heard Burt say three words except in response to Rosa the entire time he was with him before, and now he was making conversation.

A shocked Zack said, "Yes, thank you, Burt. Everything was fine at the office. Just too much work to catch up on, but everything is okay. How is everything with you?"

Burt responded with a grunt as he pulled out into traffic, and there was no more conversation.

The car slowed, and Zack recognized the neighborhood from when he had taken Rosa home from the quiet bar where they had spent the evening. That seemed years ago. A flood of hot memories jammed through his mind as he pictured her that evening.

A big wrought iron electric gate opened automatically to the push of a button in the car, and Burt maneuvered the car around the side of the house and parked under a large covered patio. It was completely out of sight from the street or from any neighbors, who also kept their cherished privacy behind high security walls. Zack didn't wait for Burt to say anything. He got out of the car and said, "Where should I go, Burt?"

"Through the gate there, senor, to the patio," he said as he pointed to a large wrought iron gate covered by an arbor of bright red bougainvillea that where tied and shaped to form a perfect arch. Zack could see a large backyard, a profusion of color of flowers of every kind, and a large swimming pool with many poolside tables and chairs. He'd seen hotel pools and gardens smaller than this. The sweet smell of gardenias and other flowers moved on the quiet air as he passed through the arbor.

As Zack walked through the gate, a young lady in a black-and-white maid's uniform motioned for him to have a seat under an arbor overlooking the pool area. The flowering arbor was an extension of the house, with large carved stone pillars supporting the trellis from one end of the house to the other. Overstuffed patio furniture and three decorator-style umbrella-covered wrought iron tables with six chairs each made up several conversational areas.

"Rob, welcome to your house. It's so nice to see you," said Rosa as she exited a large sliding glass door and walked onto the patio.

As Zack stood up, his jaw almost dropped in amazement. She wore a full-length rust-colored dress with a slit up the right leg to midthigh. The clinging material rode her like rippling water. The spaghetti strap top went over her bare shoulders, connected to the back of the dress, came around, and tied tightly under her ample bust, accentuating her bust and firm body. The color enhanced her red hair, which was pulled smooth into a French roll on the right side of her head. Her makeup was picture-perfect. *She is downright gorgeous*, he thought.

Zack had to clear his throat before he spoke. "Rosa, you said you looked a fright. Christ, you're gorgeous. It looks like you even lost some weight, not that you needed to. I feel downright tacky next to you."

She came up to him, put her arms around his neck, and held him so close that he could feel her body heat through the thin material. He put his arms around her, pulled her as close as he could, and kissed her. Her warm full lips parted, and he could feel her warm breath enter his mouth as her hot tongue caressed his lips. She moved her body ever so slowly against Zack, and he could feel himself getting aroused.

Zack pulled back, still holding her, and said, "Rosa, we'll never get to dinner at this rate."

"Oh, Rob, who cares about dinner. You did miss your Rosa after all, didn't you?" she said with a sly, knowing smile as she slowly pressed against him.

"Maybe I didn't realize until just now how much I did miss you, Rosa. I'm already a wreck. Let's sit and have a drink and let me just look at you. You are truly beautiful tonight."

"Thank you, Rob," she said as she reluctantly sat in one of the overstuffed chairs. As she crossed her bare legs, the dress slowly and silently slipped away to the top of the slit. "Tell me how you're feeling and what you've been doing. I have a lot to tell you, but this time I'm going to let you do the talking while I do the watching."

"Well, I've just been very busy in the office, and I had to make a couple of business trips. Just the mundane life of a financial planner. Nothing very exciting, that's for sure. How about you? It's just nice to see you again. I sometimes wish it was under different circumstances."

"Forget about the circumstances for now, Rob. Let's just enjoy tonight. We can talk about things later. Tonight is for us," she said as she slowly recrossed her long legs. "What would you like to drink?"

"Canadian, if you have it, on ice, and a lime would be great."

Rosa rang a little silver bell on the coffee table, and the same maid came out to the patio, took their orders, and promptly brought the drinks with a selection of hot and cold hors d'oeurves. There was enough shrimp alone to make a meal. Zack wondered about the maid. *Is this the job Veronica had?*

When they had their drinks, Rosa said, "Would you like to look around?"

"I'd love to. I didn't see much of it last time." He smiled. "This is a fabulous place. I can't believe you're going to sell it."

She took Zack through the large living room and connecting dining room, both of which were a decorator's dream. She said, "I told you what I'm going to do. It's already sold. I'm just waiting for the buyer to get his money together, and then I have sixty days to move out and close escrow. I'm not going to tell anyone but you where I'm going. The furniture goes with it, so I won't have to worry about that. All I take is a few personal things and my clothes. Quick and easy, as you Americans say."

"Well, something like that, yes."

They made their way through a surprising number of rooms, including a small suite, obviously unused, that adjoined the huge master bedroom.

Zack asked, "What do you use this suite for?"

"It hasn't been used in some time. It used to be used for my personal maid," she said absently as she moved him into the master bedroom and quietly closed the door behind them.

The room was dominated by a king-sized bed on a three-step platform with off-white marble columns that went to the ceiling. The columns were capped with Grecian capitals that connected a thin sheer white overhead canopy that ran the full length of the wall. The entire curved wall at the head of the big bed was a Grecian mural that gave the impression that you were looking out through a marble pillared patio across the Aegean Sea. White sails, gulls, and potted plants that blended into the greenery in the painting gave it a three-dimensional illusion that was visually perfect.

The entire room was done in white with various gray and blue Grecian accents. Soft gauze curtains moved in the light breeze that passed through the room. Soft fluffy pillows lay everywhere—on the bed, in the chairs, on the chaise lounge, and in front of the white marble fireplace. Zack was spellbound looking out across the sea in the highly detailed mural. Rosa moved up behind him, put her arms around him, and said, "Now I have you right where I want you." She slowly turned him around.

Zack held her closely in his arms and caressed her firm body against him. He felt the heat start to rebuild in him. He slowly moved her against the foot of the high bed and lowered her onto her back. The soft dress slid back as she slowly raised her legs and her hot eyes said, "Yes, yes, yes." Zack slowly ran his lips down the inside of her soft perfumed thigh, while Rosa moaned in pleasure and anticipation.

They were lost in the heat of the moment. Neither of them had time to completely undress. When Rosa was moaning with pleasure, Zack moved inside her as she lay on the edge of the bed.

They both laughed when they were finally spent from the ferocity of their lovemaking. Zack was more than surprised at himself. He had gotten more than carried away. *So much for control*, he thought. *This room is more than a bedroom. This room oozes sex.*

They moved back out onto the patio and refreshed their drinks. Now neither one was interested in going out to dinner tonight. Zack finally got around to telling Rosa the plan as he knew it, but he did not tell her that he had a private agenda. Rosa would pass the plan on to Rubin, and they would be ready to go in three days. She was encouraged to get as many of her people on the boat as possible and to have Ruben get as many of his men on the boat as he could, and Ruben had to be one of them. Ruben's boat would take one day to get to Mazatlan, stay there overnight, make the run across to La Paz late the next day, weather permitting, and make the run for the pickup the next afternoon. If the weather was good, they just might do it the first night out of Mazatlan.

"We want to make that as late in the afternoon as possible," said Zack. "The ferry is gone, and the fishing boats will have returned home by then. We can then go to La Paz or come directly back to the mainland. There should be no traffic, so it could be an easy run. You and I get off at the first opportunity, and Ruben can get off or go wherever he wants. That's up to him. Do you think we can trust him?"

"I think so, Rob, but I really don't know. He's not a person to be trusted. I hate to think of being on a boat with him too long after the pickup. I would like to be gone as soon as the pickup has been made, but I guess we could live together for a few hours. But that bothers me. If we have a lot of people on board, it will probably be safer that way. I'll call him tomorrow and talk to him. Tonight, I have other things on my mind," she said with a sly little smile.

Early the next day, a tired Rosa called Ruben and explained the plan as Zack had told her. "That's the way they want to play it, Ruben. They don't trust either of us, and they have the merchandise in place, and the gringo knows where and how to get it. He says he will give you the coordinates when we leave."

"What does he expect me to do? Ride around in a boat for a couple of days, carrying a load of stuff that could send us all to jail forever? The damn fool must be crazy and must think we are too."

"Ruben, you can get off on another boat that night, go to La Paz, catch a plane, send the merchandise out by plane … Do anything you want. I'm just telling you where it is and how we get it. You make your own decision as to what the hell you want to do when you get your hands on it. I just want to get paid on the boat, and the gringo wants to get paid on the boat as well. How he's going to handle it, I don't know. That's his business. He has to live with the same thing we do. He has no control over it either.

"What we have going for us is that no one, including you or me, know where it is, and no one as of this moment knows when we're going after it. We're pretty secure when it comes to picking our time, and no one can beat us to it. The gringo suggests late in the afternoon, just before dark so we can move afterward and go any place we want in the dark. We're going to have to trust each other, Ruben. Remember, Ruben, you and only you will decide when we make the pickup. No one will know but you."

When Ruben hung up the phone, his lead man Chico smiled as he leaned back on the big couch in Ruben's office. "Boss, it's ideal," he said. "We can arrange for a pickup as soon as we have the stuff, and we still have the bitch and the gringo with us. We can do what we want at that point. Hell, we may be able to put them both in the water on the anchor and come home without a problem. We can pull into a cove by La Paz and get off with the case and send it along by air that night. It's perfect. From La Paz they can fly up the Gulf, cross over in the same spot as before, and drop it up in Arizona, south of Interstate 8. It couldn't be better. We can have it picked up there and on the way before daylight. The car could be in Chicago the following day. I love it. I'll get the boys ready to go when you say."

"Maybe you're right, Chico. Put together the plane and the pickup in La Paz, and I'll decide what to do with Rosa and her gringo. You may have the right idea," he said as he swiveled around in his big chair, smiling from ear to ear.

"We're set to leave the day after tomorrow, Eduardo," Zack said as soon as Eduardo picked up the phone. "It's in motion. Ruben will take his boat out fishing. How many will be onboard, I don't know."

"We'll be ready, Zack. Ricardo assures me everything is in order."

"Eduardo, do you have the information as to how the snatch is going to be made after we make the pickup? I think Ruben will want to split up as soon as possible."

After a too long silence, Eduardo said, "Zack, I really don't know. Ricardo tells me that everything is handled and not to worry, but you know him. I don't know who is involved other than Ricardo or if there *is* anyone else involved. We've not picked up any calls from him to Mexico City. I don't know if he's connected to the Arabs or not. He doesn't say much about it. I'm sorry I don't have any other information for you. I don't know what to tell you. It's your decision here, Zack, if you want to go through with it or not. Ricardo wants you to finish this very badly. Why, I don't know, but it didn't sound like an option to me. That's why you're the only one who has the GPS coordinates. He wants you in on this for some reason. I don't like it, but I don't have any answers for you."

"If everyone has a lot of people onboard, they may not want to start a shooting match. Who knows who would get killed. That could be a real plus for everyone. I'll get you covered when you are onshore like a blanket, but I can't say how they're planning to get you off the boat. Ricardo says they will move in so fast that you will not have to worry. Just pretend you are as scared as they are, and you'll be arrested with the others."

"Right. I'm working on something, Eduardo. I just can't tell you about it. "

At 3:00 a.m. on a cool brisk morning, Emerson made his move. At last he was doing real undercover espionage work. He was going to make his name as a player tonight. He smiled as he slipped out into the empty hallway and eased down the hall to the outdoor stairway, making sure no one saw him leave the hotel. He made his way down the alley from the hotel to the waterfront. There were supposed to be guards on duty at all hours, watching over the boats, but from his past surveillance, he knew at this hour they weren't going to be very vigilant.

He could see the blinking light of the small TV in the guard shack as he opened the security gate with the key he had been given. Then he eased through the entrance and quickly went down the bank to the water, where the small skiffs and dinghies were tied at the small dock; it was as far away from the hotel and the guard shack as he could get. Out of sight, he sat on the dock and took off his black Reeboks, dark slacks, and dark shirt that covered his gray camouflage wet suit, and put them in one of the skiffs that was gently moving against the dock. After a quick look around and seeing no one, he slipped quietly into the water. As an experienced scuba diver, he considered this just an exercise.

He dove under the first dock and stayed about three feet under the surface with a slow, quiet kick and breaststroke while he breathed through his small rebreather device. He never made even a ripple on the surface as he slowly made his was across the small boat channel, watching his compass to bring him under the docks that moored the big yachts.

Zack's rental, *The Maria*, was only four boats away from Ruben's big boat, the *La Playa*, at the overnight facilities. Emerson eased up on the rear swim platform of *The Maria*. Slowly slipping through the transom gate, he raised his head above the boat's side and looked up and down the dock to see if anyone was walking the dock or visible on any of the boats. Keeping as low as possible, he quietly let himself into the salon with his key.

He quickly dried off and put on white boat shoes, a white T-shirt, and white shorts over his wet suit. These would be the hardest to see against all the white boats that lined both sides of the dock, and if he was spotted, he would look like he belonged there. A white movement against a white background would not easily be picked out at night. He picked up his small bag of hand tools and parts that was stashed in *The Maria*. He thought he had everything he would need and started for the *La Playa*. He didn't know if the crew was onboard or not. If they were, he hoped they were sleeping off a load of beer.

Keeping low, he slowly eased onto the center of the swim platform of the big boat to minimize any movement in the water. He knew if he stayed low as he slowly crossed the cockpit and eased up the ladder, he would not be seen even if someone woke up and came on deck. They would have to get up and walk around the bridge console to see Emerson in the fly bridge. With a small Phillips screwdriver, he removed the front of the VHF radio and slipped it out of its holder.

He deftly took the case off, located the power supply, checked the model number, and cut it out of the system. There were only three companies that made power supplies for the VHF radios, and he had them all.

His battery powered soldering gun made quick work of the new connection. The new power supply was set to fail upon receiving the correct VHF signal. A small wire now ran from the new power supply to the connection for the big VHF antennae. He checked his watch and smiled. He was done in less than ten minutes.

He quietly made his way down the interior staircase to the pilothouse in the salon and repeated the job with that radio. Both checked out, receiving his test signal strongly.

Emerson was drying off back in his room by four o'clock and sleeping ten minutes later with a big smile on his face. He had showed them tonight.

A soft knock slowly made its way through Zack's heavy sleep. He finally realized it was coming from the door to his room. He tiptoed over to the door, looked through the peephole, and saw the maid standing in the hall with her cart full of laundry, soap, and shampoo. "*Mas tarde, por favor*" (Later please), growled Zack.

The quiet grumpy voice said in English, "Open the damn door or I'll knock it down."

A surprised Zack looked through the glass viewer again and saw the maid standing there staring at the viewer. "What did you say?"

"It's me. Open the door."

Still not sure just who it was, he opened the door on the chain and looked out at the maid in her Flamingo Vallarta Hotel maid's uniform. He finally recognized her as Victoria.

"Christ, I can't believe you. Come on in. It's not even six o'clock yet. What are you now, a maid? You look just great in your new uniform."

She looked Zack directly in the eye and said, "I want to be on that boat. Tell them anything you want. Tell them I'm your secretary or that you picked me up in a bar in La Paz. Just get me on that boat."

"I'll have to explain it to you later. But right now you'll have to take my word for it that I don't want you on that boat."

"Why not? I think you may need me on that boat. For Christ's sake, Zack, it could be very dangerous. I don't know what's going to happen. It's the dumbest plan I've ever heard of. I'm not sure just who is making the decisions for Ricardo, but I've never heard of an exchange like this, and I don't like it. I know you don't have an option at this point, but I sure don't want you out there alone."

Zack put his hands on her shoulders and looked her directly in the eye.

"Victoria, you are very important to me. I just don't know how to explain it with all that's going on. Please take my word for it. I have an option, and I'm taking it. No questions asked. I'll explain later. When we leave tomorrow, you head for home. That's important, okay? If you see anything going on that's different than you thought it was supposed to happen, don't tell anyone—and I mean no one. Please, you must keep it a secret. Then you'll know why I don't want you on that boat."

After a long serious look, she said, "I hope to hell you know what you're doing." Her eyes were misty. She gave him a desperate hug and a quick kiss and then glanced at his undershorts as she walked out the door, shaking her head.

They all met in the dining room for breakfast as planned. After introductions, the obviously partied-out Ruben looked at Zack from across the table with rheumy eyes and said, "Okay, Bobby, ready to go?"

"Absolutely," he retorted in a controlled voice.

"We're about five to six hours from where we need to be. We'll leave here and go northwest at speed for a couple of hours. We're heading to a position southeast of Baja. It's in the middle of nowhere. We'll put out poles and act like fishermen while we check the radar and sonar. If it is clear, we'll go to the pickup spot. If we see or hear anything, we'll pass it by. We want to arrive well after dark."

"I'll meet you at your boat at four o'clock sharp. I'll fill you in when everyone is onboard. First things first, however. I need to see the money and know you have it with you."

Ruben signed the tab and said, "Come on up to my room."

The large Samsonite briefcase was packed solid with one hundred dollar bills. Zack picked up a stack and flipped through them as if he knew what he was looking for. Then he took out another stack and repeated the charade. At least there weren't any blank ones. They all looked real. It was the most cash he had ever seen.

"Their legit. No problem."

"Okay, Ruben. See you at four."

Zack watched through binoculars from his fourth-floor veranda as they all arrived at the Flamingo Vallarta marina. He had a clear view of the entire marina. There had to be twenty people getting on that boat. Interestingly enough, there were no Arabs. Why would anyone want so many people on one boat? It made no sense at all. It could end up a shooting gallery.

Zack waited until everyone was on the boat before he got there. The low rumble of the engines said they were ready to move. Zack, still standing on the dock, called Ruben out.

"Okay, Ruben, here is how it goes. You're going to go out in your boat with all your people and your chemist, and I'm going to lead you out in another boat."

"What do you mean you're going to lead me?" he interrupted with a suspicious glare.

"Wait until I'm done talking, and then you'll know. My clients had a boat delivered here to me. It's a charter from somewhere. They've entered the information regarding the coordinates into the GPS on that boat. I don't know what they are, but the boat does."

"Why don't we just go on my boat as planned?"

Zack had been afraid that he would come up with this logical argument. "I can't. I have my instructions, and the coordinates are already locked into the GPS on my boat. I will call you on the CB radio. When I cross over the point, all you have to do is follow and watch your sonar. You can't miss it. Now, Ruben, I don't want you running off with the money and the merchandise at the same time, so I want half now, and the other half you'll put in this waterproof plastic bag, tie to one of your white fenders, and throw over the side. I'll come back and pick it up. That's how it's supposed to go. That's how they want it," he said as he handed Ruben a big heavy plastic bag.

"Are you crazy? How do I know you won't just run off on me with the money I give you?"

"Because you know you and my clients can do a lot of business together, and you know I have to have the rest of the money for my clients. We're going to be about a thousand meters apart all the time. We will talk by CB radio only. That's important. The CB has a very short range, and people won't pick us up very easily with that. If we are on VHF, they could pick us up miles away. You pick the channel, and we'll use it."

"Let me talk this over with Chico."

Zack signaled for Rosa to come with him, and a very confused woman got off the boat and said, "What the hell is going on?"

"Do as I say," he said under his breath, looking her directly in the eye. "Just do exactly as I say. Don't say anything. Don't ask questions. Just wait right here."

Ruben and Chico walked out of the salon, and Chico stood in the cockpit doorway while Ruben crossed the swim platform to the dock. Ruben was sweating heavily in the afternoon sun. The beer was starting to leak out of every pore in his corpulent body, and he was mopping himself profusely with a handkerchief.

"Look, Bobby. I don't like this arrangement at all. Let's just get the information from your GPS, get on the boat, go out, and get the stuff."

"Ruben, we're running out of time. I didn't make these rules, Ruby. I just follow them. The coordinates are locked in, and if we try to get the data off the GPS, we will lose the coordinates permanently. If we don't pick it up today, my clients say someone else will in the next few days. I am under the impression they have several 'floaters,' as they call them in the Gulf of Mexico. You just happen to be the buyer of this particular one. It's you or someone else. I don't have anything to do with that. Your choice, Ruben. It's been a very successful practice for my people. No one knows where it is or when it's going to be picked up until it happens."

A very hungover and uncomfortable Ruben said, "Okay, okay. But I'll give you one-third now, and I'll send Dos along with it. That's it. You can drop him off back here, and he can fly home. Where the hell is Rosa going?"

"She's my insurance, Ruben. If you don't pay up, I have your partner." He just let the thought hang in the air. "What channel do you want to use, Ruben?"

"*Ahhh,*" he said, thinking, "channel twenty-one."

"Okay, twenty-one it is."

"Make it thirty-nine," he said, changing his mind.

"Okay, thirty-nine. Send this guy Dos with the money and tell your captain to get on channel thirty-nine and to stay there. For now, you follow me in my wake by about a thousand meters. Get your fishing lines out and look like fishermen. I don't want anyone to think we're anything but fishermen."

Zack took a hesitant Rosa by the arm and steered her to *The Maria*. At least they were off the boat. He could worry about Dos later.

"What the hell is going on?"

"Just do as I say, Rosa. No questions, because I don't have any answers," he said as he maneuvered her into the salon. "Now just sit there on the couch, out of sight, until we're out of here."

The monster Dos waddled down the dock in hard leather-soled street shoes with a big brown duffel sack under one arm. When he stepped on the swim platform, the boat dipped noticeably lower in the water, sloshing water on the big man's shoes. The dock boy spotted the forbidden shoes and looked at Zack, raising his eyebrows.

The man's bulk barely fit through the transom door, and he walked directly into the air-conditioned salon, loosening his top shirt buttons. He threw the bag on the floor by a big chair that he immediately plopped into, overfilling it. The fat man maneuvered his foot up toward his huge midsection, removed his shoes and socks, and squeezed the water out of his sock onto the carpet; his eyes never left Rosa as he quietly mumbled complaints.

Zack talked to the dock boy from the bridge and got turned loose. The big yacht moved slowly down the boat channel, and Zack nodded at the captain of *La Playa*. He knew what to do.

When they were well into the Gulf and heading north at nineteen knots, he engaged the *master and slave* switch, which allowed the boat to operate using one control lever only to operate both engines and transmissions. Then he engaged the autopilot. He hit the kill switch Emerson had given him. Hopefully it worked.

Zack walked into the salon and was surprised to see Dos sitting on the settee with a beer in one hand and two empties on the table. The other hand held a black automatic.

"What the hell do you think you're doing, Dos?"

"I'm watching you, gringo, and I'm thinking about taking the *puta* here to one of these bedrooms," said an almost-drunk Dos. "Got any objections?"

"Yes, I do, asshole. If you have any doubts about what you are supposed to be doing over here, I suggest we call Ruben and have him explain it to you. We have a job to do. I'm driving the boat and running the electronics. When I tell you, you're going to get your fat ass up topside and look out for airplanes and other boats. Do I make myself real clear? Ruben said he could do without you, and that's why you're with us. If you want to keep your job, then I suggest you keep your mouth shut and follow directions."

Zack picked up the mic to the CB and held it out to Dos, hoping the bluff would work. Dos just shook his huge head and said nothing. Zack took another Tecate out of the refrigerator, threw it to Dos, and walked out the salon door and to the cockpit. He could see why they called the big man Dos: for *dos tunas* or two tons. Damn, he was big.

"Let's see the bag, Dos. I want to make sure everything is as it's supposed to be."

The bleary eyed Dos belched and looked at Rosa for help.

"Give it to him, Dos!"

Zack looked in the big duffel and began counting bundles. It looked like it was all there. He took the bag and put it in a locked storage locker in the salon. Then he looked at Dos.

"It's time, Dos," said Zack. "Come with me and I'll tell you what to do." He led the half-drunk, sweating Dos up the rear ladder to the bridge. "Sit here. There's beer in the refrigerator over there. Help yourself. Your job is to watch in all directions for airplanes or boats. If you see something, you holler at me and I'll take a look in the binoculars. Don't walk around up here, Dos. Your street shoes are death on the fiberglass, and they're damned slippery. You'll have to be careful. You stay here until I tell you to come down. And put that damn gun away. It may go off and hurt somebody," he said as he went down the stairs to the pilothouse and locked the door behind him.

"Would you tell me what the hell is going on?" an exasperated Rosa said under her breath.

"All I know is that I chartered this boat because I didn't think you and I were safe on that boat. I don't care how many of your people are on that boat. It'll be better here. Believe me."

"Look, I had my best men fly to Puerto Vallarta, and they are on that boat because I was worried about all of Ruben's men. They could have taken care of us. I don't trust Ruben, and now we have this crazy with us."

As he sat staring at the radar, he said, "We don't have time to worry about all of them right now, Rosa. We're getting close to where we need to be."

"*La Playa, La Playa*," he called on the radio. "Let me talk to Ruben."

In about fifteen seconds, a fretful Ruben responded, "What's the matter?"

"Nothing's the matter, Ruben. As a matter of fact, everything seems to be going quite well. Are you all watching the radar, and are your lookouts outside watching?"

"Should they be?"

"Ruben, I am only going to talk to you on this radio. This thing only has a range of maybe five miles out here, and we don't want anyone else listening in. You pass all the instructions on to your men. Now get your guys outside, and get your captain's eyes glued to the radar. We're early on this pickup, and that's good. You can go anywhere you want during the night.

"From my GPS reading, we are getting close, Ruben. Get your diver suited up and get your sonar or fish finder on so you can locate the buoy. It should be only about thirty to forty feet underwater, so slow down so you don't miss it."

"Christ, we're way out in the middle of the ocean. There's nothing out here, and its dark. What are we looking for?"

"Talk to your captain, Ruben. Relax. We'll be there shortly. Just keep your eyes open, and keep the radio on all the time. I'll call you when I cross over the buoys."

"Mr. Marquez, my VHF radio doesn't work, and I can't reach Emilio in La Paz," said an excited captain.

"Well, what's wrong with it?" Ruben asked.

"How do I know? They were both fine when we left, and now they are both deader than hell. We must have gotten a surge through the antennae or something, because they are both out. I took one apart and looked at it, and it seems that power supply is fried."

"What can you do? We have to reach Emilio."

"Does the CB have the same power supply? Can we change it over to the VHF and then switch it back to the CB?"

"No, they are entirely different. If we take the power supply out and try it in the VHF, we may lose that radio as well, and we need it. It's our only contact now."

"Ruben?" Zack's voice came back over the radio.

"Yes, Bobby?"

"I'm crossing over the buoys now. You stay on the radio at all times. Don't leave it. Tell me when you see the blip, and tell me everything that is going on all the time so I can help you if necessary. Do you have your white fender ready to throw over?"

"Yes, it's ready, my friend. I'll throw it in once we've checked everything out. We see it now. We're stopping and going after it. I'm going to be off the radio for a few minutes. I'll be right back."

"Damn it, Ruben. You stay on the radio all the time. Don't lose contact. I repeat, don't lose contact. It's important. Do you understand?"

"Yes, but I have to go to the bathroom."

"Then go in your pants, Ruben. You just stay on the damn radio until this is over. You can still loose that thing, you know, and we're the only help you have."

Zack was worried about that. Ruben obviously had a backup plan that wasn't working without the long range VHF radio. Emerson had gotten the job done.

La Playa stopped dead in the water as *The Maria* slowly continued to pull slowly away from her. Zack was madly watching the radar and the sonar and looking out the window in all directions. He saw nothing. Rosa was standing in the sliding glass door, watching the *La Playa*. Dos was silent topside. They were more than a thousand meters apart now, and *La Playa* was still dead in the water over the retrieval sight.

"What's happening, Ruben?"

"He's got a line on it, and we're getting ready to pull it in," Rueben replied.

"There is a big weight on two lines attached to the bottom. When you get the container in the boat, cut the lines and let the weight go. No need to wrestle with that," said a helpful Zack.

Rosa was standing by Zack, listening to the radio and looking out the rear of the boat at the fading silhouette of *La Playa*.

"Let's hear about it, Ruben."

An excited Ruben said, "We have it onboard, and we've cut the line. We have it inside in the light, and we're opening it now. It's wrapped in plastic, but they're cutting that off now. It looks like it's dry, and they're getting the case open now. What the—?"

La Playa turned into an orange-and-white ball of fire, and the shock wave slammed into *The Maria*. In the bright flash, Zack could see flaming boat parts flying in every direction. The diesel fuel, propane gas, and ammunition only added to the explosion. Whatever was in that case had contained a high potency explosive; *La Playa* literally disintegrated on the spot.

Zack and Rosa had been staring at *La Playa* in rapt fascination for a few moments when Rosa let out a scream. "No no no, you knew this!" she said with wild eyes.

Zack could hear Dos overhead, stamping across the sundeck, headed for the rear ladder, yelling and hollering in Spanish. He could never manage the big man now. He would be completely and wildly out of control. Rosa was crying and moaning as she clung desperately to him, and Dos was coming for them.

Zack slammed the master control lever forward, and the two big Caterpillar engines roared with power, churning the two huge four-bladed props in the water. The props clawed at the dense saltwater for propulsion, and the big yacht lurched into life. The bow jumped up, and the boat surged ahead as six hundred horsepower was turned loose.

Rosa flew off her feet and crashed into the rear bulkhead. Dos was caught off guard as he dashed across the sundeck in his leather street shoes. The sudden surge of power threw him off balance. He was propelled rearward, sliding on the fiberglass surface in his street shoes, and hit the upper deck rail about midthigh. The last Zack saw of the giant was when he fell from the sundeck. His head and shoulder smashed into the transom as he disappeared into the churning sea behind the charging *Maria*.

Oh shit, oh dear, thought Zack as he saw a stunned Rosa lying on the floor, whining incoherently. The yacht was surging and crashing into the swells with its' unleashed power; he had to get control of both of them and fast. He pulled on the master control, dragging the RPM down from thirty-one hundred to five hundred. Then he ran for Rosa.

He grabbed Rosa's pretty face as she wildly looked around the salon, yelling with a stunned look. He forced her to look at him. Their eyes were six inches apart. "Damn it, Rosa. I don't know what happened any more than you do. Remember, I took you off that boat. I just knew it wasn't right. I don't know why, but I wanted us both safe. Now for Christ's sake, get ahold of yourself. We have to go back and see what happened."

Rosa slowly started to calm down, but she was shaking like a leaf.

Zack hurried to the console and punched the autopilot to turn the yacht around and send it back the way they had come.

"My god, I had all those men on the boat. Oh my god." She shuddered. Her eyes popped open as big as saucers, and she said, "Where's that crazy fat man? I haven't seen him."

"Don't worry about him. He jumped in the water. He won't be bothering you. Just relax."

"He jumped in the water?"

"Something like that," he mumbled.

He scanned the radar. Nothing. *Hell, they never were coming,* he thought, *whoever they were. They were just going to eliminate all the loose ends at once. Everyone just disappears, including me, old expendable.* Now he knew Ricardo's agenda. That bastard had the drugs and was putting together his own deal. *He knows. He has to know about Ivan; otherwise, he wouldn't go to this extent to eliminate everyone who's been involved. He just cleaned house. I've got to find Ivan now, and fast.*

There was burning debris everywhere, and burning fuel was spreading on the surface of the water but rapidly burning out. The big engines had already hauled the hull toward the bottom. This was not the place to be.

He grabbed the purse Rosa had been carrying, took out her credit cards, but left her driver's license and other personal items, including mail. He then closed the zipper on the purse and threw the bag in with the floating debris.

He turned the now-darkened *Maria* east, punched the destination into the autopilot, and set the throttles to move as fast as the sea would allow.

"You and I are the only survivors, Rosa, but I don't think we were supposed to survive either. I don't know what happened or who did what. I think this is a good time for you to retire. Just slip off to your little place on the beach. Have your attorney quietly close up your affairs in the city, and forget it."

"What happened out there?"

"I don't know, Rosa. Possibly a fuel explosion, and with all the propane, who knows," he lied. He knew damn well what had happened. Someone was trying to get rid of all of them, and he couldn't very well let on to Rosa what his suspicions were without giving away his real identity and role in this whole thing. "It's possible, Rosa, that your friend Ruben brought some explosives onboard for one reason or another. Perhaps he was planning on scuttling the boat later and needed some explosives and they went off. It was one hell of a bang. That's for damn sure."

"Maybe … I never did trust that bastard," she said with glassy eyes. "Why did you change boats? Where did you get it? Why bring me onboard?"

"I just had a feeling. That's all. I took you along because you are important to me, and I didn't want anything to happen to you," he said as he stared into her eyes.

Rosa stared out the back of the boat at the distant burning *La Playa* for a long time and said nothing. Finally, she turned back to Zack and said, "What are we going to do now?"

"We're going to Mazatlan, and I'll put you off. You can catch a bus there and go south for a while. I don't want to go anywhere near that explosion site just in case someone is snooping around. Let your attorney close out your affairs and send you the money, if you trust him. Go to your little hidey-hole you said you wanted to live in, and have the good life. Stay out of trouble. No one knows you're alive, and I think we have convinced people you're dead. I took the liberty of throwing your handbag in the water with some of your identification. I took out your credit cards and photos but left the usual things you women carry and your driver's license. Someone will pick it up, and the word will travel around that you're dead. Leave it at that."

"Thank you, Rob. Oh, how can I ever thank you?" Rosa said as she put her shaking arms around him and laid her head on his shoulder.

"You'll think of something, I'm sure," he said with a smile. "The weather looks good, and we'll have very little moon after eleven o'clock. It's on the wane now. I want to get away from here as fast as we can."

Zack went up on the fly bridge so Rosa couldn't hear him and called Emerson in Guadalajara on the encrypted satellite phone. He relayed the results of the pickup.

"My god, Zack," Emerson barked. "That was meant for you. That man's crazy, for god's sake. How did you know to stay off the boat?"

"More on that later, Jeff. I can't talk right now. I don't know if he's crazy or not, but he sure as hell was cleaning out his closet of all the dirty linen. That was his agenda all along. He's in it alone now.

At least he thinks he is, and that means there is a hell of a lot more money for him. What's happening in Guadalajara? There were no Arabs on the boat or even in sight. They were all Hispanics."

"The same Arabs are here. They've been partying constantly like there is no tomorrow, and they can't get enough. Our guys are worn-out just watching them. I thought they weren't supposed to do that sort of thing."

"I think something is about to happen and soon. Don't let those guys out of your sight. I'll be in Mazatlan tomorrow. Get the plane in Vallarta to Mazatlan for me. I'm coming back to Guadalajara."

"Do not, and I repeat, do not tell anyone I'm still alive except our team. I'm the only survivor, and I want to keep it that way," he said in a demanding tone.

"Okay. Okay, it's done. I'll call Mickey and fill him in. What are you going to do in Guadalajara if you're dead?"

"I'm working on that. Tell Mickey I'll call him as soon as I can."

Zack came into the salon after docking the boat and put his arms around a very nervous Rosa. "I think I can fix it through my clients that you're dead, Rosa. I'm sure they'll spread the rumor, and you can start a whole new life."

"Rob, I want you to come with me. I need you. I really do," she purred as she pressed herself against him and laid her head on his shoulder. "Please come with me. I'll be good to you. I promise," she said in a pleading voice.

"Rosa, my love, you don't need me. You're one hell of a beautiful woman, and you'll do just fine. If you want you can tell me where you are, and one day I'll call or come and see you. We can talk then. I have a lot of explaining to do to my clients, and I just don't know how that's going to turn out right now, and I'll have my hands full for some time. You catch one of the cabs and head for the bus depot. Stay out of the airports. I'll give you a cap and a parka. Keep your head covered all the time and that beautiful red hair of yours out of sight."

A teary Rosa kissed Zack good-bye, pulled the hooded blazer he gave her over her red hair and cap and had started to get off the boat when Zack said, "Rosa, don't forget your bag." He handed her the duffel bag, which was tied at the top. Even as disheveled as she was, she was still one dynamite woman.

A confused Rosa opened the drawstring and looked inside. Rosa gasped and looked at Zack.

Zack said, "You may need that. Save some for when I come to visit."

"Oh, Rob, thank you. I really do love you. I'll save it for us," she said as she looked back in the bag at the packets of money Ruben had sent with Dos.

"Good luck, Rosa."

CHAPTER 19

Zack arrived in Guadalajara in the early evening aboard the private jet. His first order of business was to call Victoria, so he went out in search of a pay phone in a convenience store.

An almost hysterical Victoria shouted, "Zack, is that really you? I've heard so many stories, I don't know what to believe. Where are you? Are you all right? Oh, Zack, I was so worried about you. I didn't tell anyone. Just like you told me. But I've been terribly worried."

"Whoa, slow down, Victoria. Yes, I'm all right, but everyone else is dead. I don't know what you know, but this is what happened." Zack told the obviously shaken Veronica about the trip that had ended in the total destruction of the yacht *La Playa* and all onboard. "Now you know why I didn't want you on that boat. It just didn't smell right. I don't know why, but I've learned to follow those feelings."

"Zack ... I don't know what to say. I heard rumors and was sick about it but ... but I must confess, I saw you on that other boat and knew you weren't on *La Playa*. What do you think happened? Did the navy do it? That damn Ricardo has to be involved."

"In time, Victoria. What have you learned on your tapes?"

"Not much, but he's out of the office a lot now, and he's meeting with Jorge a lot. I've been following him. I think he's up to something. His phone calls are pretty normal, and he seems happy as a lark. What the hell happened, Zack? Was the navy there?"

"Hell no. I watched the radar constantly, and there was not a blip anywhere at anytime. That wasn't an accident either. It was one hell of an explosion. It had to be Plastique or some other high-powered explosive. It went up in a fireball. There was nothing left, and I mean nothing. I want you and Eduardo to keep an eye on Ricardo 24-7. If something is going to happen, it will happen soon. Don't tell anyone but Eduardo that I'm alive."

"Where are you?"

"At a pay phone in the city. I didn't know how secure your cell phone is.'"

"It's okay. Remember, it's not in my name. No one but Eduardo and you have the number."

"Okay, I'm going to the Hilton with the rest of the team. There are three guys and one gal here now, watching the Arabs, plus Emerson on the scrambler."

"Is that safe?"

"It's fine. I don't see them, and they don't see me. We're in telephone contact only. Victoria, call me at any time. It's going to happen soon. I can feel it. We know that. Everyone is out of the way, and there is nothing holding Ricardo back now. Watch for it."

Later that night, he was sitting in his room, watching late-night television. He had packed his gear and was getting ready to go to bed when his cell phone rang. He looked at his watch. Ten fifteen. It was Victoria.

"Yes?"

"Zack, he's on the move. I'm sure of it. He left Guadalajara for Lake Chapala. He has a vacation home just east of town in a large complex in the hills. He picked up Jorge, and the two of them are on the way. I'm sure something's going to happen."

"What makes you think that?"

"Two dark blue Suburbans just picked him up and are following him. They are all headed out together. I can't see who is in the other cars, but I'm sure they're all together. I'm following them."

"Oh boy, it sounds like you might be right, but for god's sake, don't let them see you."

"No, I won't. I'm way behind them in traffic. The three of them are easy to follow."

"How do I get there?"

She gave him detailed directions on how to find Ricardo's house. He made careful notes on the hotel notepad by the phone. He repeated several items and now had it clear.

He called the team room, and Emerson picked up the phone on the second ring.

"We're moving. Are you dressed?"

"Hell no, I'm not dressed. I'm in bed. What do you mean we're moving?"

"Get dressed. Put on the darkest clothes you have. Be ready in fifteen minutes. I'll be waiting for you guys in front of the hotel in exactly fifteen minutes. Don't be late."

"But—" Emerson protested.

"Move!" Zack said as he shut down the cell phone.

Fifteen minutes later, the car quietly idled outside the hotel as Zack nervously checked his watch. The waiting was the hard part, he knew. He read his notes over again, putting everything in memory.

Emerson burst through the front door in a dark blue suit, a blue shirt, and a red necktie still askew around his neck. He looked up and down the street as if he was expecting someone. Then he got in the passenger side of the car while Zack openly stared at him.

"Where the hell do you think your going? Out dancing?"

"These are the darkest clothes I have."

"The necktie is beautiful. Take it off. Where are the others?"

"That's what I was trying to tell you. They're not here."

"What the hell do you mean they're not here?"

"They went disco hopping to watch the Arabs. I tried to call them, but either their cell phones are off or they can't hear my calls in those noisy places. They must be inside somewhere. Do we need them? Where are we going? We can look for them."

Zack had moved into traffic and headed east, shaking his head. It was going to be just Emerson and him.

With only the parking lights on, they slowly cruised the neighborhood without driving down the narrow lane in front of Ricardo's estate. The roads were nothing more than dirt trails with ten-foot-high walls and huge steel doors enclosing the grand estates. By the length of each wall, the estates ran between five and ten acres each.

They noticed all the estates on the street where Ricardo lived butted up against hills that rapidly turned into mountains. All of these homes facing the mountains had short rear walls so as not to block the view.

They looked everywhere for Victoria's car. The streets were empty. All vehicles were safely inside the secure estate walls.

They stopped at the end of the street, about two hundred yards from Ricardo's, turned their lights off, and slowly pulled into a cemetery overgrown with weeds. They drove slowly around the rutted dirt road that circumnavigated the bright stone orchard, looking for a place to park. Zack let the car coast to a stop behind a large crypt so the brake lights would not go on. He shut off the engine and sat quietly, waiting.

Emerson said, "What the hell are we doing here?"

"Shut up and listen," he answered in a whisper. "Don't talk unless I talk to you. If you hear something, touch me on the arm. Don't talk again."

Ten minutes passed. It was deadly silent in the old rotting cemetery. No one had noticed their arrival except some nighttime ground creatures that squeaked like rats. Emerson was as nervous as a cat on a hot tin roof, and his head swiveled around like it was on ball bearings.

Zack whispered. "Here's the plan, Emerson. You're going to stay here in the cemetery. You'll be able to see the entrance to the estate from behind one of the tombstones. You don't leave this place until I call you on your cell phone and tell you to. You got that?" Zack demanded.

"What are you going to do?" Emerson said in a fearful tone.

Looking Emerson in the eye, he said, "This is my bailiwick. You'll have to trust me on this. I'll have my cell phone on vibrate and will call you when I want you to come in. You don't leave this place until I call you, no matter what you hear or what you think. Do you understand that? You're the communications guy. When I communicate, you come, and not before."

Zack got out of the dark blue four-door rental and quietly opened the trunk and unzipped the duffel he'd thrown in at the hotel. He'd broken the trunk light at the hotel when he'd removed the interior lights of the car. He donned black sneakers, black camouflaged pants, and a thin long-sleeved turtleneck shirt. The black color was broken with dark greys and deep tones that broke up his silhouette. He popped open a can and started smearing his face, neck, and hands with black and dark green camouflage paint. He pulled a navy watch cap over his head that was heavy and nonreflective, and strapped on two black fanny packs, holstered both Glocks, and looked into the fearful face of Emerson.

"You stay here and keep quiet, Emerson. This is not the place for you."

"Yes, but maybe you'll need some help here."

"Believe me, you will not be of any help and only a hindrance. I'll keep my cell on vibrate, so text me if it's a real emergency. You stay near the front of the cemetery and keep an eye on the entrance. You can see the little Judas door that's in the big iron door. You'll know what's going on. Don't worry. I'll call you. Stay away from that house. Do you understand?"

"Look, let's call in for some backup. I think maybe we're going to need it."

"What backup? You mean the local police? You couldn't even get them out of bed this time of night, and you can bet the people behind these walls own them all. Our backup is out dancing tonight, remember? You're it, Emerson. So buck up. You're on.

"I don't need other people wandering around the place. If I'm alone, then I know everyone is the enemy. If other people start showing up, then the edge is taken away. I know you probably don't understand this, but that's the way it is. You sit tight." With this, he quietly moved off into the shadows.

Emerson softly closed the trunk and walked around the crypt to argue with Zack, but he wasn't there. He scanned the white tombstones jutting out at different angles and into the blackness, but damn, the man had totally disappeared.

This was his territory, his domain. This is what he was trained for. This is what he did. Too many years spent honing a deadly skill. He could survive here.

As he slowly worked his way through the brush-cluttered foothills behind the big estates, the numerous Special Ops missions he had been on flashed through his mind like a fast-forward DVD. He could see the jungles, the bush, the anxiety … but best of all, the night. The ever-present darkness. He could wear it around him like a shroud. With skill, it allowed him the ability to remain invisible until the last second when it was too late for the quarry. He realized then that he loved this work. He had just been out of it too damn long.

He wasn't here now for good or for bad. He'd learned that lesson a long time ago in Southeast Asia. There was no right or wrong. It was only in degrees, the lesser of two evils. He realized the truth in an old saying he had heard once: when we found the enemy, the enemy was us.

Many people feared the dark of night, and some reveled in it. He was one of the latter. He could blend in to any shadow and wait until he had worked out each move in detail in his mind so that when he struck, he was preprogrammed to move swiftly, quietly, and accurately. He would be ready to accept what lay ahead, whatever it was.

He lay quietly in the black shadow of the tree. Black on black. Slowly gimballing, his body and mind down to reach that lower level of mind, that sensory awareness, that sixth sense he'd worked years to hone to razor sharpness.

The estates he'd passed were all dark. Either these were weekend retreats like Eduardo's, or all the residents were in bed. Eduardo's house was the only one showing life. It had light showing through several windows on the bottom floor overlooking a large veranda.

When he finally reached that lower level of mind, his senses approached an animal-like quality. He could smell the grass and earth, detect the slightest movement of shadows, and block out all sounds except what he wanted to hear. He was ready now: observe, analyze, act, and survive. It was time.

He lay in the grass under a big tree for several minutes and detected only one person in the yard. The man was leaning on one of the three Suburbans parked by the big front door to the mansion. He was the guard, and he would be grossly inadequate to accomplish his duty. They were obviously not expecting anyone tonight.

Zack had moved to within ten feet of the man and was lying in the shadow of a big flowering hedge, waiting. When the right time came, he uncoiled like a quiet spring, and the man leaning on the front fender of the Suburban only felt a body press against his back, a hand cover his mouth, and another hand grab his chin. The only sound was a dull cracking sound like breaking a small twig.

Zack pushed the man under the Suburban and lay alongside him, watching the night. The man wouldn't be seen here under the car. Neither would someone trip over him in the dark and give away Zack's presence. He was out of the way ... unless someone drove off in the Suburban. The small sliver of a moon had already moved behind the big hills, and the only light came from the stars and the big house.

He crawled like a night snake up onto the veranda and peered into the well-lit room through poorly closed vertical blinds. It was a large high-ceilinged rustic room on the left side of the house with a huge fireplace made from native stone on one forty-foot wall on the left side. Ricardo sat in front of the fireplace in an open-necked white golf shirt. He was at a large table that obviously doubled as a desk, talking to a beaming Jorge, who stood to his left.

Two lean dark men of Near Eastern extraction were sitting on a large leather couch on the far wall, facing Zack's direction, with a moaning Victoria bound and gagged between them. Both were dressed casually in white golf shirts and tan slacks. They were laughing and pawing at their frightened quarry, playing with her.

Two more men sat at a poker table to Zack's right in deep conversation, going over a brochure or pamphlet. One man facing Zack was a bearded Arab, and the other was a thick-bodied pale-skinned gray-haired man facing away from him. In the center of the table was a large aluminum camera case.

As Zack rapidly scanned the room, he saw another man, a guard standing to Zack's right on the left of a closed heavy door that obviously opened into the main hallway down the center of the house. He was well over six feet tall and weighed close to three hundred pounds. His eyes were half-shut, but his eyelids twitched as his eyeballs moved, and his head moved slowly, constantly scanning the room. There were eight people in the room, including Victoria, but the guard would be Zack's first and biggest problem.

He had both Glocks ready to go. He could see down the well-lit center hallway through the glass sidelights at the now unguarded front door. The hallway was empty, and the door was unlocked and moved easily on the huge hinges. He quickly looked in each room off the main hall—all except the great room that stood behind the closed heavy wooden door.

He could hear several muted conversations as he moved up to the door. He held one gun in his left hand. The big guard was on that side. He tucked the other gun in his waistband and very slowly and carefully turned the door handle with his right hand. If he made any sound or if someone saw the big knob turning, he was dead. He could hear the muted conversations in the room and had to hope that everyone had remained in place.

He slowly and gently pulled the door to release any latch pressure and then very slowly turned the knob. When the latch was fully pulled back, he moved the door a very small fraction of an inch to make sure it would open and was not locked from the inside. He took a deep breath and shoved.

The big man was three feet inside the door and hadn't moved before Zack came in. He went down in a heartbeat as he turned, grabbing for Zack. Zack pulled out the second Glock, and the next two shots sounded as one as the two men with Victoria sat back down on the couch, each with a small red hole in the center of his white golf shirt.

A surprised Jorge had a gun out now, but it was too late. Zack tapped the trigger twice to make sure the heavily muscled man stayed down. He moved the automatic in his left hand to cover a startled Ricardo, and with his right hand gun covered the two men at the poker table. He never took his eyes off them and watched Ricardo with his peripheral vision. Ricardo was the least of his worries.

"Hi, Ricardo. Keep your hands on the table. Who're your friends?" he said as he backed into the big door, closing it quietly.

Ricardo could only mumble. He was too startled to see Zack alive.

"Yes, I missed you too, Ricardo. Nice place you have here. Must cost a lot of money to have a country house like this. Nice place for a private meeting."

The gray-haired man never took his eyes off Zack. He calmly folded up the pamphlet with thick farmer hands. The rest of him matched the hands. His thick, blunt features had Russian written all over them. If he had a gun, he would have used it by now. He was a cool, controlled man who didn't appear to be the slightest bit afraid. This was a man who was familiar with death, a man who had seen a lot of it.

"Victoria, are you okay? Looks like your two boyfriends are out of the meeting."

She vigorously nodded, and Zack could see tears running down her face.

"Ricardo, it looks like I interrupted your meeting. Sorry I'm late. Perhaps you can bring me up to speed."

"Zack, is that really you? I don't know what to say."

"Well, hello would be nice. Yes, it's me, Ricardo. A little surprised to see me after the big yacht party you threw? Who're your friends?"

With this, the Arab sitting at the table with the Russian started fanatically yelling at the top of his voice in a language Zack couldn't understand. The man jumped up and pulled out some kind of curved throwing knife out of some hidden pocket in his blousy shirt. He dropped on the heavy tile floor during his windup, still mumbling in the same language. The heavy man never flinched, and his eyes never left Zack.

"My name is Tomas." He pronounced it *Tomash* in a husky, guttural voice. "I am a diplomat. I have papers. You cannot arrest me, and if you hurt me, you will have the international authorities to deal with. I am here doing business." The man spoke with conviction and confidence. He was cool and knew what he was doing.

"Tomas what?"

"Tomas Vladsnok is my full name."

"Well, sir, you won't have to worry about that. I'm not here to arrest you."

Relief showed on the man's face.

"I'm not with any police department or government. I really don't care if you're a diplomat or whatever. Yes, I know you. It's Major Tomas Vladsnok, isn't it?"

A little smile crossed the man's heavy face, and his bloodshot black eyes twinkled. He sat up straighter in his chair and jutted out his chin in pride. "Yes, you have it right. How do you know who I am? I'm impressed."

"Major, I read your book on tank warfare. I found it interesting that you were a student of the Rommel tactics. You used a lot of his theory in planning your tank maneuvers."

"You read well, Mr. Zack. I believe your friend Ricardo called you that."

"I found your analysis of Erwin Rommel and of the tank genius Guderian very interesting. You were a student of the great tank commanders, I could tell. What brings you to sunny Mexico, Major?"

"I'm here doing business, but it seems you have eliminated my customers. Perhaps you and I can do some business."

"What do you have in mind, Major?"

Ricardo broke in and whined, "Zack, I'm really not a part of all this. I want you to know that. I didn't have anything to do with that boat business. I swear. These people are important foreigners who wanted to meet in a private place, and this was the only place I could think of. You carry on here, Zack. I really need to get back to the city."

The Russian looked at Ricardo like he would look at a cockroach and muttered something under his breath. Whatever it was, Ricardo understood.

"Sit where you are, Ricardo. You're not going anywhere. Just keep your hands on top of the table where I can see them. Just what did you have in mind, Major?" he said, turning back to the Russian.

In very proper English with a course Russian accent that sounded like a growl, the man said, "Well, things have changed a great deal in the last few minutes. I think you and I can come to some kind of an arrangement. I have the last payment of ten million US dollars here and the merchandise. We could become partners, you and I. I have many other customers for my wares." He waived a hand toward the aluminum suitcase. "We could split the money and go our separate ways."

"How do I fit in, Major?"

"Fifty-fifty. I think that's fair. We can sell the merchandise to some other people, and for a fast sale we can get perhaps twenty million, as we don't have to be too fussy now. That gives us thirty million to split. I have arrangements in South America, where life is good and easy. You could even join me there, and with your share you could buy what you want, live like a king."

"Sounds like you have it all planned out, Major."

"Of course I do. Everything is arranged. I leave tonight for Rio."

"Somehow I don't think that's going to happen, Major."

"Let me show you what we have to sell. May I call you Zack? I believe that's what that maggot of a politician called you." The modulation of his voice never varied. He acted like nothing had happened at all in this room and like he hadn't heard anything Zack had said. He was a salesman now.

"Of course."

The big man gently pulled the aluminum case toward him and snapped open the two locks. He slowly opened the case, but his eyes never left Zack. As the case opened, Zack saw a stainless steel cylinder inside, settled in Styrofoam and with the unmistakable international radioactive symbol on the side. This was Little Ivan. It was the first Zack had ever seen, but it probably didn't vary much from the US version, he guessed. They both did the same thing: made one hell of a bang. The only difference in appearance with this one was that it had been built to fit in a cylinder but was now modified for the case. It had a bundle of wires that came out of one end and went into a small black box that was also imbedded in the foam lining of the case.

"This, Zack, is the business end of a 152 mm artillery projectile. Probably the finest and most sophisticated atomic warhead ever built in it's time. Very small, very clean and lightweight, but very efficient."

"Just how efficient, Major?"

"This is a seven megaton device," he said as he studied Zack.

"What did your customers have in mind with their purchase, Major?"

"They were going to have a barbecue, Texas style, they said. I believe it was to be held in California. Silicone Valley, I think."

"How were they going to get this up there?"

"Oh, your friend Ricardo had that all taken care of. It seems he has good connections with the border guards on both sides of the border. He's quite proficient at moving things and people across the border. We've used him several times in the past when we wanted to get an agent into the United States. Now you can see how he can afford such a nice country home. I think we've paid for this place many times." The major chuckled as he watched Ricardo squirm in his chair.

"You see, since Mother Russia no longer needs some of her things, a few of us are selling them to other people. It is better than having them fall into disrepair or disintegrate entirely, I think."

"What do you have for sale, Major?"

"Well, we've sold a few helicopters, lots of small arms and ammunition, of course, and a few components of special artillery rounds. The CIA in America has been a big client."

"What do they buy?"

"They bought a lot of small arms and several helicopters. They use them in their covert operations. A Russian helicopter in the Near East goes unnoticed, but an American helicopter will draw fire from everyone. No one likes the Americans." He chuckled.

This disclosure brought a broad smile to the man's pockmarked face. Zack could see a steel tooth glinting at him from the left side of the man's mouth.

"You see, there were a lot of things missing when the boys went home. Inventory wasn't very good; we saw to that." He fondly patted the aluminum case and said, "The 152 is a wonderful design. It is not too difficult when you have the proper technicians to open the shell and remove the warhead. Many times they were shipped separately, and they easily got lost in the system. That was the easy part. Finding customers with the money, now that's the hard part."

"I believe they were having the barbecue in Silicone Valley. They knew it would destroy a lot of the tech business and the fallout would scare the shit out of the Americans," he said, shaking his big head with a smile.

"I thought you said this wasn't a dirty bomb?"

"It isn't. That's where the barbecue comes in. They add some nuclear waste material with it that they already have in the United States and put several bags of charcoal that the Americans use for their barbecue around it. When it goes off, the carbon absorbs radiation, and of course hopefully you get a nice black cloud that has radiation in it that would cover perhaps a few miles downwind. That would pretty well shut down Silicone Valley, and the economic fallout would be spectacular."

That's the third time he's looked at his watch, Zack thought. *Something is about to happen, or he's waiting for …* Zack dashed across the room and flattened himself against the wall alongside the big window with the faulty blinds he had peered through earlier.

"Both of you look at your hands and don't take your eyes off them. If you even glance at me, it will be your last look. Ricardo, turn the lamp off on your desk."

He was to Ricardo's right now and slightly behind him, and the only light in the room was the big halogen touchier in the far corner behind the Russian.

"Who are we waiting for, Major? Victoria, get on the floor and roll over behind Ricardo's desk. Stay out of sight and be quiet."

"Ah, it was the glance at the watch, wasn't it? You're a very perceptive man, Mr. Zack. Indeed, a good adversary and a better partner, I think."

"Who are we waiting for, Major? I won't be asking that question again."

"Well, I believe our friend Ricardo has invited some others to this party. They should be here any minute actually."

"Who are they?"

"They're the ones who are buying the heroin in that case over by Ricardo's desk. They're the ones who were going to pay the balance of what is owed to me for the 152. I believe they're from Tijuana and are a nasty bunch, but they have the money," he said with a shrug.

"How many are coming, Ricardo?"

"I'm not sure, Zack. Probably three or four," he stammered.

"Mr. Zack, why not let this deal go through? We will have the money and the 152, and then you and I can sell it again as partners. We can sell it anywhere in the world, and when that's over, I'm going to go to my little home in the south, and you can go anywhere in the world. What do you say?"

"Major, who do you think would buy this thing? Who else has the kind of money you need to sell it?"

"The Middle East is ripe, my friend. Sadaam Hussein was a client. He was building that marvelous rifle barrel to shoot all the way to Israel. The Brits and Germans made the barrel, and the Germans made the projectiles. I don't think they were too worried about what Sadaam was going to shoot into Israel. No love lost there either, you know. Of course, he would probably only get off two or three rounds before the rifle was located, but he would have accomplished his goal. All of the Arab nations and half the world would be happy. Yes, no love lost there, I think," he mumbled. "Yes, my friend, the Middle East is where we sell it," he said, leaning back in his chair like a corporate executive but still looking at his hands.

"I thought NATO and the coalition searched Iraq for weapons of mass destruction."

"You see the size of this weapon?" he said, gently patting the aluminum case again. "You could lower it a few thousand feet down a dry oil well, put it in a cave, or haul it in a donkey cart. It could be carried in a knapsack or backpack and across the border into Syria or anywhere else. It has a very small radiation signature. Rest assured whatever was there was promptly moved elsewhere. These Arab gangs are everywhere. One day it will come out of hiding, believe me. I think—"

The room exploded.

Emerson was wringing wet with sweat, even in the cool evening. This was the first time he'd ever been exposed in the field like this. He usually was far from harm's way in a secure trailer filled with electronics. He didn't like sitting in a cemetery with squeaking rats. The place even smelled bad in the chilly night air. He was shivering, either from cold or fear; he didn't know, and he didn't care. He just wanted out of this place. He was thinking that it was too damn quiet when he heard the motor.

He flattened himself against the whitewashed wall of the gate and peered down the broken road in front of Ricardo's house. A car was moving slowly with its lights off. It quietly rolled to a stop in front of Ricardo's gate. The doors opened, and three men got out holding short assault rifles. They looked up and down the street and, apparently satisfied, went in through the Judas door in the big gate.

He didn't know what to do. Zack had told him to stay put, but Zack wouldn't know about the three men who had just arrived. He had to do something. But what? He couldn't call him on the cell phone, but he couldn't wait and do nothing. Zack may not even look at a text. He'd go help. He would sneak up to the house and arrest these men. Damn right. He'd help Zack.

A few minutes later, Emerson eased himself through the Judas door in the gate and saw all three men looking through open slats in a large window in the front of the house. He drew his gun. It was the first time he had ever drawn his gun except at the agency shooting range. He wasn't even sure he could kill a man. He didn't belong here, and every part of his body told him to turn and run. He crouched low and rapidly moved to the nearest Suburban in the driveway. Just as he reached the car, all hell broke loose. In a panic, he dropped to the ground behind the big car, and his breath caught in his throat with horror. He was staring into the glassy eyes of dead man ten inches away who was lying underneath the vehicle.

He tried to bring his gun up to shoot but couldn't move; his muscles had frozen. Even in the poor light, he could tell the man was staring at him with a kind of wild look, and his jaw and head were hanging ajar. The noise at the house was terrific. Guns roared, glass broke, and bullets crashed into things.

The window exploded. The vertical blinds were torn off the wall and scattered around the room. Glass flew everywhere. There were two automatic weapons firing indiscriminately into the room. Bullets slammed into everything and ricocheted off the big stone fireplace wall. Pieces of plaster and dust danced in the air. Glass flew. The bullets were tearing the room to shreds. Zack squinted through his hands, which held his two Glocks, and waited. His time would come.

He could hear two guns firing into the room now, and the muzzle blasts winking through the disintegrated window confirmed they were immediately outside. Ricardo went down with the first burst, but the wily old Russian had disappeared into the hallway with Little Ivan with the first burst of gunfire.

The shooting stopped as abruptly as it started, and Zack heard magazines being released and dropping on the tile porch. His time had come.

Emerson stood up behind the Suburban and peered through the window. Two men were spraying the room with bullets through the gutted window, and a third man went through the front door, shooting down the hallway. He knew he had to move now, but how?

The shooting stopped at the window while the men jammed in new clips for the automatics. It was then that he saw a black shadow and only a shadow move across the window. He would think it a trick of the light except two guns roared twice in its passing, and the two men on the front porch went down. This was not the place to be. He remembered the man's words now: when I'm alone, everyone is the enemy. Crouching, he turned and ran for the Judas gate.

Zack moved across the window as a black flash with both Glocks ready and double tapped two rounds into the chest of each man. Their faces were lit by the big torchiere behind Zack, and he could see the startled looks on their faces as he passed. Zack saw one go down, and the other jammed over the railing into the yard just as another automatic started hammering in the big hallway. The Russian didn't have a gun that Zack knew of, so it had to be another of the new arrivals.

He made his way to the open door leading into the hall and waited. There was only one gun firing, and it was tearing up everything in the hallway. The firing stopped for a clip change, and Zack peered around the doorjamb with one Glock, pumping out rounds into the lone man standing just inside the big front door. The Russian and Ivan were nowhere to be seen.

Zack looked up and down the hallway and up the big staircase leading to the second floor. No major. He couldn't have made it up the stairs in the time he'd had, so he had to be on the main floor. Zack moved down the hall away from the front door and peered into each room over the barrel of a Glock.

It was the third room. It was a bathroom, and the major was sitting on the floor in a pool of blood. Little Ivan was propped up on the toilet seat. The case was open, and as Zack entered, he saw the Russian flip a black toggle switch. A red digital panel lit up as Ivan whined into life. Something was moving inside the bomb, and a red digital number display rapidly scrolled down from three digits to two. They were so fast that they had to be tenths of a second. The Russian's pale face glanced at Zack for only a moment. Smiling, the old man looked back at the case and lifted a small clear plastic window. Underneath the window was a red toggle switch. The Russian's finger rested on the red switch as he watched the numbers rapidly decline. Ivan was arming itself.

This was the timing device the major had described. When it got to zero, a person could set the time. When it got to zero, it was ready to go off, and with the major's finger on the red switch, he wasn't going to set the time. He was going to turn Ivan loose and decimate this quiet countryside.

Zack started into the room, but the numbers told him he would never make it; they were single digits now. It was going to happen in a bathroom in Mexico.

The major toppled over with a little smirk on his face. The two small holes just over his right ear appeared just before the digital sequence hit zero.

It was then that Zack realized he'd been holding his breath. He let it out with a *huff*. He slowly walked across the tiled room and looked at Little Ivan for the first time. It was a simple-looking device, the cylinder and a black box that housed the timing device.

He carefully closed the clear plastic cover over the red toggle switch and examined the device. There were only two switches—one black and one red. He flicked the black switch, and Ivan quietly whined again as it disarmed itself and went back to sleep. He closed the case, picked it up, and returned to the big room after checking the three men from Tijuana.

Victoria had survived the hail of lead from the two men on the porch. She was sobbing hysterically. Zack cut her loose and held her while she cried herself out.

"At least we got Little Ivan, Victoria. You don't know how close it was, but Little Ivan was a heartbeat away from evaporating this neighborhood. I want you to know that I learned you are very important to me, and I'm happy you didn't get hurt in this fracas," he said in a quiet tone close to her ear as he held her. "Let's get out of here." He punched the autodial on his cell phone.

Zack called in Emerson. When he arrived, he was ashen and shaking like a leaf. "What the hell's the matter, Emerson? You okay?"

His head swiveled from one side to the other as he walked into the big room. "Jesus, Zack. I've never seen or heard anything like this. Oh my god, look at the bodies."

"Get a grip. We've got a lot to do. Get Mickey on the satellite phone and see how they want to handle things."

"They're not going to like to hear about all these people who are dead. That's for sure."

"Hells bells, Emerson. They don't give a damn about these guys. We have Ivan, and that's what counts."

CHAPTER 20

While Emerson was trying to explain to Mickey what had happened, elaborating on the house of carnage he was standing in, Zack took the shaking Victoria by the hand and led her out the door into the cool evening. They walked away from the house and stood in the cool grass, away from everything, and Victoria started to calm down. Zack took her in his arms and just held her while she held him in a tight security grip.

"It's going to be all right, Victoria. You and Eduardo will have to figure out a story that will work. I don't think there are any other people involved other than Ricardo and his bunch, and they are all gone now, so you can probably say anything you want. You're going to have to leave out Ivan, of course, but it would look good that you two solved a large drug sale and eliminated some very important players. It's just another high-level drug operation that was solved by good police work and cooperating governments. It would look good for everyone. Eduardo will have to figure out how to handle your involvement, but I'm sure he can say that special undercover agents worked with him on solving the problem."

Zack looked her in the eyes, held her close, and said, "I'm going to miss you, Victoria. We hardly got to know each other, but I'd like to get to know you a whole lot better. You've become really important to me. You said you've never been fishing, so when this is all over, why not come up to San Carlos and I'll take you fishing? I think you'll like it."

Victoria let out a shaky breath and leaned against Zack, holding him closely. "Zack, I'm going to miss you too. I think I'd like to try fishing. I think that sounds like a great idea. I'm going to look forward to it," she said. She reached up, pulled his head close to her, and kissed him hungrily on the mouth.

Then Victoria called Eduardo and told him what had happened. They talked for a long time, and the more Victoria talked, the calmer she became. She was all undercover agent now. Zack noticed her looking over at him from time to time as she talked with a little smile on her face.

Zack and Emerson loaded Little Ivan and the heroin and left the money for Eduardo to show for their efforts and then drove to Guadaljara to catch their plane, which was being readied as they left. Eduardo's team would clean up the mess at the country house. Several of the CIA and DEA operatives would meet them at Davis Monthan Air Force Base in Tucson. They were cleared through customs as a military consulate flight from Guadalajara direct to Davis Monthan. Everyone looked the other way.

The sleek Learjet whistled its way up to and into a designated hangar and rolled to a stop as the big engines whined down and the hangar doors rumbled shut. Zack had never seen so much security. There were armed personnel everywhere, and none of them were looking at the jet. They each had their objectives.

"Zack, you did great. Get Ivan inside pronto and tell us about him," said an exuberant Mickey as he slapped Zack on the back.

"I had a lot of help, Mick. Our girl Victoria gets a hell of a lot of credit. Believe me."

"How was Emerson when the chips were down? Did he perform well?"

"He did exactly as he was supposed to do, Mickey. He did good."

Mickey smiled and shook his head as he glanced over at a disheveled and nervous Emerson. "Get that damn thing inside, and let's have a look at it."

Seven megatons in a briefcase; it was frightening. How many more of these things were on the loose? God only knew.

The bomb expert Harry Wong walked into the small room. He looked like he was a teenager in jeans and a golf shirt that was too big. He just glanced at Zack and Mickey and nodded to Emerson as he walked directly to the aluminum case. He looked the Ivan apparatus over and said, "Boy, it's damn simple, guys. It's meant for a dummy to operate." He looked at Zack and Mickey with a grin.

He slowly eased the gray foam lining away from the sides of the case and finally tilted the foam up on one end, exposing the wires underneath.

"Emerson, look at this! Hold the light for me."

Emerson flashed the mini Maglight under the foam and moaned. "How about that? They have a fail-safe device in here."

Mickey asked, "What's a fail-safe device?"

Wong looked over at Zack and Mickey and said, "It's a trap. If one of you old guys tried to cut any wire, this little transistor box that's powered by a small nine-volt battery would trigger the bomb. It would arm itself and go off. There would be no stopping it. It's meant to keep the bomb from being tampered with."

"So what are you going to do?"

Wong looked at Emerson, and they went to work. Emerson held the foam and light, and Wong disconnected the battery and dumped it on the table. A curious conspirators' exchange was made between Wong and Emerson, and Wong said, "The problem now, Emerson, is that the transistor box is still hot and has to be disconnected safely." He reached under the foam with small wire cutters.

Emerson mumbled, "Be careful which wire you cut, as the thing could go off, you know. Seven megaton ... Well, they were thinking of closing this base anyway, I think. No, don't cut that one. Never the middle one. It has to be one on the end. I'm not sure which one, so you pick one. Hey, fifty-fifty, right?"

"Okay," Wong mumbled under the foam. "I'll give this one a try."

Zack was staring at Mickey by this time. *Just what the hell is going on here? I thought this was supposed to be an expert. They sent a kid to do a man's job. He's going to blow the whole damn place up.*

"Here goes, Emerson," Wong said as the small wire cutters disappeared into the rat's nest of wiring. There was dead silence in the room now. No one was even breathing. *Snick.*

"*Bang!*" Wong yelled.

Zack jumped back with an *unngh*, and Wong and Emerson laughed hysterically. Mickey knew these guys, and he started to laugh too. Zack had been had by Wong and Emerson, who both thought it was terrific.

"Mickey, I'm going to shoot these two. Give me your gun! I want to shoot them right now."

Wong and Emerson skillfully cut wires and removed all the components, putting them in separate Ziploc bags as they continued to chuckle.

The DEA took the drugs, and the CIA took Ivan and the components, and they disappeared into the night in their heavy black Suburbans with only a nod to Mickey and Zack.

Mickey looked at a still-disturbed Zack and said, "Let's go to your place, Zack. Walker will be here within the hour, and he wants to debrief you. Zack, he wants to hear everything, and I mean everything; besides, I think we both need a drink. So let's go," he said as he took Zack's elbow and moved him along.

Zack put his arm on Mickey's shoulder as they walked off, and gave him a happy shake, looked at him with a grin, and said, "We're old guys?"

Late in the afternoon three months later, Zack was sitting on his big leather couch reading and listening to satellite music in the salon of his boat *The Seaduecer,* when his vibrating cell phone started to jiggle around on the coffee table. He set down his Tecate beer and picked up the cell with no plan of answering it. He just wanted to see who was calling. It was his friend Mickey O'Leary. He wouldn't miss this call.

"Hey, Mickey, how's the world of espionage and intrigue going?"

"Funny thing you should ask that, Zack. We have a situation we need to talk about."

ABOUT THE AUTHOR

Royal Bouschor, born and raised in Duluth, Minnesota, is a retired judge and semiretired attorney and businessman living in Tucson, Arizona. He is an international hunter and traveler and the cofounder of The International Wildlife Foundation, that built one of the world's premier wildlife museums in Tucson, Arizona. He has lived in Sonora, Mexico, for several years.